D1577073

700040485505

THE REVISED FUNDAMENTALS
OF CAREGIVING

the REVISED FUNDAMENTALS -of- CAREGIVING

a novel

JONATHAN EVISON

HEAD of ZEUS

First published in the United States of America in 2012 by Algonquin Books of Chapel Hill, a division of Workman Publishing, New York.

Published in the United Kingdom in 2013 by Head of Zeus Ltd.

Copyright © Jonathan Evison, 2012.

10 9 8 7 6 5 4 3 2 1

A CIP catalogue record for this book is available from the British Library.

ISBN (HB): 9781781851753
ISBN (XTPB): 9781781851760
ISBN (E): 9781781851784

Printed in Germany.

Design by Anne Winslow.

Head of Zeus Ltd
Clerkenwell House
45-47 Clerkenwell Green
London EC1R 0HT

www.headofzeus.com

For Case,

a genius and an inspiration . . .

THE REVISED FUNDAMENTALS
OF CAREGIVING

hooked on mnemonics

I WAS BROKE when duty called me to minister to those less fortunate than myself, so maybe I'm no Florence Nightingale. And maybe in light of all that happened with Piper and Jodi, I'm not qualified to care for anybody. The fact is, at thirty-nine, with a gap in my employment history spanning the better part of the technological revolution, I'm not qualified to do much anymore.

But don't get the idea that just anyone can be a caregiver. It takes patience, fortitude, a background check. Not to mention licensing and a mandatory curriculum of continuing education, as evidenced by my certificates in Special Needs in Dementia 1, Positive Crisis Management, and Strategies in Nonverbal Communication. The bulk of what I learned about being a licensed caregiver, I learned from the Fundamentals of Caregiving, a twenty-eight-hour night course I attended along with fourteen middle-aged women at the Abundant Life Foursquare Church right behind the Howard Johnson in Bremerton. Consuming liberal quantities of instant coffee, I learned how to insert catheters and avoid liability. I learned about professionalism. I learned how to erect and maintain certain boundaries, to keep a certain physical and emotional distance between the client and myself in order to avoid burnout. I learned that caregiving is just a job, a series of tasks I'm paid to perform, as outlined in the client's service plan, a binding care contract addressing everything from dietary constraints, to med schedules, to toiletry preferences. Sometimes, that's a lot to remember. Conveniently, the Department of Social and Human Services has devised dozens of helpful mnemonics to help facilitate effective caregiving. To wit:

Ask
Listen
Observe
Help
Ask again

I had a head full of these mnemonics and a crisp certificate when, three days after I completed the course, the Department of Social and Human Services lined me up an interview with my first potential client, Trevor Conklin, who lives on a small farm at the end of a long rutty driveway between Poulsbo and Kingston, where they do something with horses — breed them, sell them, board them. All I really know is, that Trevor is a nineteen-year-old with MS. Or maybe it's ALS. Something with a wheelchair.

I've got one more cash advance left on the old Providian Visa before I'm cashing out the IRA, which will only yield about fifteen hundred after penalties. For a year and a half after the disaster, I didn't even look for work. All told, I can hold out another month before I'm completely sunk. I need this job. My last job interview was eleven years ago, before Piper was born, at the *Viking Herald*, a weekly gazette devoted primarily to Scandinavian heritage, pet adoptions, and police blotters. The *Herald* was hiring an ad sales rep at the time — a telemarketing gig, basically. I met with the head of sales in his office at the ass end of new business park on the edge of town. Right away I forgot his name. Wayne. Warren. Walter. Not so much a salesman as a miscast folk singer, someone you might find strumming "Tom Dooley" in the shadow of a cotton-candy stand on a boardwalk somewhere.

"Have you ever sold anything?" he asked me.

"Muffins," I told him.

I didn't get the job.

This morning, I'm wearing one of the button-down shirts my estranged wife, Janet, bought me five years ago when it looked as though I'd finally be rejoining the workforce. Never happened. We got pregnant with Jodi instead.

I arrive at the farm nine minutes early, just in time to see whom I presume to be one of my job competitors waddle out the front door and down the access ramp in sweat pants. She squeezes herself behind the wheel of a rusty Datsun and sputters past me up the bumpy driveway, riding low on the driver's side. The sweatpants bode well, and even with three missing hubcaps, my Subaru looks better than that crappy Datsun.

The walkway is muddy. The ramp is long like a gallows. I'm greeted at the door by a silver-eyed woman roughly my own age, maybe a few years older. She stands tall and straight as an exclamation point, in bootleg jeans and a form-fitting cotton work shirt. She's coaxed her flaxen hair into an efficient bun at the back of her head.

"You must be Benjamin," she says. "I'm Elsa. Come in. Trevor's still brushing his teeth."

She leads me through the darkened dining room to the living room, where a tray table on wheels and a big-screen TV dominate the landscape. She offers me a straight-backed chair and seats herself across from me on the sofa next to the reclining figure of an enormous brown cat showing no signs of life.

"Big cat," I say.

"He's a little testy — but he's a good ratter." She pets the cat, who bristles immediately. She strokes it until it hisses. Undaunted, she forges on until the beast begins to purr. I like this woman. She's tough. Forgiving. The kind that sticks it out when the going gets rough.

"My neighbor has a cat," I offer.

"What a coincidence," she says. "So, tell me, do you have any other clients?"

"Not at the moment."

"But you have experience caregiving, right?"

"Not professionally."

She's unable to suppress a sigh. Poor thing. First the lady in sweatpants, now me.

"But I've worked with kids a lot," I say.

"Professionally?"

"Not exactly."

"Do you have children?"

"No. Not exactly."

She glances at the clock on the wall. "Do you mind if I ask what led you to caregiving?" she says.

"I guess I thought I might be good at it."

"Because . . . ?"

"Because I'm a caring person. I understand people's needs."

"Do you know anything about MD?"

"A little bit."

"And what did you think of the class?"

"Honestly?"

"Honestly."

"I thought it was . . . uh, pretty informative."

"Hmm," she says.

"I mean, a lot of the stuff was common sense, but some of it was pretty eye-opening in terms of, you know . . . just different methods and approaches to . . ." I've lost her.

"Benjamin, I've taken the class," she says.

At last, Trevor wheels into the living room, a good-looking kid in spite of an oily complexion and a severe case of bed head. He's sporting khaki cargoes, a black shirt, and G-Unit low-tops. The disease has left him wafer thin and knobby, slightly hunched, and oddly contorted in his jet black wheelchair.

"Trevor, this is Benjamin."

"You can call me Ben."

He shifts in his seat and angles his head back slightly. "What's up?" he says.

"Not much," I say. "How about you?"

He shrugs.

"Trevor is looking for a provider he can relate to," Elsa explains. "Somebody with similar interests."

"So what kind of stuff are you into?" I say.

His hands are piled in his lap, his head lowered.

"He likes gaming," says Elsa.

"What games?" I say.

"Shooters, mostly," he mumbles.

"Oh, right, like, uh, what's it called — *Mortal Combat*?"

He rears his shoulders back, and hoists up his head, moving like a puppet. "You play?"

"No. A guy on my softball team is always talking about it."

He lowers his head back down.

"Tell Ben about some of your other interests," says Elsa.

The instant she calls me Ben, I feel like I've gained some small bit of ground.

"Yeah, what else are you into?"

Trev shrugs again. "I don't know, not much."

"He likes girls," says Elsa.

"Shut up, Mom," he says. But she's managed to coax him out of his shell. For the first time, he looks me in the eye.

Elsa rises to her feet. "I'll leave you two to get acquainted." And without further comment, she strides across the living room and through the dining room.

After a moment of awkward silence, Trevor whirs closer to his cluttered tray table.

"So," I say. "Girls, huh?"

He casts his eyes down, shyly, and I wish I could take it back. Poor kid. Bad enough he's all twisted in knots — people are always putting him on the spot, pushing him out of his comfort zone, pretending that everything is normal, as though he can just go out and get a girlfriend, ride the Ferris wheel with her, and feel her up in the back of a car. Look at him, staring into his lap, wishing he could disappear, wishing everybody would quit pretending. But it's all just a ruse. Because when he lifts his head again, he swings his chair round clockwise and checks the doorway. Jockeying back around, he smiles and looks at me unflinchingly. There's a glimmer in his eye, a flash of the evil genius, and I understand for the first time that I may be dealing with someone else entirely.

"I'm crippled, not gay," he says. "Of course I like girls."

I check the doorway. "What kind of girls?"

"Any kind," he says. "The kind who want to get with a guy like me."

"You mean because of your . . . because of the wheelchair?"

"I mean because I'm horny. But yeah, that too. Do you have a wife?"

"Not exactly. Well, technically yes, but — long story."

"Is she hot?"

"She's hot."

He leans in conspiratorially. "Would she get with me? Do you think she'd get with me?"

"Uh, well, um . . ."

"I'm joking," he says. "Why do you wanna work for nine bucks an hour, anyway?"

"I'm broke."

"You're gonna stay broke working for DSHS."

"Does this mean I've got the job?"

"Sorry, man," he says. "But I haven't met all the candidates yet. I like you better than the fat lady, though."

CLIMBING INTO MY car after the interview, my hopes are buoyed by the sight of a dented white Malibu bumping down the driveway as another candidate arrives from DSHS. The front bumper is all but dangling. The tabs are expired. The guy behind the wheel has a spiderweb tattoo on his neck.

the pro

NOW, FOUR MONTHS after the interview, I spend anywhere from forty to sixty hours a week with Trev. We're way past the awkward toiletry stage. Beyond the honeymoon stage. I've been Asking, Listening, Observing, Helping, and Asking again for sixteen weeks, a gazillion waffles, eight trips to the shoe store, endless hours of weather-related programming. I passed the burnout stage about three months ago. That's not to say I don't like Trev — I do, tyrannical streak and all. I feel for him.

His father ran off when he was three years old, two months after he was diagnosed. Funny how that works. Trev is currently enrolled in the college of life, though his mom is encouraging him to take community college classes. Elsa ought to wear a cape. She runs the farm sixteen hours a day, makes dinner, cleans house, and still finds quality time for her son. She sleeps about three hours a night, and even then, she's up every half hour to turn Trev.

It's not MS or ALS but Duchenne muscular dystrophy tying Trev in knots, twisting his spine and tightening his joints so that his ribs all but rest on his hips now. His legs are bent up toward his stomach and his feet point downward and his toes curl under, and his elbows are all but locked at his sides. A pretzel with a perfectly healthy imagination. But I'm not going to ennoble Trev just because he's looking death in the eye. Really, what choice does he have? We're all dying, Trev's just dying faster than most. But I've seen faster — a lot faster. The truth is, for the last month or so, at least half the time, I'm downright annoyed that Trev doesn't take more risks, that he willfully imprisons himself inside of his routines, that he consumes life by the measured teaspoon. And for what? So he can milk a few extra years watching the Weather Channel three hours a day, eat a few hundred more flax-seed waffles? Piper should have been so lucky. Jodi should've had such opportunities. Sometimes I want to let Trev have it.

Aren't you tired of doing the same ten things over and over! I want to say. *The waffles, the Weather Channel, the mall and the matinee on Thursday? Don't you ever just want to free yourself from your compulsive routines, and go out in a blaze of glory? Or at least order something besides fish-and-chips every single time we go to the Lobster!*

But of course, I never do these things, or say these things. Because in spite of the burnout, I still cling to my professional credo:

Professional
Reliable
Objective

According to the Fundamentals of Caregiving, Trev doesn't need to know what happened to my daughter or my son or why my wife left me or how I lost my house. Or how I contemplated killing myself as recently as last week but didn't have the guts. My guilt, my self-contempt, my aversion to other people's children, Trev doesn't need to know about any of them. Trev needs only to know that I am here to serve his needs. Try spending sixty hours a week with one person under these circumstances. Everything about him will bug you before long. Once you've recognized all his quirks and idiosyncrasies, once you can predict (or think you can predict) his actions and reactions, he'll start to drive you crazy. Once you're forced to endure his routines time and again, you'll want to strangle him. For instance, Trev's very particular about his shoes. All his pants are khaki cargoes and all his shirts are identical black tees with a left-breast pocket (which is annoying in itself). Even his boxers are an identical royal blue, as though by dressing the same every day, he might stop the clock or at least sneak a few extra days under the radar. But his shoes are a different matter entirely. He buys a new pair at the mall on the second Thursday of every month and aligns them (that is, I align them) neatly on three shelves running the length of his double closet: footwear for every conceivable occasion. Shoes are a morning ritual. Even before the five pills, the two waffles, the eight-ounce Ensure with the bendable straw, even before the Weather Channel informs him of the weather he's not likely to venture out into.

"What'll it be today?" I'll say.

"I don't know."

This is my cue to start Asking, to start Listening, to start Observing. "What about the white Chucks?" I'll say.

"Nah."

"Black Chucks?"

"Nuh uh."

"Docs?"

"Nah."

"The All Stars?"

"I don't think so."

Round and round we go. I reel them off. He declines them. It's our daily exercise in independence, something I might have done with Piper when she was four years old.

Thursdays are something of a highlight, particularly that hour before the matinee, when we come to the food court at the mall to ogle women. Few spectacles are more conspicuous and ungainly than the masculine figure in crisis. Trev, at least, has youth in his defense. I'm just pathetic, I guess. From our preferred vantage opposite Cinnabon, we objectify, demystify, belittle, and generally marginalize the fair sex, as though we weren't both completely terrified of them.

"Look at the turd-cutter on her," he says, of a poodle-haired blonde in tight jeans. "Would you tap that?"

"In a heartbeat," I say.

Lolling his head to the side, he looks me in the eye. "I'd give her a Gorilla Mask."

"I'd give her a Bulgarian Gas Mask," I counter.

"I'd give her a German Knuckle Cake."

"That's fucked up," I say.

"Thanks," he says. "Should I ask her out for a pizza and a bang?"

"A bang and a pizza."

"How about just a bang?"

"No, trust me, the pizza part is classy."

Poodle Hair breezes by toting two Cajun corn dogs and some curly fries, with a boyfriend trailing in her perfumey wake. They take a table in front of Quiznos and begin eating together silently, as though they've been eating together their whole lives.

"What is she doing with that tool?" says Trev.

I wave them off. "She's probably a psycho."

"Yeah, they're all psychos."

We lapse into silence, and I wish I had a smoke. Strip away our routines, and we are little more than our hypotheticals. Last year, in this same food court, I asked Trev what he'd do if he awoke one morning with all of his muscle functions, which is about as hypothetical as it gets since his condition is progressive and incurable. I was thinking: Climb a mountain, run a marathon, chase a butterfly down a hill. He said: Take a piss standing up.

Poodle Hair and I exchange brief glances. Or maybe I'm imagining it. When I go fishing for a second glance, she is evasive. She's getting cuter by the second. She looks good holding a corn dog. I'm now convinced I could spend the rest of my days beside her. Then we lock gazes. And for one delicious instant there is a spark of possibility. Possibility of what? Of getting my ass kicked by a two hundred pound cuckold? Or more pathetic still, the possibility of being loved again, by anyone?

Now Poodle Hair is whispering something to her boyfriend who lowers his corn dog midbite. I was wrong — he's at least 220. He's staring holes in me. All I can do is look at Trev's checkered Vans and feel the heat of my face.

"What?" says Trev.

"Showtime," I say.

And without further delay, we stand to leave — I stand to leave, anyway, acutely aware of the boyfriend's eyes in my back like daggers.

Trev hunches his shoulders to buttress the weight of his head, clutches his joystick with a knotted hand, and whirs around in a semi-circle, piloting himself toward the exit.

"Regal or Cineplex?"

"Regal," he says.

It's always the Regal.

o-fer

DOING ANYTHING with Trev is slow, no matter how many times we've done it before. There's the matter of the ramp, along with all that buckling and unbuckling, the fact that he's a slow eater, and the fact that he likes to make me wait. But at least we always get a good parking spot. Thursdays are tight for me schedulewise, depending on the movie. Usually, by the time the matinee is over and Trev's had his fish-and-chips, and I drop off the van, I've got just enough time to put on my navy blue sweats with the drawstring and the elastic cuffs, my knee braces, my jersey, my cleats, and my hat.

My softball team hasn't lost a game in three seasons. It helps that we play the same two teams over and over—helps *us*, anyway. Line us up, and we look like any other stooping, paunchy, hobbled men's league roster from here to Casper, Wyoming, but we hit line drives all day long, and our defense is strong up the middle. Me, I can't seem to buy a base hit the last two seasons, not when it counts. Back in the day, I was a line-drive machine. Back when my skin was elastic and I wasn't so soft around the middle, and people used to tell me I looked like Johnny Depp, I played a nifty center field. I was a vortex where fly balls went to die.

Nowadays, the last thing I want to do after a week of caregiving is strap on some cleats and make a spectacle of myself in front of my peers (and worse, their wives and children), by going 0 for 4 against a guy who recently sprained his back making an omelet. But I soldier on for the team. And it is with the same sense of duty that I agree to accompany Forest and a few of the guys to the Grill on game nights to celebrate our victory.

Forest is my best friend. I roomed with him freshman year at the U. Even back in those days, he was gently trying to show me the way. Years later, he was my best man when Janet and I got married.

Forest is about six foot, 230, with big arms and a little bit of a gut in recent years. The crotch of his red sweats is starting to ride uncomfortably high — uncomfortable for everyone involved. We call him the Grape Smuggler because — well, use your imagination. Forest is the backbone of the O-fers. He pitches, bats cleanup, collects the fees, makes all the pregame reminder calls, fills out the lineup card, and is the undisputed (though unspoken) team captain. Few things inspire like watching Forest round third in the late innings with a head full of steam and two bad knees, his spare tire heaving violently beneath his snug jersey, just as the second baseman is fielding the relay.

"Run, Forest, run!" we yell, from the dugout. It never gets old.

Tonight at the Grill, it's cricket. Forest and I against Max and Teo. Max has a mustache of the biker / leather fag variety. We call him Lunch Box because he always brings his hustle. He may not look like a player with his straggly locks and stovepipe legs, but he hits ropes all day long, and though he runs like a man who is angry at the ground, he can actually motor. Pretty good at darts, too. He and Teo are currently smoking us. I'm not helping matters with my short-arm delivery.

"Good darts," Forest says, patting me roughly on the shoulder.

He's lying, of course. I've managed only a single 20, and I've left 17 wide open. Triple 17 used to be my sweet spot. I was money on 20. I've lost my steady hand. Teo is raping us on 17s, and I'm letting Forest down again. But the truth is, it's hard to care for very long. The world flows right through me like a human dribble glass.

I know I should be counting my blessings: Forest, for starters. The guy is solid. Then there's the fact that I get to see a matinee every Thursday for free — how many people can say that? I should be doing my work. I should be plugging those holes, healing myself, filling myself back up like a jug. It's been over two years. But I'm still stuck in that driveway, my arms loaded with groceries, looking back helplessly over my shoulder as my universe implodes.

"Yo, Benjamin," Forest says to me, handing me the darts. "Why don't you focus on bull's-eyes, and I'll work on closing those seventeens?"

"I'm on it," I say.

Having just scored a double bull, Max is grinning like a chimpanzee. I know I'm a loser because I'm always happy for the opponent.

"Good darts," I say to him.

Forest slugs me on the shoulder. "Bear down," he says.

And I do. Adjusting a not-so-snug flight, and tightening a tip, I toe the line and narrow in on the bull's-eye. It actually looks pretty big tonight. I can still see it when I close my eyes. I tell myself I can hit it. Forest is probably telling himself I can hit it, too, but like me, only half believing it. Finally, leaning forward on my right foot, poised like a marksman, I let the first dart fly.

And, well, you can probably guess the rest.

the long way home

On the way back from the Grill, I do what I haven't done in months. I take the long way home. I don't know why I decide to take this backward step tonight of all nights. Maybe because Piper's birthday is approaching. Maybe because I can't bear the apartment tonight — or the *com*partment, as I often refer to it. No matter how many nights I spend in the compartment, it continues to defy the expression "lived in." The place smells of hand soap and new carpet. I eat from paper plates. Nothing new accumulates, no call from the outside world eludes compartmentalization. To the tune of several hundred dollars, I've purchased from Rite Aid hard plastic vessels of every shape and size to contain the bric-a-brac before it spreads. I stack them in the master closet, three and four high. Beneath one of those glacier blue lids, nested like a matryoshka within an envelope, inside of a folder, within a container, you will find my unsigned divorce papers.

Had I gotten shit-housed at the Grill tonight, had I matched Max beer for beer, shot for shot, I probably wouldn't be taking the long way home. But that would've been a backward step, too. Everywhere I step seems to be backward.

The drive home down Agatewood is still so familiar that my muscles know every wooded bend by memory. I could drive this stretch without headlights. Indeed, in those agonizing months following the disaster, after Janet ran off (or rather, walked away), I frequently drove this stretch from the Grill to the house so gooned I might've pissed myself and not known better. Those were the nights without Forest, the nights before serving Trev had imposed any shape back on my life. The other nights I was in Forest's care, too selfish and shortsighted to consider that I was robbing him of his own family. For a year he tried to coax me to dinner at his house. But I always insisted on going out. Nights I spent with Forest were moderate nights by comparison — a few pitchers for distraction, a ball game, a pizza, and yet those occasions are no less blurry. By my count, I lost eighteen months to the blur. Eighteen months in which I could not move myself to seek employment, even as my small nest egg dwindled. Eighteen months in which I may well have been inhabited by somebody else or nobody at all. I participated in hundreds of conversations of which I have no memory. I forgot my birthday. For eighteen months I was awash in a sea of faces, some of them concerned, some frightened, some even repulsed, to which I can attach hardly a single name or context, at least not from where I'm sitting now. I made friends I don't remember, collected numbers without names, made promises based on good intentions that were not my own. My life, if it could be called one, bled mindlessly through the hours like ink on a blotter. It's a miracle I didn't start smoking again.

There's somebody living in the place now, finally. For over a year after the foreclosure, the house stood vacant, and that doesn't happen around here, even in a slumping market. You'd think the place was haunted all those months. But not anymore. It's a home again, that much is clear. There's a jungle gym in the side yard, which I can just make out by the ghostly light seeping from the upstairs bedroom. The old greenhouse is gone. Piper's bottle tree is gone. The tenants have erected a cedar fence between the driveway and the ledge, a great big sturdy thing. They've planted boxwood to obscure it. How can I help but wonder how things might've been different had I erected such a fence? But the truth is, I was remiss in so many other ways the fence is irrelevant.

And what was I thinking in that instant just before the world went icy black, as I strode toward the front door irritably beneath my mountain of groceries? That the ice cream was melting? That if I hurried, I'd still have time to put away the groceries, take a shower, and preheat the oven before *Iron Chef*? That I wished like hell the kids would go to bed early, so I could have twenty minutes and a beer to myself before Janet got home? Maybe I was thinking about those hundred feet of waterfront on Discovery Bay. Thinking about buying a skiff. What thought so consumed me in that moment, what matter was of such pressing importance in my life, that I could be so absent? And the answer is: I don't remember.

The car is still idling. I see that a light has come on in the foyer, and now a face peers out the window at me. I pull away from the curb slowly, resisting the urge to look back.

adventures in cartography

On Fridays, Trev and I work on the map for ninety minutes. The map was my idea. It was inspired by one of those "America's back roads" type of travel channel shows where the host goes to some rotting seaside burg and learns how saltwater taffy is made, or he travels to some dark hollow in Appalachia where the hoecake was invented. Except in this particular show, they went to places like the Two Story Outhouse, in Gays, Illinois (alternatively known as "the Double Dumper"), or the Spam Museum in Austin, Minnesota, or the Wonder Tower in Genoa, Colorado. The host, with his overactive eyebrows and tall hair, was impossibly irritating, but the unique destinations made the show worth watching. You wouldn't believe what's out there. They've got an actual stuffed jackalope in Wyoming. There's a Virgin Mary in a stump in Salt Lake City. Liberace's ghost is haunting an overpriced Italian restaurant in Vegas. The town of Bedrock actually exists. Yabba-dabba-doo!

We started the map early in the spring, as a sort of survey of North American roadside attractions, from double dumpers (of which we've cataloged no less than sixteen) to Hitler's stamp collection, which purportedly resides in Redmond, Oregon. I suspect the ongoing project appeals to Trev for the same reason that the Weather Channel appeals to him; it's an opportunity to note conditions he will never experience himself. We've devoted the better part of a living room wall to our AAA road map, which Rick down at Kitsap Reprographics was kind enough to enlarge by 400 percent for us in spite of certain copyright infringements — and at a nifty price, too. People will do most anything for a guy in a wheelchair as long as he doesn't have food in his beard. Working on the map means a lot of Googling and pushpins. Of course, I, being of fine digital health, do all the Googling and pinning. Trev delegates like a field general from his wheelchair. Lately, we've been focusing our survey on Muffler Men. We've cataloged over four hundred of these giant fiberglass humanoid relics coast to coast. They are a diverse lot from Loggers, to Vikings, to Cowboys, to Indians, to a former Big Boy in Malibu who's been made over into a Mexican, complete with serape and burrito platter.

To keep track of everything, we use a color-coding system. Muffler Men are red. Museums are blue. Mystery houses, vortexes, crop circles, and other unexplained phenomenon are green. Dead celebrity parts (Einstein's brain, Napoleon's johnson, etc.) are black. Everything else is yellow — this would include anything from ghost towns to two-headed farm animals, to Thomas Edison's last breath, which, technically speaking, should probably be cataloged as a dead celebrity part. Somewhere behind all of this pinning and mapping, there lingers the vaguest of notions that we will someday visit some of these places. Needless to say, it'll never happen and we both know it. The map is just another exercise in hope. Next comes the slow, steady deferral of that hope over the coming months.

After we conclude our mapping for the day, Trev whirs to the bathroom, urinates into his plastic vessel for what seems like an inordinate period of time, whereupon I dump his pee (which is invariably too yellow by my estimation), flush the toilet, rinse the jug out, and replace it on the counter. This I do efficiently and respectfully, like a waitress, in strict adherence to my sensitivity training. I do not stand by tapping my foot as he struggles to liberate his dingus after I've unzipped his fly. I do not say things like *Gee, you really had to take a squirt,* or *Why does it dribble out so slow?* or *Try not to get any on the rim.* I do not grimace when I wash the vessel, nor do I wrinkle my nose on those occasions when he's evacuated his bowels and I must clean him with baby wipes, as he leans helplessly forward with his face buried in my inner thigh for support. This is my job. I'm a pro.

From the bathroom we move on to the Weather Channel, where our host, a chubby blonde with a Rachel cut and big hooters, informs us that it's not a good day to be wearing flannel in Charleston, that

Portlanders might consider carrying an umbrella this afternoon, and to "think layers" if you live San Francisco. Meanwhile, out the window, the clouds are burning off, and I have no idea what the temperature is.

"I'd hit that," Trev observes, matter-of-factly.

Trev is a hopeless chubby chaser, as I once was, before Janet broke the mold. Maybe it's because he's withering away to nothing — he was 103 pounds at his last checkup. Whatever the case, he likes his women generously proportioned.

Trev flashes an evil-genius grin. "She'll go crazy for my Big Mac cologne."

"You'll know it's over when she starts singing."

And so the hours pass. When I first started working for Trev, he whiled away these same afternoon hours with his wheelchair two feet in front of the computer, gaming online at full volume. First-person shooters. I used to sit on the couch with the cat in my lap and watch stupidly, marveling at the bloodbath. Or try to read Edith Wharton in spite of the racket. Now and then, I'd sneak a little one-eyed nap. But then a couple months ago, Trev's digital functions started deteriorating rapidly. Imagine somebody putting screws through your finger joints and tightening them one turn at a time until your fingers can no longer move. Gaming suddenly became an exercise in frustration for Trev. The more he played the game, the less proficient he became. Finally, he hung up his joystick (threw it away, in point of fact) and turned his attention to the weather. Lately, I've noticed that even the TV remote is giving him problems. To change channels, he has to contort in his wheelchair with his head lolling heavily to one side and his forearms dangling out in front of him like a tyrannosaurus. The remote looks as though it weighs ten pounds.

Now more than ever, as his fingers turn to stone and his heart weakens, I want to push Trev to new places — if not to the American back road, then at least to Quiznos for a change of pace.

"You wanna go to Quiznos and get a sub?"

"Not today."

"What about IHOP? They've got waffles."

"Nah."

"Mitzel's?"

"No."

"Mickey D's?"

He's stony silent. My pushing annoys him. It makes him uncomfortable. I can tell by a slight flush in his face as he rears his big head back toward the Weather Channel, where he leaves it until it stops bobbling. He stares straight ahead as the color continues to suffuse his cheeks.

I want to say KFC. God, I want to say KFC.

But I don't. As it stands now, he will exact his revenge in some trivial way by defying my will to push him into new places. Maybe he'll send his message by shrinking our world still further. Maybe there will be no matinee next Thursday, no food-court gazing, no fish-and-chips. Maybe next Thursday we will sit right here in the living room and watch storm systems gather along the Gulf Coast while Trev eats waffles. Could it be because we both know he's stuck with me, and that quality care is hard to find at nine bucks an hour, that I push him so? Do I make it my business to force Trev's hand daily because I care about him deeply or because it vexes me that he refuses to live when Piper and Jodi no longer have the chance? I suspect it's neither, but because I know that no matter how safe one plays it, no matter how one tries to minimize risk, to shelter oneself or one's charge from the big bad world outside, accidents will happen.

any other day

June 12, 2007, begins like pretty much any other day in the Benjamin household. Toilets flushing, footsteps up and down the carpeted stairs, Buster scratching at the door to get out.

Janet's running late for surgery. She'd skip breakfast if I let her.

"Have you seen the keys to the Jetta?" she calls down.

"Check in your coat pocket!"

Piper pads into the kitchen in slippers, the hem of her bright red cape dragging on the linoleum. Yes, my child is wearing a cape — this is not unusual. Her hair is in a sleepy jumble. But already she's bright-eyed at 7:45 a.m. During the school year, I had her up at 6:10 every morning, and she was a trouper.

"Jodi's got a runny nose," she announces.

On cue, Jodi rumbles into the kitchen barefoot, every inch a boy, despite the grief I've taken for giving him a "girl's" name. I should have named him Sylvester the Cat, to hear him talk. I can't understand a word he says. Without Piper, his communications would be lost on all of us.

"Squish-squish-squishity-squish," he says.

"He wants cereal," Piper explains.

"Too late," I say, skillet in hand. "Besides, we're out."

"You were right," says Janet, dropping the keys in her purse as she strides into the kitchen.

I corral them all around the breakfast table and dish them up just as the toaster pops. Piper promptly refuses to eat her eggs on the grounds of runniness, and Jodi begins feeding Buster his faux bacon.

"Jodi, stop that," I say.

"Buxuxer," he says, grinning out from beneath his mountain of curly hair.

I plate the toast and set it on the table.

"Pretty crummy weather for summer," says Piper.

"It'll burn off," I say.

"That's what you always say."

Janet sips her grapefruit juice and nibbles briskly around the edges of her unbuttered toast, as she scrolls through the *Times*.

"Daddy, can I have yogurt instead?" says Piper.

"Fine," I say. "Just put the plate by the sink. And don't give your bacon to Buster. He'll poop on the floor."

Jodi laughs, and snot runs out his nose. "Poop poop," he says, then something else jumbled I can't understand. When do we start talking about a speech pathologist?

Piper carries her plate to the sink, lobbing Buster some bacon on the sly.

"Do you have to read at the table?" I say to Janet.

"You're right," Janet says, pushing the paper aside, even as she finishes reading her sentence.

"Thank you," I say.

She glances at the clock, takes a courtesy bite of her eggs. "So, what are you doing today?" she says, though I'm pretty sure I already went over it with her last night in bed. I suspect she's just making conversation so she doesn't seem like she's in a hurry to leave.

"Taking the kids to your mom and dad's."

"Leaving them there?"

"Just visiting."

"Are you shopping?"

"Yeah, afterward."

"Don't forget Kleenex."

"I won't."

"What about the rest of your day?"

"Probably not much. Maybe go to the park if there's time."

"Sounds nice," she says.

"What's that supposed to mean?"

"It's not supposed to mean anything. It just sounds nice."

"You know, you're welcome to stay at home, Janet. I am employable, you know. At least marginally."

"I didn't mean anything by it."

"Well, I sort of resent the implication that my life is easy just because I'm not performing colon surgery on a shih tzu."

"It's a Lab. And it's intestinal."

"This is not as easy as it looks, Janet. Especially not when Jodi is sick, and Piper is home, and —"

"I know how hard you work, Ben. I didn't mean anything. You're just being defensive."

She's right. I've been defensive for weeks — ever since she found me sleeping on the job a couple of Fridays back. She came home for a surprise lunch and caught me snoozing on the sofa with my fly unzipped, a half gallon of Rocky Road in my clutches, and a Cat Stevens CD skipping. In my own defense, I was exhausted. Jodi hardly slept the night before. It wasn't a big deal, and anyway, I was only asleep for a minute. Piper was still at school. And Jodi wasn't farther than four feet away, sequestered in his Pack 'n Play. I'm not even sure Janet saw me sleeping, or if she just thought I was lounging. I think it was more that Jodi was chewing on the nail clippers that got to her. She didn't say anything about any of it, but I felt her disapproval. A couple days later, she found my weed pipe in the gardening shed and accused me of being developmentally arrested.

"What do you mean?"

"I mean, you're sitting around smoking pot and eating ice cream and listening to Cat Stevens, Ben. Isn't that what you did in college?"

"I didn't eat ice cream in college. And I'm not sitting around," I explained.

"Daddy, can I show Grandpa my rat, today?" Piper says, peeling back the seal on her peach yogurt.

"Wait until Grandpa and Nanny come over, sweetie," says Janet.

"But I asked Daddy, not you," she pleads.

"Your mom's right, honey. We can't bring the cage with us in the car. We need to go to the store afterward."

"I asked *you*, not Mommy," Piper says. "How come Mommy's always right?"

"She's not," I say.

"Well, whenever she talks first, you always say the same thing as her. Like an echo or something."

Janet chuckles.

Sometimes it feels as though there's a conspiracy afoot.

crossing the line

Elsa is made of impressive metal. She is resigned to her grief, breath by breath, day by day. Meanwhile, it is the suddenness of my own that has left me reeling. I crave Elsa's strength, her resolve, the shelter of her self-assurance. I'm convinced I could love her, with her sad clear eyes, her starched work shirts, and the scent of timothy and manure that trails in her wake.

Two of her lessons have canceled, so she's at home this morning, sweeping the kitchen, folding laundry, and emptying wastebaskets while Trev sleeps with the door closed and the baby monitor beside him on the nightstand. When I hear Elsa filling the sink and stacking dishes, I leave my post on the sofa and, without asking, station myself beside her at the sink. Sunlight floods the kitchen from the east, so I can see the downy hair of Elsa's face, otherwise invisible. In silence, she washes, I dry. I could stand all morning in this square of light. Now and again, I look up from my plate or my dish or my mug to sneak a sidelong glance at Elsa squinting into the sun. It feels good to be standing next to somebody, hip to hip, almost touching. After years of being climbed on, and jostled, tugged at and embraced, I am needy. I ache for human touch, if only the graze of an elbow.

"You can only push him so far before he starts pushing back," she says.

My scalp tightens. She's caught me totally off guard. I'm not sure if the statement is an observation or a reprimand.

"I learned the hard way," she explains. "The way I learned everything else. Do yourself a favor, Ben, and use a little finesse."

"I . . . It's . . ."

"You don't need to explain yourself," she says. "Just take my advice — it'll make the job easier. For everyone." Her tone is not critical but matter-of-fact.

"Thanks," I say. "You're absolutely right."

"You're welcome."

She likes me. She wants me to stick around. And who knows, maybe not just for Trev's sake. "I guess that's true of everybody, right?" I say. "Push them too far, and they'll push back?"

"Some people absorb better than others," she says. "When you're a parent, you learn to absorb."

She's left me no choice but to tell her the truth. "Elsa, look, there's something I . . . In the interview when you asked if I had any . . ."

"I know," she says.

"About . . . ?"

"Yes. Word travels fast." She fixes her eyes on the murky dishwater, scrubbing absently beneath the surface. "I'm sorry, Ben. Very sorry." Then she turns and looks up at me, squinting in the sunlight. And before she can say another word, I seize her about the waist with both hands and pull her toward me. Instantly, the world turns to ice as Elsa tears herself free of my clutches, glowering. It's tough to say what all is written in her expression as she backs away from me across the kitchen, but surely there is a hint of ambivalence. She can't look me in the eye.

"I think you better go home for the day," she says.

"I . . ."

"Please," she says, just as the baby monitor squawks out Trev's summons.

the whistle stop

When Elsa encounters me in the kitchen the next morning, she is business as usual, starched work shirt, efficient bun, tack bag in hand.

"I may be a little late today," she says. "Can you stay until six?"

"Of course," I say. And I can only marvel at her capacity to move on.

I'm mid-crossword when Trev calls me to the bedroom two hours early. Assuming he needs to be turned, I peel back the blankets to reveal his wasted figure, which fails to stir as the cold air greets it.

"I'm ready to get up," he says.

"Bathroom?"

"Just up."

His curtness makes me think he knows. Suddenly, I don't want to lose this job. I begin to dress him on the bed, beginning with his gold-toed socks. When I've managed to wrestle his cargo pants up around his knees, I hoist him out of bed and prop him on my elevated knee, and with one hand I work the pants the remainder of the way up before nesting him in his wheelchair.

"White Chucks today," he announces, even before we've assumed our post in front of the double closet. "High-tops."

Chucks are shallow-bottomed and narrow shoes. Which also makes me think Trev knows about my pass at his mom, because Chuck high-tops are a pain in the ass to put on, and he knows it. The high-tops need to be unlaced most of the way to accommodate his gnarled feet. They can't be comfortable with his buckled toes and high arches.

"Would you do Charlize Theron?" he inquires, much to my relief.

"Duh."

"What about in *Monster*?"

"Oof. No way," I lie.

By the time we move to the kitchen, I know I'm in the clear. I'm about to uncap his Ensure and pop his frozen waffles in the toaster when he catches me off guard once more.

"Let's go out to breakfast," he says. "I'll buy."

He must know. Either he heard us, or Elsa told him. He never buys, except for the matinee, and that's his mom's money. Suddenly, it occurs to me that Trev may be conducting me to the neutral confines of a restaurant for the purpose of firing me. But then who will drive him home?

"You pick the place," he says.

And so, after three Digitek and two Enalapril, a morning piss, a brushing of the teeth (his, not mine), and two swipes of deodorant under each arm, we make for the van, where I lower the ramp somberly and buckle Trev into place as one might secure a piece of rented power equipment.

Forced to choose, I pick the ancient diner downtown for my last meal as a caregiver, the one that looks like an old Airstream splashed with neon.

"Listen," I say as we bump up the driveway. "About yesterday . . ."

"My mom already told me."

"She did?"

"As long as it's just allergies, I'm not worried," he says.

A warm sense of relief washes over me. "So, uh, why are we going out to breakfast, anyway?"

"I fucking hate those waffles. They taste like cardboard."

"For real?"

"My mom makes me eat them. They're healthy as shit."

"Ahhhh."

He bobbles his head toward the side window. Still, I can see in the mirror the suggestion of a grin playing on the corners of his mouth. "Fucking flaxseed goes through me like birdshot."

"Ah man, why didn't you say anything? I could've made you something else on the sly — smuggled you some Frosted Flakes or whatever."

Craning his torso to one side, Trev does his best to wave the subject off, offering a little flipper motion with his right hand.

The Whistle Stop is so packed that the windows are fogging up. The tiny parking lot is at capacity but for the disabled spot. Unfortunately, a black Escalade is spilling over into the ramp clearance, so I'm forced to leave the van idling in the middle of the lot as I crawl around undoing the four buckles, circle the car, and lower the ramp, making Trev's entrance all the grander as the platform eases him gently onto the wet pavement. It's an entrance worthy of Queen Victoria. A few curious diners have pressed their faces to the window. On the pavement, Trev whips a three-point turn and waits off to the side in the rain as I raise the ramp, circle the van, and guide it in the handicapped spot, leaving a loogie on the driver's door of the Escalade, as is my custom when somebody blocks the ramp clearance.

No sooner do we reach the entrance than I note the three cement steps and the absence of a disabled ramp.

"What the fuck?" I say.

Our predicament is not lost on the proprietor, a morbidly obese gentleman in a white apron with a film of sweat on his forehead visible from thirty feet. Just as Trev is whirring a one eighty, and I'm mentally preparing myself to jockey the van around, he rushes from behind the counter, waving madly at us, and drawing to our little drama the further attention of his patrons, who are now as attentive as any Greek chorus.

Bursting through the glass door, the fat man huffs and puffs as he beckons us back with his spatula. "Come! Come! Around back!"

Here we have no choice but to oblige. We circle the shiny structure and arrive at the back door between two Dumpsters, where the fat man greets us urgently.

"Just one little one," he says, indicating the single cement step.

Before anyone can object, the services of the dishwasher have been employed to lift, and Trev finds himself hefted wheelchair and all, rotated, tilted, and generally finessed like an oversized sofa through the narrow doorway. Slightly unnerved but safely on the ground, he whirs past a stupefied line cook and through the kitchen, where he appears to the diners as a severed head gliding smoothly across the countertop.

By the time we emerge from the kitchen into the dining room, we are nothing less than a curiosity. People are craning their necks. The waitress and the busboy are clearing a booth furiously to accommodate us. Obviously, Trev's not going to fit in a booth; thus his place is being set on the end of the table, where his wheelchair will occupy the better part of the narrow aisle, creating a clusterfuck for not only the waitstaff but anyone who wants to use the john. Adeptly, with a series of clicks and lurches, Trev finesses himself into these tight quarters. Almost instantly, a curious toddler in a baby blue onesie attaches himself to the back of Trev's chair, where he begins exploring the hydraulic guts of the thing with chubby fists. Soon he is rooting around by the battery compartment.

I can't tell who the child belongs to. "Psst," I say. "Get lost, kid."

But the boy is only encouraged by my attention. The little fellow is pretty excited, goggle-eyed and bubbling at the mouth. He's got a tiny yellow bruise on his forehead, where no doubt his curious wanderings have met an abrupt end against a table edge or some other obstacle.

The toddler has now moved onto the tactile mysteries of the back right wheel. Trev, who is amused rather than annoyed by the attention, struggles to crane his neck in order to investigate matters, but his body won't allow it. He is smiling nonetheless. The instant he rests his gnarled hand on the joystick, before I hear the mechanical click, I see the darkness descend, though I'm powerless to utter a sound. In a chilling flash the toddler is screaming not eighteen inches from Trev's ear, and still Trev can't see why or even where precisely the child is situated. He looks utterly helpless and confused as he backs his wheelchair up still farther with a click, whereupon the child's caterwaul reaches a bloodcurdling crescendo. People are converging on us in a terrible instant. Somebody's got coffee on their breath. Trev's wheelchair is jostled and wrenched carelessly about, and finally it's jerked off its right wheel to liberate the screaming toddler, who appears to be in one piece, though still terrified by his own vulnerability, as he is swept up in his mother's arms. I want to berate her for not paying attention, for letting her child wander into peril's way, for causing all of this.

Goddamnit, you can't take your eyes off. Not for a second.

Poor Trev is mortified, his oily face has gone as red as a stop sign. I'm glad that he has diverted his gaze, so he doesn't have to see the scowl on the mother's face.

"Watch your kid," I snarl.

profiles

According to Janet's Facebook, she is currently "cooking eggplant Parmesan and listening to John Prine."

Her networks are Portland, Oregon, and Oregon Metro Zoo. Her status is "in a relationship," though it should say "married," because I still haven't signed the papers.

Somebody named Jim Sunderland has tagged her in a note.

Somebody named Polly has written on her wall: "Yeah, I know what you mean. Those are the worst."

Yesterday Janet "lit a candle that smelled like orange blossoms."

She "liked" Jim Sunderland's status update.

She became a fan of Jane Goodall.

She wrote on Jim Sunderland's wall, and Jim wrote back: "You're on, but only if I get a head start."

Who the fuck is Jim Sunderland? He sounds like a real-estate agent. All I know at this point is that he wears glasses, has good teeth, and looks a few years older than me. He's verging on handsome, I guess, in a beady-eyed way. But he looks like an NPR listener. He looks like he'd bore you at a party. I can just tell he's one of those laid-back people with hidden agendas. One of those mild people who simmers beneath the surface. A fucking little prick who preys on vulnerable women. I want to write on his wall "Fuck you, Jim! You big fucking phony!"

But I don't. Instead, I friend him.

And what will Jim Sunderland think of me when he views my profile? It's doubtful he'll mistake me for Johnny Depp. Jim will see that I have no status, no network, and that I haven't cooked anything or lit any scented candles in months. He will see that nobody writes on my wall except Forest, who posts things like: "You okay? Give me a call,"

"Remember what I told you," and "When are you going to update your profile?"

Janet looks good in her most recent photos. She's aged about the eyes, and her smile looks as though it takes some effort. But her color is good and she's managed to maintain a certain radiance. I guess that makes her a survivor. In an album titled "Cannon Beach," I find pictures of Janet on the beach with Jim Sunderland and a ten-year-old kid so hopelessly plain-looking I can't even tell if it's a boy or a girl. Whatever it is, the kid is doomed by the Jim Sunderland gene. Doomed to be unremarkable. Who's to say that the world wouldn't be better off without his kid instead of mine?

Not three minutes have elapsed before Jim Sunderland has accepted my friend request. Things are even worse than I thought. Jim is currently "listening to Strauss II and drinking Sauvignon Blanc."

Jesus, Janet, what were you thinking?

Jim's networks are Portland, Oregon, Portland Metro Zoo, and UC Irvine Alum. He is a fan of Powell's Books and Koko the Gorilla.

He belongs to the groups *This American Life* (I knew it!) and John Prine.

Jim's friend confirmation arrives in concert with a message: "Do I know you?"

"No, we haven't met. I'm just a fellow Irvine Alum and fan of Strauss, especially the waltzes."

How long before Jim realizes we have one mutual friend — Janet — and begins making connections? How long before he realizes I don't know anything about Strauss except what I learned in three accordion lessons when I was thirteen?

Now Jim IMs me: "Go Anteaters! LOL. Have you heard Wein Weib and Gesang by the Vienna Boys Choir?"

Boys choir? This guy gets creepier by the minute. "Haven't heard that version, I'll have to check it out."

"Do. It's transcendent."

Transcendent? Who talks that way? What the fuck is Janet doing with this guy? And who does he think he's fooling with all his transcendent bullshit, anyway? I know he's a heartless little fucker deep down. *I fucking see you, Jim! You're not fooling me with your Bordeaux wines and your boys choir bullshit!* And if Janet were awake enough to see you through the splintered glass of her broken life, she'd recognize you, too.

"Fuck you, Jim!" I want to type. "You little fucking prick!"

But I don't have the guts to post it.

pins and needles

Trev is back on waffles. Our recent dining disaster has probably set us back months. I can hardly blame him for not wanting to venture out into a world that refuses to cooperate. Pushing pins into a map is so much easier. We like to tell ourselves that we might someday actually make Livermore, California, our destination, for that is where we would find the world's longest continuously burning lightbulb. Or maybe we'd keep driving south to Monrovia to see the Wizard of Bras. Or maybe we'd go for broke and head clear to Smithfield, Virginia, to see the World's Oldest Cured Ham, which from all reports is quite impressive and looks like a petrified gunnysack.

It's ninety-four degrees in Orlando. Seventy-one in Minneapolis. Today we learn how to make pineapple chutney. Today we learn how to upholster an ottoman. We learn more about Richie Sambora from E! Entertainment than we care to know. Once you surrender to this routine there are certain comforts. To wit, Rachael Ray is cute but not so cute that it's impossible to imagine being with her, and the fact that her arms are a little chunky and she's carrying a little pooch above the waistline makes her all the more real. There's a certain comfort in knowing that the Ottoman Empire survives, if only to rest our feet on. With double Doppler and round-the-clock coverage, even the weather is predictable. And it's good to know that Richie Sambora is still out there, because it means there's hope for me. But where is the comfort for Trev? Sit Rachael Ray naked in his lap, and what could he do with her? Try giving a Bulgarian Gas Mask when you can't even stand up. Maybe ten years ago he could've propped his legs on an ottoman. While Richie Sambora is pushing fifty and still banging Heather Locklear the last time I checked, Trev may not see twenty-five. Trev's life is subtraction. At twenty, he's aging in reverse. It's only a matter of time before he's helpless as an infant once more, and slicing his waffles into thirty-six pieces will no longer be enough. Eventually somebody will have to feed him the forkfuls. And yet what choice does he have but to mark the time?

Around two, our routine is interrupted by the ringing of Trev's cell phone. Retrieving the phone from the nylon pouch near his arm rest is no simple task for Trev, and it's frustrating as hell to watch. But watch I must, for nowhere is it outlined in our service plan that I should answer his phone. It is among those tasks, technically speaking, that he can still perform on his own. In this way, I am helping Trev help himself — simply by sitting on my ass.

For leverage, Trev is forced to arch his back and roll his head to one side and lean slightly forward before he can go fishing in his pouch with his inflexible right arm. Once he's got a purchase on the phone, it dangles precariously in his clutches as he raises it to his ear like a human steam shovel. Trev hates talking on the phone. And watching the way he's forced to bow his spine and loll his head to execute the task, it's easy to see why. Everybody understands this implicitly, so nobody calls Trev unless it's a logistical matter of some import. Nobody but his dad. The timing of his father's calls adheres to no schedule or routine, which further irritates Trev. That his father does not know enough about Trev to accommodate his need for structure is irritating even to me. Trev could easily ignore these calls — he's got caller ID. But he seems to savor these opportunities to make his father work. What's more, he even seems to savor my audience.

"Hello?" he says, as though he doesn't know who's calling.

"Oh, it's you," he deadpans.

And from there it is a stilted and awkward dance, all the more so because I am witness to only one side of the conversation — and it's the mostly silent side. I can only imagine — as the cat sleeps curled in my lap, and Hurricane Dean sweeps silently across the screen in satellite — that his father's part consists of false starts and errant stabs at small talk, inquiries into whether Trev got this message or that, whether he ate turkey for Thanksgiving, whether it's humid in western Washington. And when his inquiries attempt to delve deeper into Trev's life — yielding nothing but the most cursory yes or no answers — he is forced to share the details of his own life in Salt Lake City.

Meanwhile, Trev's end of the conversation consists of little more than the occasional withering commentary on his father's failures, jagged remarks along the lines of "Well, that figures" or "Hmph, that's a first" or "What did you expect?" And who can blame him? How dare a father deign to engender intimacy from halfway across the country with a child he forsook. How dare he grope around in the dark years after the fact, grasping for forgiveness. How dare he wish to undo what can't be undone.

bernard and ruth

My real father, Benjamin Benjamin Sr., sired me at the venerable age of sixty-two. He died of natural causes two years before I dropped out of college. He was the father who threw the football underhanded, when he threw it at all. He was the father so far removed from the cultural currency of the day, so oblivious to the pulse of all things immediate, that you could smoke pot or steal his liquor or have sex right under his nose. I always believed that this ignorance was willful, that he chose not to notice, that my father looked upon me as though I were some baffling new technology he wanted no part of, something he stubbornly ignored, like call waiting. It's not that I didn't love my father. The fact is, I hardly knew him. I probably had more heart-to-hearts with my high school gym teacher than with my dad.

Not until I married Janet did I get a taste of the sort of fatherly propriety for which I'd always secretly yearned. Her father, Bernard, has been a revelation, with his smiling eyes and shoulder squeezes, and hair-mussing affections. For eleven years now, he's called me son. I blush to think how much I enjoy this familiarity, how right it feels to be claimed by Bernard, to recline in the den beside him on blustery Sunday afternoons in the fall, with the wind rattling the panes and the central heating rumbling up through our slippered feet, sipping scotch (a drink I normally hate) and watching football (a sport I normally hate) and talking about things that normally don't interest me: the economy, history, civil engineering. What matters is that sitting beside Bernard, I belong. In my hopelessly romanticized conception, our sequestered Sunday afternoons have the weight and substance of presidential summits. Our manly forays seem all the more momentous because of the life buzzing all around us outside that den, the plenitude that surrounds us: Janet and her mother happily engaged preparing a feast, Piper thumping up and down the carpeted stairs, squealing with laughter. Jodi howling with delight from his playpen at the bottom of the stairwell. The smell of ham hanging so thick and tangy in the air that you can taste it. The clink of silver, the ease of our own unhurried voices marking the hours. Surrounded by such bounty, it is impossible not to feel like a man of consequence.

Today, of course, it's just the kids and me going to visit Bern and Ruth. Janet is probably elbow deep in a Lab's intestinal tract. Great day for it—the visit, I mean. As I predicted, the marine layer has burned off, and the afternoon promises to be mild and the sky blue. On the drive over, Jodi fidgets in his car seat, garbling away, while Piper is too busy sulking about her rat to translate any of it.

It's 11:37 a.m. by the dash when we roll up the driveway. Ruth is working in the front garden. She removes her gloves as she walks to greet us, brimming with grandmotherly delight. Trailing her red cape, Piper jumps out to greet Grandma, leaving me to unbuckle Jodi, who is kicking his legs spastically.

"Squishity-squish, Na-nana," he says, pushing his way past me, and rumbling out the door toward Nanny.

"How are you, darling?" Ruth says to me, as Jodi clutches her.

"I'm good, thanks."

"I'm so glad. And how is Janet?"

"She's great. Busy."

"Well, that's good. Bernard's in back," she says. "Tying those stupid contraptions. Frankly, I'm sick and tired of vacuuming the darn things up. And I'm terrified the kids are going to step on one. Or the cat's going to eat one. I've been telling him he should look into model making, but he complains he can't do it outside. Well, I'm not convinced. Would you like me to bring you back something to drink?"

"No, thanks."

"Oh, darling, I've got an entire pitcher of Arnold Palmers, and you know the kids will only drink lemonade."

"That'd be great," I say.

"What about a sandwich?"

"I'm good, thanks."

"Bernard has a sandwich at noon — let me make you a sandwich."

"Honestly, Ruth, I'm not that — "

"No, really, Ben. It's no trouble. I'll make you a sandwich, and you can just nibble on it."

"You know, a sandwich would be great."

"You kids come inside," she says. And without need of further persuasion, she spirits them away, no doubt to the kitchen.

I find Bernard in the backyard, under the umbrella, tying flies, his newest obsession (though I've never known him to fish). Mostly, I think, he just dreams of fishing and enjoys the busy work with his hands. So he ties flies and gives them names: Horse Hair Special. Belle of the Ball. Green Skunk Butt #5. Ask him what they're good for: "Beats me," he'll say. "They look like insects, though, don't they?"

Some of his finished flies wind up dangling from his fishing hat. I have no idea what happens to the rest of them — those that don't go the way of the vacuum cleaner. There's a little pile of them on the side table next to his untouched Arnold Palmer and his ancient transistor radio. He's listening to the M's pregame show.

"Ahoy, Bernard," I say, lowering myself into a padded Adirondack.

"Sit down, Ben," he says.

"Afternoon game, huh?"

"Chicago."

"What's that you're tying?"

"Haven't named her yet."

"How do you know it's a she?"

"Good question."

Ruth must've sprinted from the kitchen, because already she's arrived with my Arnold Palmer. She clutches the half-full pitcher, signaling me to drink up.

"I need the pitcher," she explains. "You too," she says to Bern, who sets his fly aside with a sigh to take a long pull of his Arnold Palmer. Ruth promptly refills our glasses and hurries off.

"How are you, son?"

"Ah, you know. Little stir-crazy. But good."

"No shame in being a father."

"Oh, nothing like that," I say. "It's just that when you're living on a steady diet of fruit leather and Nickelodeon, it's hard to feel like a grown man sometimes."

"What's Nickelodeon?"

"Television."

"Like this high definition I keep hearing about?"

"No. It's a network. Children's programming."

"Ah," he says.

"The idea is, I am what I eat, Bern. And everything in my life is made for children's consumption."

"Have Ruthie make you a sandwich."

"No, Bern, I mean I just want to work at something. I want to feel productive outside my home. I don't even care if I get paid anymore."

He pauses in his fly-tying duties, lowers his reading glasses, and sizes me up for a long moment until he begins to nod his head sagely. He's about to say something fatherly, when the kids spill out into the backyard. Bernard smiles contentedly as Piper wraps her arms around his neck and kisses him on the cheek.

"You're it," she says.

And here comes Jodi bounding toward his grandfather with a head full of steam, all but knocking him out of his Adirondack. Bernard delights in Jodi's boyish roughness.

"Get this boy a helmet," he says.

Ruth stands nearby, knowing that I could use a break. "You kids come play on the grass," she says. "Let Daddy and Grandpa talk."

And once again, the kids spring obediently into action, rushing toward Bernard's fastidiously kept lawn.

"You're a lucky man, Ben Benjamin."

"I know that, I do."

He resumes his fly tying. "But I think I understand you, son. You want to see beyond one day at a time. You want to engage a larger slice of life."

"I just want to get out of the house."

"You're out of the house now."

"No, I just brought the house with me."

He smiles. "I see your point."

"Watch this one, Grandpa," Piper yells, and proceeds to execute a perfect somersault, cape and all.

Bernard sets his fly in his lap and applauds her. "Atta girl!"

"Watch *this* one!" she calls.

And as Piper does one nifty somersault after another, Jodi tries desperately to win his grandmother's attention, clumsily aping Piper's every move. But his efforts are mostly fruitless. No sooner does he execute a respectable somersault than Piper moves onto cartwheels and handsprings. Ruth does her best to split her attention, smiling this way and that, but Piper commands attention. Sometimes I wish Piper didn't crave the limelight so much, if only because Jodi could use some center stage. Bad enough he can hardly talk.

"What you need, son, is to build something," Bernard says, having resumed his fly tying. "I mean, build it with your own hands. Something that will last. Something you and Janet and the kids can enjoy long after Ruthie and I are gone."

"You're talking about one hell of a tree house," I say. "We're mortgaged to the hilt, as it is."

He leaves off tying once more and lowers his reading glasses. "What if I told you I bought three acres on Discovery Bay? Hundred feet of low bank. Already got a building site, a well, septic approval for three bedrooms, and electricity to the road — what would you say, then?"

"You didn't?"

"No, not yet, but I'm seriously considering it."

"Dock?"

"It's a teardown. *But.*"

"But?"

"But we're lucky it's there, because we can use the footprint. Otherwise, we'd never get a permit. Same goes for the boathouse. We can use the footprint." He leans forward in his chair. "Think of it, Ben. Whole weeks of summer out on the bay. Christmas, Thanksgiving."

"Weekenders," I say.

"Exactly. Three tiny bedrooms, a big dining room. But rustic. Cabiny. Even one of those cedar kits. We build it with our own hands. There's a creek out back. We build a little footbridge over it. Make a gravel path. Rebuild that dock."

"Sounds like a dream, Bern." And it does. The whole enterprise. All that work.

"Could be a reality," he says. "If we can only make Ruthie see."

"She doesn't like the plan?"

"The place. Says it's muddy. Can't see the whole picture. Wants something closer to town."

"How can we persuade her?"

"Beats me. Something to think about, anyway. For the future."

technicalities

Technically, at least on paper, Bernard is still my father-in-law. But since the disaster, he has not squeezed my shoulder once or mussed my hair or called me son. There is no longer a trace of the fatherly propriety that once shone in his gray eyes, only reticence beneath those bushy eyebrows. But today is his birthday, and I'm determined to honor Bernard as though the universe were still in balance. He is at his desk in the den, constructing a scale model of the Brooklyn Bridge. Or maybe it's the Williamsburg Bridge. He does not stand to greet my arrival, though Ruth has announced it and promptly retreated back to the atrium, where she tends to her tropicals.

I'm clutching a fifth of Talisker in one hand and a box of stubby black Onyx cigars in the other.

"Hi, Bern."

He doesn't look up. "Mm," he says, fastening a tiny stanchion in place.

God, but the house seems so silent, so dead without the kids, all the thumping and howling.

"Model making, huh?"

"Just bridges."

He's not going to make this easy on me, but I'm determined to stick it out.

"Came to pay my birthday respects," I say.

"Mm. Well, thanks. You can set that stuff there." He indicates the bar with a slight jerk of the head.

I welcome the opportunity for retreat and fall back to the bar, where I set my offerings.

"Drink?" I say.

"Little early," he grumbles, fingering a tiny cable, as he references the instructions.

I forgo my own drink and turn my attention to the wall of family photos behind the bar, from which I'm noticeably absent, save for my right arm, which I recognize steadying Piper's shoulder as she perches on her new bicycle in front of the Christmas tree.

"So, then, how have you been?" I say.

"Fair," he says, still peering over the rim of his reading glasses at the instructions.

I drift a little closer to him, as though drawn by curiousity. "Brooklyn Bridge?"

"Manhattan," he intones.

There was a day when my slightest curiosity would've been met with a soliloquy to the Manhattan Bridge, an ode to the engineering genius of Ralph Modjeski, a poetic inventory of spans and dimensions. Now it seems there's no bridge big enough or strong enough to span the distance between us.

"Eighteen nineties?" I venture.

"Nope," he says, without further explanation.

"Ah." I fall back again to the photographs, as Bernard studies his schematics. I'm just glossing over the photos now, as I might gloss over photographs of somebody else's life. The man in the fishing hat is not Bernard. The woman in the wedding gown is not Janet. The child being steadied by the ghostly right arm is not Piper.

"Nineteen oh nine," Bernard says, after a long silence. "The bridge."

"Wonder if the Yanks won the series that year."

"They didn't," he says. He looks up at me for the first time. "Ben, why are you here?" His gray eyes are not without pity, but the cruelty of the question takes the breath out of me. I don't have an answer, not a sufficient one. All I can do is stand there, exposed and aching dully like a giant tooth.

"Go home, Ben," he says. "Move on."

the horse

Forest is convinced tonight is a big step for me. Like Janet and everybody else, he thinks it's high time that I set my grief aside and get back on the old horse. It's Saturday midmorning, and despite his invitation for french toast with Melissa and the girls, I've pulled Forest away from his family yet again, this time for coffee in Poulsbo at the Poulsbohemian, where I'm too anxious about this evening's events to pay the cute counter girl much notice. Upon prior sightings in the food court with Trev, we've discussed in no small detail the possibility of giving this counter girl a Dirty Muskie or a Gaylord Perry. But today I am too consumed with the possibility of getting back on the horse.

"Relax, Benji. Lord knows I'm not telling you to go out and get hitched. I'm talking about a hookup here — maybe a booty call. What's it been? Three years?"

"Two," I say into my coffee cup.

"Tonight's the night. Everything will work out great," he says, clapping me firmly on the shoulder. "Hum now. No reason to be nervous. She's not expecting a marriage proposal, and she's not expecting Brad Pitt, either."

I lower my coffee midsip.

"No offense," he says.

"None taken."

"Besides, I've met her ex-boyfriend and he's a total goat roper. Just don't go getting all, you know, needy and stuff. No crying."

"Got it. No crying."

"What about the papers? Did you sign the papers?" He can see I haven't signed the papers. He closes his eyes and shakes his head grimly, then sighs. "Tomorrow you sign the papers. Tonight you get laid, tomorrow you sign the papers. Got it?"

"Got it."

I know that Forest has only my best interests in mind, and I also know that he's absolutely right, that immobility is slowly draining the life out of me, like a car left to sit in the driveway too long. For all my mall gazing and talk of Rusty Trombones and Alabama Hot Pockets, it has never actually occurred to me to take decisive action with a woman since Janet left. The idea of ever seeing the world through somebody else's eyes again — as I saw it through Janet's or Piper's or little Jodi's — seems neither possible nor compelling to me.

I will not be needy, I tell myself, piloting my dented Subaru south on Highway 3. I will not cry. I will not mention Janet. My shirt hasn't seen an iron since the Clinton administration. Forest says to work the caregiving angle. Forest says to be myself. He says ask questions — but not too many.

Her name is Katya. Forest has briefed me as to some of her particulars — the fact that she's twenty-nine, that she recently dumped the aforementioned Goat Roper, and that she's "pretty cute" and "really nice," which doesn't necessarily bode so well. The one piece of compelling information which Forest provides is that Katya works as a trapeze artist at a casino dinner theater in Tacoma. A trapeze artist! Who better to bedazzle me with her high-flying antics? Who better to defy the stultifying gravity that is my life?

Katya's eyes are as big and dark as avocados. You could hide a Cuisinart in her voluminous hair. Though her skin is a little on the bumpy side, her bone structure is remarkable; high, wide cheekbones and a plunging jawline. We are building our own Mongolian stir-fry at Colonel Lee's in Bremerton — her pick. I've decided to be up front with her.

"Just so you know," I say, tonging some bean sprouts. "I'm only using you to get to the sword swallower."

She laughs. Already, a great weight has been lifted from my shoulders. I do not feel needy. I will not cry. Janet who? I avoid the frozen chicken and pork as I move down the line, stacking my plate with cabbage and bamboo shoots and julienned carrots. I'm wary of the raw meats, even if they're frozen, because Jodi once went volcano on some frozen chicken. But I won't mention that or anything about the kids tonight.

Having performed the early show before meeting me, Katya is still in uniform beneath her long tan coat. "Sorry about all this," she says of her jewel-encrusted blue leotard. She's wearing a pair of running shoes that look like they might've belonged to her father — they're huge. "Misty was late," she explains. "So I didn't have time to go home first."

"I think you look adorable," I say.

Her face pinkens like a sunset. I should've said hot — adorable is too familiar. But the sad truth is, already she feels familiar. I'm restless to be with her, impatient to hear the intimate details of her life. My neediness is not a hole to be filled but something beneath the skin scratching to get out.

Katya absorbs this trespass gracefully. "So, Forest said you're a nurse. That's really cool."

"Not exactly. I'm just a caregiver."

"What's the difference?"

"At least fifteen grand a year."

She smiles. "Who cares about money, anyway, right? It's all about freedom. Hey," she says, as we arrive at the hissing grill. "You totally forgot your meat."

I CAME OUT tonight expecting awkwardness and ultimately failure. I came with my exit in mind, armed with excuses. Still, I'm determined to stay on the horse as long as possible, so that next time, next horse — if there is another — I might stake my purchase a little longer. And in this manner I will inch my way toward manhood again. But things are not unfolding as I expected. At our table in the corner, beneath a frameless print of a Mongolian market scene at once reminiscent of Gauguin and Hanna-Barbera, in the shadow of a potted plastic monkey tree, my evening with adorable Katya unfolds swimmingly. Aside from a near slipup, when she asks me if I smoke and I almost tell her my wife made me quit, I'm pretty sure I'm holding my own. She seems charmed by my brief (and I'm pretty sure botched) recitation of Rimbaud.

Once she starts talking about aerial dance and static trapeze, and the difference between a double cutaway and a triple cutaway half, I know that I could love Katya. As she regales me with the details of her job at the dinner theater, I playfully press her for information regarding the sword swallower. I press her for information about her family, her dreams, her future. I want to know everything, every sad little detail, all the ways in which she's been broken or mishandled by life. My Katya does not disappoint. She is forthcoming with the details of her life — her childhood in Connecticut, her stint as a stripper, the profound freedom she feels letting go of the trapeze bar — a bit of reckless verve that makes me want to lean over and kiss her big chapped lips. I am fascinated by her life, mostly because I've been granted access to it.

The empty Tsingtao bottles begin to congregate near the center of the table. I haven't had four beers coursing through me in months. I will not surrender to their downward pull tonight. If I've retained a shred of dignity after the fall, I owe it to the wisdom that it's better not to tempt old Bacchus with my mental and emotional instability and risk running that blurry gauntlet once more. I am here, at least in part. I am in the now, to some degree. I am engaging the circle of life. Hopefully, I'll remember it tomorrow.

"You totally remind me of someone," she says, considering me over the rim of her green bottle. "Like someone famous. Wait! I know who it is!"

I'm dreading the answer. "Who?"

"Johnny Depp."

I am in love with this girl.

KATYA'S APARTMENT BUILDING would've looked right at home in East Berlin. Situated directly behind an old hospital, colorless and hemmed in by concrete, the floodlit complex evokes a desperation familiar to me. I follow Katya up the walkway, through the heavy glass door and down the brown carpeted corridor, clutching a six-pack of Henry's. The interior of her studio is no less stark than the outside. Sparsely furnished, walls unadorned, there is little sign of life here. The wood floors are painted gray. The windows look out over the empty hospital parking lot.

Katya sets her purse on the kitchen counter. "I'm never here," she says, as though she could hear my thoughts. "I used to mostly stay at Todd's."

Todd must be the Goat Roper, I figure. Katya looks different now in the glare of the apartment. Her hair seems less voluminous. Her skin is scalier. Her big eyes look less sultry and a little more bulgy. She looks crazy in her raincoat and leotard. Somehow I like her better for all of this.

"Go ahead and put those in the fridge if you want," she says, removing her raincoat. Kicking off her clown shoes, she retreats to the bathroom.

I stow the beers in the barren fridge, crack one open, and stand around to no purpose in the glare of the kitchen for a minute or two, planning my next move. I wonder if my breath is bad and swish a little beer around in my mouth, just in case. The overhead light fixture is a gallery of dead moths. You can practically smell their singed wings. The lone decorative flourish is a picture of a dog stuck with a magnet to the door of the fridge. It looks like a border collie or some kind of cattle dog, nuzzling curiously right up into the camera lens.

"That's Timber," she says, emerging from the bathroom in jeans and T-shirt.

"Yours?"

"Was."

Drifting toward the living area, I take the only available seat on the edge of the futon under the window, where I prop an elbow on the sill and gaze out over the lighted parking lot, hoping I strike a thoughtful pose.

"Sorry, I don't have any music. I mean, I *have* music, just nothing to play it on."

"I know how you feel."

"You wanna beer?"

"Got one," I say, hoisting the bottle.

When she moves to the kitchen, she doesn't move like my idea of a trapeze artist. Her movements are tentative. She considers the contents of the refrigerator before selecting a beer. She briefly straightens the photo of the dog, before joining me on the edge of the futon, where we share a moment of silence. I pretend it's an easy silence, and I suppose it's easier than most, but I can still feel my neediness scratching to get out.

"You're nice," she says at last.

Taking this as an invitation, I lean over and kiss her chapped lips. She stiffens but does not resist. Her mouth is cold and tastes of metal, but I don't mind, because she tastes human. She runs her cold tongue over my teeth. Our hearts begin to gallop, and we are breathless as Katya begins to wrestle the shirt off my back. Then suddenly she stops herself. I can't say exactly what stops her, whether she recognizes my hunger as something more than sexual, or the force of my neediness is pressing in on her, but I can feel her pity like a warm stick of butter sliding down my esophagus. She lets go of my shirttail and looks right at me, her big avocado eyes inviting me to share her sadness. Smoothing the back of my shirt, she pecks me on the cheek and offers me a little apology by way of a smile. Part of me is grateful, though I know that her pity alone cannot sustain me.

For the next three hours we sit shoulder to shoulder, upright in bed, talking and not talking. We dance around my past as though it doesn't exist. Even in the silence, it hovers there. I'm certain by now that Forest has briefed Katya about the disaster and perhaps even my role in it. I can hardly blame her for wanting to know the details. I don't doubt that knowing them, she would only wish to comfort me. A bigger man than I would at least acknowledge it, so we could both stop pretending there's nothing wrong. But she doesn't push me, and I'm grateful for that. However, I'm beginning to suspect I could really use a push. Tonight, though, with Katya asleep on my shoulder, and her kinky hair grazing my face, I'm content to pretend.

poetry

Monday morning, Trev wants a full report with his Ensure.

"So, did you give her a Moroccan Meatball?"

"Nope."

"Fishhook?"

"Nope."

"Pasadena Mudslide?"

"Hey now," I caution. "She's a classy girl."

"C'mon," he persists. "What'd you give her?"

"I really shouldn't kiss and tell."

"Disappearing Panda?"

"No condom."

"Pittsburgh Platter?"

"No coffee table."

"Change Machine?"

"Only had bills."

"C'mon, I give up. I know you gave her something."

"Okay, okay," I relent. "I gave her a Minivan. I would've given her a Snowmobile, but she lives on the bottom floor."

"But seriously, did you bang her?"

"Of course." But I'm too slow to answer.

"Did you even come close?"

"Yeah," I say, lamely. "Pretty close."

The truth, of course, is that I didn't even get so much as a Raspberry Beret out of the deal, but I'd be lying if I said I haven't been clinging to a certain desperate hope in the thirty-six hours since Katya's trapeze act swung into my life. That this crazy-haired girl with her clown shoes and her leotard and her love of a dead dog invited me into her sad little apartment, if only to pity me, means that there is still hope for me.

While Trev was sleeping this morning, I Googled the name Katya down many a blind alley, without so much as a last name. I Googled dinner theaters in Tacoma, trapeze acts in the greater Puget Sound region. I learned about straight jumps and bullet drops and whip-to-saddle swings, about inverse double suicides and half turns, along with a dizzying array of departures. With the cat curled in my lap, I was even moved to write Katya a little note of gratitude, a poem of sorts, really.

Adorable Katya,

    May you live your life like a trapeze artist, by letting go and describing your graceful arc with confidence and ease, knowing that your grip will not fail you on the other side.

Yours,
Ben

While composing this little missive, I begin to mist over at the nobility of my own gesture, knowing, even before it's finished, that after work I will drive to Bremerton and slide the note under the door of her apartment, and Katya will see that I'm worth loving.

guess who's coming to dinner

I've finally submitted to dinner at Forest's house, albeit shamefully late. I'm sitting in his driveway behind the wheel of the Subaru, working up the nerve to make my entrance. I can see him at the window impatiently waving me in. I should've brought wine, dessert, something. Instead, I've arrived empty-handed, smiling sheepishly as I mount the steps, where Forest greets me at the front door with a clap on the back.

Though I am some eighteen months behind Forest's timeline, he is apparently sticking with his plan to facilitate my redomestication by degrees, for soon after my arrival — before Melissa has even emerged from the kitchen — I learn that the girls have been packed off to a friend's house. While it embarrasses me that he's made such provisions, part of me is grateful not to have to see the girls, particularly Maggie, who at ten and a half is precisely the age that Piper would be. And I'm not sure how I'd hold up under the force of their curious gazes.

The house smells of curry. Melissa is lovely with her cherubic cheeks and plump arms. She flutters from the kitchen on butterfly wings and wraps me in a hug.

"So good to see you," she says. "God, I haven't seen you in ages."

Melissa is generous with her familiarity, in spite of all those rebuffed dinner invitations, in spite of the fact that for two years I've avoided her like a creditor.

"You look great," she says. "Have you lost weight?"

"Nah. Actually, I think I've gained some."

She smiles sweetly. "Well, it looks good on you."

In college, I dated Melissa. She was rock solid, even back then. She liked my poetry and my thick hair and believed, blindly, in my con-fused heart. But like a dummy, I let Melissa get away, drove her away, really, into the arms of my best friend. Knowing how good and giv-ing and loyal and sympathetic she is, it's an easy thing to regret from where I'm standing now. But she's better off with Forest, and we all know it.

"So, how's the nursing?" she says. "Are you still working with the boy with ALS?"

"MD, yeah. But I'm not actually a nurse. More of a manservant."

"I think it's wonderful," she says.

"Me too," says Forest.

"It's just a job," I say.

"Not everybody can do a job like that," she says.

"Not everybody can afford to."

The truth, of course, is that nobody can afford to. I'm twelve grand in credit card debt, and digging myself deeper every month. Before I became Mr. Mom, I had decent options. Okay, options. But the job market slowly passed me by.

"Well," says Forest. "Whaddaya say? Let's eat."

Though I do my best to uphold my end of the dinner conversation — praising the curried chicken, lauding the swiss chard, extolling the virtues of the Gato Negro as I swill more than my share — dinner is mostly a silent affair. Afterward, Forest and I retire to the shaggy domain of his basement, where we sit on the overstuffed sectional drinking Michelob, as *SportsCenter* unfolds silently on the big screen.

"You wrote her a *poem*?"

"Kind of."

"Whoa, whoa, slow down, Bob Frost. Dude! What were you *thinking*?"

I don't have an answer for that.

"I thought you gave up writing poetry for girls in college. It never worked *then*."

Only shame prevents me from pointing out that it worked on Melissa.

"It wasn't really a poem," I half mumble. "More of a note."

Forest takes a pull of his beer and shakes his head grimly. "Christ, what did she say when she read it?"

"I haven't talked to her."

"How long has it been since you left it?"

"Six days."

I've confirmed his worst fear. He closes his eyes, squinting as though to fight off a headache. Scratching the back of his neck, he asks: "Did you . . . you know?"

"No."

He winces.

"What?" I say, lamely.

I've disappointed him again. He's disappointed himself by over-estimating me. Here he's presented me with the opportunity to take a small step forward, and like an impatient child, I've stumbled.

"Just . . . forget about her," he says, waving it off.

But even now I'm tempted to drive out to the casino and watch her float through the air or to slide another note beneath her door in hopes that I might set things right. If only to smell her hair again, if only to lie next to another body for one more night.

when does now begin?

While I'm quick to fault Trev for his futile exercises, for mapping the places he'll never go, my design for a future with Janet is every bit as futile. Janet will never come back to me. Janet has moved on. She's put her grief beside her and started shacking up with Jim Sunderland and his hermaphrodite kid. As far as I know, she is standing on her own two feet, which is more than anyone around here can say.

Manning my post on the sofa with my unfinished crossword in my lap, I am more alert than usual this morning, listening to Trev's labored breathing from the bedroom. He's been sleeping considerably later than usual this week, down with a virus that threatens to settle in his lungs. A bug my body could probably beat in a day or two, but given the havoc that MD has already wrought on Trev's respiratory functions, a pesky virus like this could prove to be deadly. All week long a dark cloud has hung over the house. It doesn't matter that it's sunny in Tampa. His fear is palpable. He sits motionless in his wheelchair before the television, conserving energy, completely unmoved by Doppler images of Tropical Storm Erin, resistant to the chubby charms of his favorite meteorologist — no matter that her pendulous breasts are packed inside her blazer like a pair of baby pandas. There is no mention of giving her a Dirty Muskie or a Gorilla Mask. Trev blinks slowly like a tortoise at the TV. His lips are blue. He hardly talks at all. This morning Elsa is around the house, having canceled her lessons for the day. Last night when his breathing was shallow and frayed, she hurried him to the emergency room at Harrison, where she paced the tile floor until the wee hours.

But the ordeal came to nothing more than another sleepless night.

After two hours on the ventilator, Trev's breathing returned to almost normal. He's slept fitfully throughout the morning. Twice in the last hour, he has called for her, and she has turned him over in his bed. It is Elsa who sits beside him while I wrestle with 23 Across. I can hear her talking softly to him over the hum of the respirator, and though her words are lost on me, I know they're as comforting as words could ever be.

When she is not ministering to Trev, Elsa moves busily about the house, stacking bills and magazines, watering plants, changing laundry. On this occasion, when I hear her filling the sink and stacking the dishes, I don't budge from my place on the couch. Elsa pauses long enough in her duties to take a bite of a muffin and make a cup of instant coffee. But no sooner has she begun to stir the coffee than Trev calls for her again. From across the dining room she sees me stand, and bids me at ease with a shake of her head. On command, I sit down and pencil in *avoid* for 23 Across. Setting her coffee aside, she answers Trev's call. Again, I hear the soft drone of her voice as she turns him on his side. When she emerges from the bedroom, she takes up her coffee and walks through the dining room to the far side of the living room. She looks out the window with the sleepy eyes of a Komodo dragon and blows on her coffee so a ribbon of steam curls up her face.

"He's irritable when he's like this," she observes. "He says things he doesn't mean."

I want to go to her, to offer myself as comfort, to say the words that will smooth her wrinkled resignation, but I haven't got the guts.

"Is there anything I can do?"

"Just stay a little longer," she says into her coffee cup.

But for the muffled hum of the ventilator and the rasp of Trev's breathing in the distance, a dense silence settles in as she gazes out the window, where a rogue sunbeam flashes silver off the wet driveway. Now I see that Elsa is looking right at me with great sadness in her sleepy eyes.

"It's not our fault," she says.

battle of the blur

None of my zippers work anymore, which must be some kind of metaphor. Listing ever so slightly before the urinal, I'm not surprised to discover that my fly is already open. Tonight is Max's birthday. We're having a little party at the Grill, where happy hour ended some two and a half hours ago. I'm wearing my blue cords for the occasion (in spite of the lazy zipper) because they're the only pants I own that still manage to achieve some kind of slimming effect, an illusion, I fear, that's beginning to lose its crisp edges with every cheeseburger.

This evening is sure to end badly. Already, I can feel hints of the old blur coming on: the dull throbbing in the chest, the thick, slow coursing of blood behind the temples, the heaviness of limb which signals my approaching oblivion. Zipping my fly up futilely, I'm determined to fight the blur this evening, determined to feel and remember, to walk among the living, even though I have nothing to hope for.

Rejoining the party to the tune of Motorhead's "Fast and Loose," I see that a second larger table now abuts our own. We are being joined by five of Max's Bremerton friends. The tall guy with the trench coat and the dirty glasses is vaguely familiar. There is a short, ample redhead dressed like a witch. Her black leggings fit like sausage skins — which is appropriate because this is basically a sausage party. The other two Bremerton friends are also dudes, skinheads dressed like rappers, with tattoos above the collar, both of them with initials for names, not J. J. or B. J. but awkward-sounding ones: G. R. and C. L. or P. K. and K. W.

Full introductions are made, shots are procured, and the bar is soon abuzz with our chatter. The jukebox cycles more Motorhead, Bon Jovi, the Boss. The tables get stickier by the minute. The world is still tactile, still memorable. I'm winning the battle. The tall guy is talking to me about Atlantis, the Pillars of Hercules, ziggurats in pre-Columbian South America. I wish he'd clean his glasses — it's all I can do to resist leaning over and doing it myself. Teo is arm wrestling a skinhead who keeps calling him "bro," while Max appears to be making headway with the redhead, who giggles more than you'd expect for a witch. She's unwittingly slopped a big gob of nacho cheese on her cape. These people are slobs. I'm beginning to feel superior this evening in spite of all evidence to the contrary.

"Your fly is open," says Forest, nudging me.

"Dude, what about the Olmecs?" says Dirty Glasses.

Big Red giggles as Max leans over and shovels the cheese off her velour cape, licking his finger. A little orange string of it still dangles from his mustache but not for long. Big Red leans over and licks his mustache clean.

"I'm out, Holmes," Forest says, clapping my back as he stands. "I wanna see the girls before Mel puts them to bed." He looks around the table and back at me a little uneasily, as though he can see my future. "You sure you don't need a ride?"

"I'm good."

"He's goin' to a party with us," Max says.

And sure enough, twenty minutes later, after we've cleared the big tab with the usual confusion, the whole group of us arrive at a house party out near the Olympic College campus in a sagging green craftsman with a dead lawn. No sooner have I mounted the front steps than I'm accosted on the porch by a ruddy little pug-faced man who pulls me aside and starts breathing a fog of Jägermeister into my face. He's totally gooned, his eyes lolling around in his head.

"Dude, dude, check this shit out," he says.

"What?" I say.

He wrestles clumsily with his open cell phone until his eyes light up, and he thrusts the phone up into my face.

"Dude, check it out."

"What am I looking at?"

"Wait, wait, this way," he says, tilting the phone horizontally, and pushing it even farther into my face.

Squinting, I still don't know what I'm looking at, but it's fleshy and hairless.

"Is that your baby?" I ask.

"Dude, that's my dick!"

I push past him, and he slaps me on the back.

"Aw, man, we're cool, right?" he calls after me. "We're cool?"

Dirty Glasses Dale and I help ourselves to a beer and settle at the kitchen table, vacant but for a jumble of empties. A pair of short girls sashay into the kitchen, also talking loudly. One of them, the blonde, has the most vivid fake tan I've ever seen. She's perfectly orange. Her eyebrows are albino blond. They look like they might burn your fingers if you touched them.

"Hey psst," I say to Dale. "Look, an Oompa Loompa."

But the reference is lost on Dale, who is in earnest, still furrowing his brow at the inexplicable development of the water clock in a culture that couldn't grow beets a hundred years prior. "Gotta be Atlantis," he says. "There's no other explanation for the widespread development of technology that quickly."

"Is anyone sitting here?" says Oompa Loompa.

"Go for it," I say.

Construction cone orange or not, Oompa Loompa is smooth-faced and kind of cute. Her friend, not so much. She's got a big overbite. From the side she looks like a bottle opener. But I'm guessing she probably looks better through Dale's smudged glasses, because he's all over her right from the get-go.

"So, do you live here?" Oompa Loompa says to me.

"Nah. We're here with Max."

"Max just left," she says.

"Oh. Well, I guess we're here by ourselves."

"I'm Cindy," she says.

"I'm Ben."

Suddenly, there's a bloodcurdling scream from the bathroom down the hallway, and the pug-faced kid with the cell phone bursts out the door clutching his groin with both hands. He slumps in the threshold of the kitchen with everybody staring at him.

"Dude," he says. "Come here, come here, you gotta help me."

"Me?" I say.

"Dude," he pleads. "You gotta come here, man, you gotta." Waving me onward over his shoulder, he begins shambling down the hallway, clutching his abdomen and moaning like Tina Turner as he goes.

Warily, I follow him to the bathroom, and he shuts the door behind us.

"What's the deal?" I say.

He corkscrews his face and fresh tears stream down his cheeks. "I was smoking," he moans, releasing his crotch to expose his wrinkled red member.

"Jesus!" I say, recoiling.

"It huuurts," he says.

I reach for the doorknob, but he grabs my arm pleadingly. "Dude, what do I do? I'm serious, what do I do? It huuurts."

"Hell if I know, put a Band-Aid on it."

He looks up into my face with the most desolate and apologetic of all expressions: the expression of a guy who just burned his penis with a cigarette and wants you to put a Band-Aid on it.

"Dude, I can't do it," he says. "I'll pass out."

I heave a long sigh. Rifling through the medicine cabinet, I wonder why it is that the winds of fate have blown me here. Why in a house full of people did the little pug-faced man choose me to minister to his injured penis? How did he know?

"Hold still," I say.

He winces at first, but then sighs with relief as I apply a curlicue of Neosporin to the popped blister. His dingus feels like a salamander between my fingers, though nothing in my manner suggests that I am disgusted. I am, after all, a pro.

"You're not a fag are you?" he says.

"Nope," I say, smoothing over the Band-Aid and releasing his penis.

"That's good." He gives me a pat on the shoulder. "Hey, man, seriously, thanks."

"No problem," I say, rinsing my hands. "Do me a favor, though."

"Yeah, dude, name it."

"Stay away from me."

I can see the hurt in his little pug face. But you know what? I don't give a damn anymore. I'm developing a taste for superiority.

Rejoining Dale and the girls in the kitchen, I see that Dale is making headway, talking some crap about the Phoenicians owing their ancient trade routes to the Atlanteans. The Bottle Opener is either smitten with Dale or she's from Atlantis, because she's eating it up.

"What was that all about?" Oompa Loompa wants to know upon my reappearance.

"Guy hurt his thumb," I say, reaching into the fridge for a beer, popping it, and guzzling a third of it in one motion

"That guy's a freak," she says.

Look who's talking, I want to say. *You look like a fucking jack-o'-lantern.* "Yeah," I concur. "Total freak."

"Your fly's undone," she says.

"Yeah, I know."

Dale has produced a pot pipe from the depths of his trench coat and begins loading it. I don't know how he can see what the fuck he's doing through those glasses. He sparks the pipe and passes it around. The conversation becomes hopelessly stilted. Even Dale can't seem to string together sentences. Cindy is changing colors like a lava lamp. The tentative emergence of a freakishly overweight tabby from behind the dead ficus near the head of the hallway ultimately provides the group with a much-needed focal point. For three or four minutes we sit stupefied, sipping our beers, observing the beast's every movement without comment as it licks and circles and runs its spine along the bottom of the refigerator. I can feel my jaw slackening. I'm drained of all my drunken swagger, all my superiority. I begin to wonder if there's anywhere I belong or anyone to whom I could ever belong again — a trapeze artist, a sword swallower, Janet. Certainly, I don't belong here. A small part of me — perhaps the hopeful part or maybe the courageous part — wants to suggest that we all pile into the Suburu and go buy Slurpees. But then I remind myself that I'm a would-be divorcee, who used to be a father, and most of me wants to run from this house as though it were burning.

stations

Elsa is around the house again Monday morning, having cleared her schedule of all lessons for the third day in a row. The house is immaculate: no stacks of mail, no heaping recycle bin, no dishes glutting the sink. The carpets have been vacuumed, the pillows aired, the fishbowl cleaned. Everything smells of citrus and pine. And still, Elsa circles and sweeps and dusts.

In the three hours since I arrived with my sack lunch and my crossword, I've yet to be called into service. I've scarcely moved from my station on the sofa. How long before Elsa runs the feather duster over me? I feel obligated to stay alert on the sofa, poised for action should my assistance be required in lifting Trev or warming up the van or hauling out the recycling. Though this last task is nowhere in my service plan, today I'm willing to test the boundaries, willing to throw all those mnemonics out the window for a little occupation. The Monday crossword was a pushover. The cat is presumably out roaming the farm and can offer me no company. I've already eaten my banana and half of my tuna sandwich. And to make matters even more excruciating, the face of the dining room clock is in full view as the minutes crawl by. Somehow I can't bring myself to turn on the television. It's one thing to sit around being useless and another thing to watch television. Instead, I gaze at the darkened screen and wonder if it's another scorcher in Miami, whether it's raining in Davenport.

I should probably be thinking about the job market, as Trev's condition has only worsened over the weekend. While I was out bandaging penises and spilling beer in people's laps, the virus settled in Trev's lungs. While I was nursing my hangover on Saturday, Elsa took Trev to Harrison once more for chest x-rays and a CT. He's been on the respirator full-time ever since. Since the machine makes sleeping on his side difficult, Trev's even more restless than usual in bed. Every fifteen or twenty minutes he calls for his mother, and they talk softly as she tends to his itches and clears the sweat from his watering eyes. On those frequent occasions when Trev needs the toilet, it's Elsa, not me, who lifts him out of bed and onto the toilet, Elsa who awaits his call outside the bathroom door.

Around 12:15 p.m., Trev's cell phone starts ringing from the pouch of his wheelchair. Three times the ringing is cut short by voice messaging. When the cell finally relents, the house phone starts ringing almost immediately, and Elsa picks it up.

"What is it, Bob? . . . Yes, Bob . . . No, Bob . . ."

She waves to me across the dining room to indicate that she's taking the call outside.

I wave back, at the ready should Trev require assistance.

"Bad idea, Bob," Elsa says, closing the back door behind her. I can still hear her muffled voice as she passes below the window. "It's a little late for that now, don't you think? . . . I'll tell you how I know, Bob. Because for the past four or five . . ." Then I lose her as she drifts deeper into the backyard, though I can still see her as she begins pacing with the cordless beneath the big maple.

Poor Bob will never have closure. He'll never live down his mistake. What does he hope to accomplish with this phone call? And what is his bad idea, anyway? Does he simply want to talk to Trev, to run into the same brick wall over and over, to be judged for his failings yet again? Maybe he wants to fly out from Salt Lake City and sit at the bedside of his son, or what's left of his son, to plead his case. I can't help but wonder whether Trev might secretly relish his father's testimony. Who is to say that deep down Trev's little boy isn't still fighting to win approval? But I know beyond a shadow of a doubt that Trev will permit no such drama, and probably, in his position, neither would I. Trev will hoard his advantage until the very end, withholding the one piece of evidence that might ever absolve his father, namely, that he still loves him.

As Elsa continues her pacing in the front yard, Trev beckons her,

and it is I who answer his call. The bedroom smells of sweaty feet
and turning fruit and the inside of an aspirin bottle. The shades are
drawn against the sunlight, and the respirator hums on the nightstand beside him. A few dusty shafts of light cut across the foot of
the bed. On the sill above his head, stuffed animals are lined shoulder
to shoulder: a bear, a penguin, one of those singing grapes from the
old commercial. On the wall at the foot of the bed is a Misfits poster,
right beside a Nike poster that proclaims, "We are all witnesses." The
low dresser is completely bare on top but for a plastic box of pushpins
and a folded black T-shirt.

"What's up?" I say.

His eyes sit deep in their bruise-colored sockets. His lips are
cracked. I see no evil genius flashing in his blue eyes. I'm disgusted
by the sight of him, repelled not by his condition but by a complex
stirring of emotions I can't process.

"Where's my mom?"

"Outside on the phone."

"My dad?"

"Yeah."

He rolls his head heavily to one side, away from me, then rolls it
heavily back until he's staring at the ceiling.

"Dude," I say. "Check it out: I banged an Oompa Loompa this weekend, swear to God."

Trev doesn't offer so much as a smirk or the bat of an eyelid. "Could
you go get my mom?" he says. There's a rasp in his voice eerily like a
death rattle.

"Do you want any water or anything?"

"No. Could you get my mom?"

"I can turn you."

"I just want to talk to my mom," he says, unable or unwilling to
mask his impatience. "Could you get her? *Please*."

He lolls his head back toward the wall again, looking agitated.

I know that I shouldn't take it personally. Somewhere in the *Fundamentals of Caregiving* textbook there's a whole paragraph devoted
to such matters. But Trev's dismissal stings like a betrayal. Already I

regret the impulse to sting him back. This is not about me, I remind myself.

"You sure you don't need to go to the bathroom or anything?"

"Yeah, I'm good."

I turn to leave, then turn back. "Oh, and I was lying, you know. I didn't fuck shit."

"I know," he says.

From the dining room window, I wave to Elsa, and she begins making her way toward the house. I catch the final snatches of her conversation as she clomps up the wooden ramp and through the back door.

"Yes, I promise, I will. *Bob,* I'm hanging the phone up now."

And Elsa makes good, at least on her final promise, replacing the phone in its cradle with a sigh.

three feathers

Sharing a barren and seemingly endless parking lot with Target, the Dollar Store, Papa John's, and Office Max, the Three Feathers Casino projects little in the way of pretense. Its very shape offers no relief from rectangularity beyond a negligible slope in the cedar-shingled awning, and a pair of sad-looking totem poles flanking the entrance like panhandlers. On the outside, the giant gray edifice broadcasts none of the opulence, possesses none of the gaudy flourishes — no fountains, no doormen, no pissing cherubs — that I've come to expect in casinos. Just those hard-luck totem poles looking all the more miserable in the rain and a dented yellow cab idling out front.

Checking my fly and mussing my thinning hair, I enter the lobby, where I'm greeted by the cold stink of conditioned air and stale smoke. The riotous clanging of a thousand one-armed bandits, the pulse of garish light from all quarters, the muffled protestations of Buffalo Springfield over the house intercom — all of it is an assault on my senses. The worn carpet is a fussy and overworked pattern somewhere between Mayan petroglyphs and art deco. The patrons themselves are something out of Nathanael West: a groping horde of doughy Midwesterners, hopeful against all odds as they waddle up and down the aisles with their plastic tumblers heaping with tokens and their colons packed with reasonably priced buffet fare.

The dinner theater is none other than the Bayside Circus, opposite the buffet and behind the dollar slots. Never mind that there's nothing resembling a bay within four miles. Never mind that the place is practically empty. What impresses me the most about the Bayside

Circus is how badly the proprietors have botched the circus theme. This is not the Cirque du Soleil. Not even the Teatro ZinZanni. If Chili's opened a strip club, it might look something like the Bayside Circus. Through the narrow entrance and past the hostess station I see a slice of tawdry stage, lined with Christmas lights and speckled with glitter. Center stage, in a puddle of murky light, hangs the vacant trapeze bar. Nothing about this place — neither its busy decor nor its high ceilings nor its odor of fried chicken and mop water, nor the fact that it's too dark to see your food — is appetizing. One look at the hostess in her tight pink leggings tells me that she could use a Brazilian. No sooner has this hairy attendant greeted me at the podium than I spot Katya across the dining room in her fringed blue leotard, serving oversized cocktails to a party of revelers.

While there's nothing particularly nimble or athletic in Katya's comportment, she is not without a certain knobby-kneed grace as she circles the table balancing a tray in one hand and dealing out drinks with the other. Her big hair has been wrestled into a knot on the back of her head, presumably to keep it out of people's food and avoid wind drag. Without that mess of hair to compete with, her dramatic jawline and big avocado eyes are all the more striking, even in this dull light at a distance of forty feet. My instinct is to turn and flee before she sees me. Instead, the hostess leads me the length of the dining room, seating me not ten feet from where Katya is delivering the last of her cocktails. It's still not too late to lower my head and avoid detection, but why come this far? What do I hope to accomplish here? Am I really trying to win a girl or just unraveling my most recent failure to some pitiful conclusion so I can keep feeling sorry for myself?

Though she passes within three feet, her chin held high, Katya does not recognize me. Not until she comes for my drink order. I see at close range that her leotard has a few snags in it and looks worn about the edges. The low light is agreeable to her complexion. Her crazy hair threatens to explode the little bun on the back of her head.

"Oh. Hey," she says, almost like a question.

"I tracked you down," I say, regretting the stalkerish implications immediately. "Don't worry," I add, in attempt to right my ship. "I'm not stalking you or anything."

This doesn't seem to ease her mind. "Um, o-kaay," she says. "Well, that's good. So, can I start you off with something to drink?"

"Just a Coke, I guess."

"Pepsi okay?"

"Sure."

She scratches the order out onto the pad.

"So, how have you been?" I venture.

"Not bad. Really busy. My plate's way too full right now, with school and work and everything else."

"Did you get my note?"

She wants to say no — I can see it in her eyes as she hesitates.

"Oh, yeah, thanks," she says.

"I hope I didn't scare you off."

"No, it was sweet, thanks. I'm just really busy." She steals a glance over her shoulder to the wait station, then toward the stage.

"I didn't know you were in school. That's cool. What are you studying?"

"Just basic stuff."

"Math? Lit? What?"

"Yeah," she says glancing back toward the wait station once more. Her body language is shifty and impatient, her manner slightly hurried — all of it suggesting that she's in the throes of a dinner rush. But the place is dead. The din of the surrounding casino bleeds in through the false walls, dinging and donging, as Katya awaits my order.

"How come there's no net?" I say, nodding toward the stage.

"Huh?" she says, unable to belie what I'm beginning to suspect is annoyance.

"No safety net, I mean."

She looks to the stage, then back at the bar. "Yeah, well. It's static. So it's not like I'm flying through the air or anything like that."

"Did you ever see that movie *Trapeze*?" I venture. (I rented it two nights ago for this very reason.) "With Burt Lancaster? Totally cheesy, but some of the trapeze stuff is — " I stop myself when I see that her body is actually stiffening before my eyes, like she's drawn a deep breath and held it in.

"So, uh, do you need another minute? I can have Misty come by for your order, if — "

"I'll have the fish-and-chips," I say, without opening the menu.

"Soup or sal — "

"Soup."

"Okay," she says, dotting an *i* and turning on her heels. "Right back with that Pepsi."

What kind of world is it where you write a poem for a girl and she holds it against you? What benevolent God would conceive of a dynamic where the impulse to nurture repels? I had hoped to get beyond her pity, and it looks like I've succeeded, one way or another. It is Misty who delivers my Pepsi as the lights dim. The party behind me begins to jockey their chairs around and reach for their coats, even as Katya, in her sad garish leotard, takes the stage and approaches the bar. The wooden stage sounds hollow beneath her steps. When she turns to face the dining room, scrupulously avoiding my gaze, her tenuous beauty fails her beneath the murky glare of the spotlight. Her big eye sockets look alien. Her sloping forehead is freakish. Her bare knees look like frozen game hens. And to think she pitied me.

Katya mounts the bar, swings her legs up, and dangles by her knobby knees for a long moment, as though concentrating her energies. Her spine runs straight and dimpled down the length of her back. Upside down, all the missing sequins of her leotard come to light, exposing little piebald patches like dry skin. Arching her back in a Bird's Nest, clutching the rope a foot above the bar, Katya expertly swings herself headfirst and backward into a shaky handstand. Slowly, she collapses herself like an accordion on the strength of her stomach muscles, splaying her legs in a V as she folds herself nearly in two. By the time she swings her legs out in front of her into an L-sit, we are alone. The revelers have cleared out. Misty is probably out back smoking a cigarette while my soup grows cold. Katya cannot help but feel me there, folding my arms and hating her, as she swings a seven-twenty, reversing her hands, and comes to an abrupt stop with her back facing me. How can I hurt this woman if I can't even reach her? And why should I want to? We all run hot and cold, so why blame Katya? She spins a quick one-eighty, reversing her hands once more, and comes to rest facing me. I narrow the focus of my hatred right between her hairy eyebrows. This is for your pity. And this is for withholding it, you crazy bitch. But Katya looks right past me.

I stand, fish out my wallet, drop a twenty on the table, and turn to leave without looking back. When I hit the cold stale air of the casino, all I can feel is shame.

this is not a funeral

Before we go feeling sorry for Bob, who flew nearly halfway across the country to make an appearance at the bedside of his ailing son, let's talk about Bob's tactical errors. Number one: flying halfway across the country uninvited (nay, conspicuously discouraged), not to mention totally without warning, is just the sort of flight decision that got Bob in trouble in the first place. Moreover, showing up on the doorstep at 7:50 a.m., five hours before Trev's customary waking time, demonstrates not only a lack of consideration but a complete disregard for the order and routine that Trev stands for. And finally, the flowers.

"Jesus, Bob, it's not a funeral," says Elsa, who has canceled her lessons again.

"They're for you," he says.

Elsa takes the bouquet and tosses it on the cluttered credenza in the foyer, knocking over a mug full of pens and pencils. "How thoughtful."

"Well, are you going to let me in?"

Elsa steps aside, and Bob enters the foyer. He's dressed in pale green Dockers and a forgettable dress shirt, and he looks like Al Gore before Al Gore got fat: mild, average, palliative in his dullness. Yet for all this mild-manneredness, there is something distinctly clownish about him. Maybe it's his short legs and long torso or perhaps his oversized dress shoes. Though I'm predisposed toward not liking Bob (the guy is a deadbeat, after all), I can't help but sympathize with him — perhaps it's because we've both made such a hopeless mess out of fatherhood, or because we're both so well acquainted with rejection, or because we both yearn so badly for forgiveness. Or maybe it's just because his fly is open.

"Bob, this is Ben, Trev's caregiver."

"Hello, Bob," I say, from my station on the couch.

Extending a hand, Bob advances two steps, landing squarely on the cat's tail with one of his loafers. The cat darts behind the entertainment center, a hair-raising caterwaul and a brown blur.

"Bob Conklin," he says, proffering a business card. The business card just says Bob Conklin with a phone number, nothing else. "Pleasure to meet you, Ben." His hand is clammy, his grip a little too firm but not in a confident way.

"Likewise," I say.

Elsa rolls her eyes for my benefit, then promptly takes leave to alert Trev.

Bob looks around vaguely, as if he might sit down. "I've got a deaf neighbor," he informs me, apropos of nothing.

"Is that right?"

"Yep."

"I knew a deaf lady once," I offer.

"How about that?"

He decides to peruse our giant map, rocking ever so slightly to and fro on his big loafers, furrowing his brow in concentration as though fascinated.

"What do the pins signify, do you know?"

"Muffler Men are red, museums are blue, dead celebrity parts are black, and everything else is green."

"Hmmph," says Bob. "Interesting. Elsa did this?"

"Trev."

"Ahh, I see." But Bob doesn't really see — he looks downright puzzled. "How does he reach?"

"I do the actual pinning."

"Ahh, I see, I see. Very interesting." He runs his flattened hand over Wyoming and Colorado, as though it were a relief map, tilting his head curiously like a golden retriever confronting a quadratic equation. "What does it mean?" he says.

"What do you mean?"

"I mean why does he mark them?"

"I guess I don't have a good answer for that one. It's just something we do. Your, uh, zipper, Bob."

"Oh, yeah. Thanks." He fastens his zipper about two-thirds of the way and turns his attention back to the map. "So, what's this in Salt Lake City?"

"Virgin Mary in a stump."

"Ahh. I see."

As he ponders the map with an expression somewhere between genuine curiosity and mild abdominal cramps, it's hard to resolve Bob with the villain I've come to expect. I expected denim and a five-o'clock shadow. A slight fog of gin, maybe some tattoos. If ever a guy seemed innocuous, if ever a guy seemed benign, it's Bob. Doubtless, he's squashed a few butterflies with those clunky loafers along his life's path, surely he's trampled a few unwitting hearts, not the least of which his son's, but never on purpose, it would seem. To me, he seems no more capable of malice than he seems capable of grace. Here is a man that does not make decisions. Decisions make him.

"So, then, the whole thing is just . . . sort of . . . what, then?"

"Sort of an exercise."

"But I thought you stuck the pins in?"

"Not a physical exercise, Bob. Just something to do with our time."

"Ah, I see." He runs his hand across the mid-Atlantic, over double Dumpsters and mystery houses. Surely, he can hear the low conspiratorial voices from the bedroom, and surely he must know they do not bode well for him. It is an awkward moment. I know he means well, and I believe he's sincere; still I want to shake him by the collar.

"He's a neat kid," I say. "I wish I had half his guts."

"Hmph. Me too."

"And he's really funny. He makes me laugh constantly. "

Bob turns toward me. He's smiling, and there's nothing mild about it. "Yeah?"

"A couple weeks ago, we're mapping — the four-corners area, actually — and we come across Bingham Canyon, the Biggest Pit in the

World, and Trev says, 'I thought Clifton, New Jersey, was the biggest pit in the world.'"

Bob takes his smile up a notch just as Elsa reemerges with a businesslike comportment. Why do I feel as though she's caught us in the act of something?

"You'll have to try back at three o'clock, Bob."

Bob looks at his watch to find he's not wearing one. He looks disappointed, even beaten, but resolved to this setback. At some point during his short visit his shirttail has come untucked. The cat still eyes him warily from behind the entertainment center.

"Well, then. Uh, I guess it's three o'clock," he says. "Nice meeting you, Dan."

"Ben."

"Right," he says. "See you at three." And without further incident, Bob turns and nearly upends a floor lamp. I feel his pain. I've hit that fucking lamp two dozen times — it's misplaced to allow for the wide berth of Trev's wheelchair. Elsa heaves a sigh the minute she shuts the door on him. Through the window, I watch him bump his head as he climbs into his rental, a gray Taurus coupe, a mild automobile if ever there was one.

TREV CALLS FOR me, not Elsa, at ten o'clock. It's the first time he's called for me in a week. At this point, I'm grateful to leave the couch.

"You gotta go to the bathroom?"

"Nah. Just ready to get up."

I pull the covers back, remove the pillow from between his knees, and shift him onto his back.

"How's Jake?" he says, referring to the cat, as I begin to slide his left sock on.

"Oh, he's fine. Just gave him a spook." Slipping his right sock on, I note that Trev's toenails need to be cut, and the flaky skin around his toes needs to be scrubbed off. Though completely useless, his feet are nonetheless high maintenance.

"What an idiot," he complains.

"Your dad?"

"Yeah."

"Why, because he stepped on the cat?"

"No, because he flew out here." I see a glint of the evil genius flash in his eyes, a little more pointed than usual. He's back but irritable. Impatient. Ready to complain. Even by Trev standards, his body is stiff and uncooperative as I wrestle his cargo pants over his legs.

"He's a klutz," I say. "That's for sure."

"He's pathetic. Do you know he carries around a little scrap of his baby blanket?"

"What do you mean 'carries around'?"

"In his pocket."

"For real?"

"Seriously. His fucking baby blanket."

"Wow." I say, hoisting him onto my waiting knee, where I hitch his pants up around his waist, zip the zipper, and snap the button.

"He rubs it when he gets anxious."

"Rubs it?"

"Yeah, like in his pocket. Sometimes you can see him working at it — it looks like he's scratching his nuts."

"That's fucked up," I say, nestling him into his chair. It's sort of heartbreaking, actually — in a fucked-up way. But now is not the time to pity Bob. "Do you think he jacks off with it?"

"Probably. Or maybe he just sniffs it while he jacks off."

I lean him forward in the chair and hitch his pants up another inch, tucking the tail of his shirt beneath his nonexistent ass so it won't ball up uncomfortably. I pull the shoulder seams fast and straight, align the crew collar around his thin neck, adjust the fabric around his trunk so that his shirt hangs naturally, and finally, smooth out the breast pocket so it looks crisp. "You ready for some Eggos?"

TREV REMAINS MOSTLY silent throughout breakfast. He eats impatiently and doesn't finish his flaxseedless Eggos. He hardly drinks any of his Ensure. Beginning our day hours earlier than usual, the morning does not adhere to our standard regimen, though our television menu consists of roughly the same fare. We visit Myrtle Beach.

We track tornadoes. We learn how to cook white chicken chili with fried tomatillo salsa. All the while, Trev shifts restlessly in his wheelchair, easily annoyed as afternoon approaches. Nearly every commercial elicits a grumble. In spite of repeated attempts to distract him — everything from idle speculation as to the size of Rachael Ray's taco to the color of Kathy Griffin's bush — he is not interested in childish repartee. After three hours of channel surfing and two trips to the bathroom, Trev decides to take a nap, just in time for Bob's arrival. A minute after I put him down, he calls for Elsa, and they talk in their hushed tones.

When Bob pulls in at 2:54 p.m., I see that the front left wheel of the Taurus is one of those undersized spares. Though he's managed to muddy the knees of his Dockers, Bob is otherwise intact — shirt freshly tucked, fly tightly secured, as he walks across the yard clutching a giant bag of KFC, the bottom of which nearly gives out halfway across the lawn. Bob manages to get his hands under the bag and stop the breach before the bag ruptures completely but not before the beans start dripping down his shirtsleeve and a side of mashed potatoes tumbles out, bursting open on the lawn. He stands for a moment looking stoic like a clown, though I can feel his frustration. I'll bet he wishes he had a free hand, so he could reach for his pocket and fondle his baby blanket. Instead, he just stands there dripping at the scene of the accident for a good thirty seconds, paralyzed by indecision, looking alternately at the mashed potatoes and the house, wishing, I presume, that the problem would simply disappear. Finally, he abandons the mess and resumes his progress, trailing beans and tomato sauce across the lawn. By the time I hear his steps on the wooden ramp, Elsa is already at the door to greet him, if you could call it a greeting.

"I'm sorry, Bob," I hear her say. "You should've called."

"But you said come back at — "

"I *mean* you should've called before you flew out here. Showing up out of the blue is only upsetting him. He's in bed. And besides, don't you think it's a little late in the game to expect — " She lowers her voice here, so that Trev, or perhaps I, cannot hear what she has to say. And judging from the length of her message, she has a lot to say.

I imagine she's been rehearsing it for years as she's tended to Trev's every special need, tossed through every fitful night's sleep, while Bob was out breaking lamps and missing trains.

For his part, Bob seems to offer little protest. Craning my neck, I see that his manner remains inexplicably mild as she dresses him down. Elsa's repertoire of verbal blows seem to bounce off Bob like rubber hammers. But you know he's crying on the inside. It occurs to me that this willingness to absorb, this absence of protest, this utter lack of resiliency, is probably somewhere near the root of Bob's failure in all its guises. As if to prove my point, in the end he attempts to surrender the dripping bag of KFC across the threshold to Elsa, who refuses it. Seconds later, I watch him slop across the yard with it, a portrait of defeat. He sets the disintegrating hodgepodge on the roof of the car — where it bleeds and oozes — as he opens the door and bumps his head climbing in again. Closing the door, he fires up the Taurus and starts up the driveway. About halfway up the drive, the bag oozes off the side and bonks the side mirror on its way to the gravel, whereupon Bob clips it with a back wheel, leaving yet another mess in his wake.

the trouble with bob

When my workday ends at six fifteen, I rattle up the bumpy driveway and into the gathering darkness with a mounting sense of relief. This evening I'll answer the call of the Grill before happy hour is over. Max'll probably be down there, maybe even Forest. Cresting the rise, who should I find at the top of the drive, sitting on the hood of the Taurus, shirt spattered with barbecue sauce, fly wide open, but Bob?

"Another flat?" I say through the open passenger's window.

He shakes his head.

"You've been here the whole time?"

Casting his eyes down, he begins scratching absently at some dried bird shit on the hood.

"Are you waiting for Trev?"

He shrugs and leaves off scratching the bird shit.

"Chances are, he's not going anywhere," I say.

"I figured." He kicks his big loafers idly a few times and looks off toward the horizon.

The guy is deflated. After the rubber hammers have been laid to rest, and the midgets have all gone home, here at last is the sad clown. It appears my workday is not over, after all.

"Buy you a beer?" I say.

PUSHING OUR WAY through the big sticky door, we're swallowed instantly by the swampy environs of the Grill, where the husky strains of Bob Seger greet us, along with the rabble of two dozen patrons and the bitter bouquet of stale beer and burned hamburger meat. A quick inventory reveals that Max is indeed in the house, playing cricket with a big bear of a guy in a flannel shirt and dirty Carhartt pants. Max is wearing black sweats, the drawstring kind, and his O-fers jersey, though the season is long over. Otherwise, it's the usual suspects populating the Grill: predominately rustic males in dirty jeans and dirty baseball caps and work boots. Bob looks out of place in his Dockers and dress shirt, though he hardly seems to notice or care.

We soon join Max and his friend with a fresh pitcher and four glasses. Max introduces the big guy as Pete. I introduce Bob as Bob.

"You guys up for some doubles after we wrap this one up?" Max says, with foam in his mustache.

I look to Bob, who has already inhaled his beer and began to slump. He shrugs. "Sure. Whatever."

A moment later, while Bob is preoccupied draining his second beer, steadily and without relish, Max says to me in confidence, "So, what's with Al Gore?"

"He's my client's dad."

"You mean the retarded kid?"

"He's not retarded. He's got MD, Max."

"What's he so glum about?"

"Long story."

"You're up," Pete says to Max.

After two and a half beers, Bob is showing signs of life.

"You have kids?" he says to me.

"Nah."

"Wife?"

"Nope."

He empties the dregs of the pitcher into his schooner. "Me neither. Seems like. Don't worry, I'll get another one."

"No worries. Drink up."

"I never drink," he says, draining his glass.

"Sorry they wouldn't let you in." The apology ought to feel like a betrayal, but somehow it doesn't.

He looks me right in the eye for an instant, then looks away toward the dart board where Max has just hit a pair of triple-19s. "Yeah, well, I wouldn't let me in, either. Would you?"

"Yeah. I think I would."

"Guess that's why you're a nurse," he says, considering his empty glass.

"So you weren't surprised they turned you away?"

"Were you?"

"I guess not."

"Well, there you go," he says, wiping his mouth on his sleeve.

He clutches the empty pitcher, and rises to his feet a little unsteadily. As he walks to the bar, he stuffs his left hand deep into the pocket of his Dockers, and I wonder if he's rubbing his baby blanket in there or if he's just digging for money.

Bob and I don't stand a chance against Max and Pete. Especially not Bob, who misses so wide with every third throw that his dart eludes the board altogether. He goes through house darts like Tic-Tacs. By midgame he's already busted four tips, and we're throwing mismatched reds and yellows. The bartender is beginning to shoot me dirty looks, as if to say, *Hey, fucko, tell your friend house darts don't grow on trees.* Max has his own darts, of course: grooved brass fittings and high-gloss Confederate flag flights. He's started throwing left-handed just for sport, and it barely slows him down. He's mauling us on 17s. He looks like a walrus toeing the line with his foamy dick-duster and his big amorphous body, but the man can throw a dart. Thankfully, Pete sucks eggs. Though he's a behemoth, to be sure, maybe six four, three hundred pounds, his touch is too soft. You'd think he was throwing butterflies. The way he squints at the line and wrinkles up his big bearded face, I'm guessing he's nearsighted. But at least he hits the board. Oddly, I'm probably throwing better than I've thrown in two years. Something about being saddled with Bob takes the pressure off, I suppose. I'm not aiming. My wrist is loose. The old muscle memory seems to be kicking in. Toeing the line, I sniff the air like a predator, lock eyes on my prey, and let the darts fly without a thought in my head. I'm money on 20. But it's still not enough to compensate for Bob.

Between turns, Bob sprawls in his wooden chair with his fly wide open. Though he's curbed his beer consumption somewhat in the last thirty minutes, he can't belie the obvious signs of an amateur drunk. He's beginning to blurt things, and laugh at his own blurtings, which are as unintelligible as anything Jodi ever uttered. He'll sort of half blurt, half mumble something, and it'll sound like "Morley Safer's gooch." And when you say "What?" he'll just wave you off.

"Saginaw leatherneck," he says.

"What?"

"Old chifforobe."

"Huh?"

"Fucking-hic-boiled ham."

"What are you saying?"

The front of his dress shirt is beer-sopped, and his dart game continues to deteriorate. Bob is a man who falls apart fast. His baby blanket is hanging out of his pocket as he toes the line unsteadily, hiccupping twice, then letting a double 7 fly.

"Hum now, Bob. Think bull's-eye, buddy."

Bob straightens up — wobbling slightly, chin out. "Rusty — hic — swing set," he says.

"What the hell is he saying?" says Pete, over the rim of his Styrofoam spittoon.

"Beats the hell out of me," says Max.

When Bob's next dart hits the coin slot, Max shoots me a concerned look.

"I know, I know," I say with a double nod.

Undaunted by his failure, Bob laughs, blurts something that sounds like "knob gobbler" and lets loose an errant bull's-eye attempt, which, to the horror of everyone but Bob, pierces the waitress's neck just below the earlobe. Reasoning perhaps that she's been stung by a mutant wasp, she cries out and slaps at her neck, letting go a tray of half-empties, which caroms off a table edge and crashes to the floor.

Nice going, Bob.

Ten minutes later, Bob is yacking in the alley behind the Grill while I stand watch. When he's got nothing left but a dry retch, I guide him by the shoulders and shepherd him past his rental to the Subaru, where I pour him into the passenger's seat and buckle him in as he groans and mumbles. His hair is all mussed and his fly's still open, and his eyeballs are lolling around in their sockets. He smells like corn dogs and cheap cologne.

On the drive back to the compartment, Bob presses his face to the window and continues his sad drunk mumblings. When we stop at the signal at the top of Hostmark, he turns to me in the half-dark of the intersection, and his eyes look hollowed out.

"What would you do?" he says.

But I don't have an answer for him. I wish I did. The best I can do is deliver him to the compartment, where I make him a bed on the sofa, offer him a sandwich and a glass of water and a toothbrush, and grant him one of my flat pillows on which to lay his head. Before I can finish making his sandwich, he reclines fully clothed on top of the blanket and passes out. When I go to turn off the lamp, I see he's clutching his ragged baby blanket tightly in his fist. He looks mercifully untroubled in his leaden sleep state, almost childlike. It would serve Trev well to see him like that, I think. Or maybe it wouldn't. Removing Bob's big loafers, I set them at the foot of the sofa, and he hardly stirs. Liberating part of the comforter from beneath his dead weight, I drape it over him as best I can and snap off the light.

flight

In the morning, I find Bob — hair combed, fly zipped — standing at the compartment window looking out at the rain. There's still a little dried puke on his right loafer, and his dress shirt has apparently endured some recent and desperate attempt at laundering, for the front is visibly wet in large blotches.

"You wouldn't happen to have a hair dryer?" he says, indicating his shirt front.

"I've got a shirt," I say.

He smiles a little sadly. "Ben, you're a lifesaver."

From the back of the bedroom closet, which smells of fresh Xerox copies and lemon-scented Glade, hanging to no purpose behind a bulwark of plastic containers governing the loose ends of a life which now seems impossibly remote, I unearth the twice-worn dress shirt that Janet bought me for the express purpose of job interviews. Grid matrix on pale green. Graph paper on cotton. Very forgettable. Very Bob. And indeed, it looks good on Bob. I'd hire him.

"I'll send it back," he says. "Or I can pay for it."

"Consider it a gift. It never fit me."

Bob extends a handshake. "Well, thanks," he says, giving me a pump. "I just wanted to say thanks. I should get a cab. I've got a flight this afternoon."

"I can drop you off, no problem. You want coffee?"

"Thanks, no."

"Something to eat?"

"I'll grab breakfast on the ferry," he says, gravitating back toward the window, where he turns his attention to the rain. "The novelty never wears off."

I'm not sure if he's talking about breakfast on the ferry or the rain, which started sometime late last night and hasn't let up. "How many times have you been out here?" I say.

"I lost count."

"Do they ever let you in?"

"Twice. Once on my birthday and once when I brought chicken. That's why I always bring chicken."

I want to tell him to try fish-and-chips. But I haven't got the heart.

The radio is silent on the drive to the Grill. The rain is falling slantwise, slapping the windshield like paint spatter. The whisk of the tires and the fast thrumming of the wipers are the only other sounds, as we shoot down the hill on Hostmark past the Money Tree toward town.

"Probably best not to mention any of this to Trev," he says at last. "Or Elsa."

"Probably not," I say. But what I want to say is: *Fuck them. Quit apologizing. They don't deserve your chicken.* But I know that's not true, either.

I can see when I drop Bob at the curb that there's a parking ticket pinned like a sheet of wet fruit leather beneath the wiper of the Taurus.

"Thanks again for the shirt," he says, leaning back into the car.

"No problem. Good luck," I call after him.

When Bob pulls out behind me, I see in the rearview mirror that he's neglected to remove the parking ticket from beneath the wiper, where it traces a smudgy trail across the windshield twice before disintegrating, and I begin to understand how Bob's life works: that unpaid ticket will turn into a bench warrant and, eventually, probably even result in Bob's arrest on a minor traffic infraction, inciting the cruel amusement of his estranged son and ex-wife. And poor Bob will never know what hit him.

Arriving at work ten minutes late, I discover Elsa standing in the middle of the kitchen, tack bag slung shoulderwise. I wonder if she knows about Bob and me, or whether my tardiness is the source of her impatience.

"Morning," I say. "Sorry I'm la — "

"I've got a nine o'clock," she says. "Remind me I need to talk to you about the first week of September. We need to make arrangements."

"Got it."

"He's up early," she says. And without further pretense, she crosses the kitchen and walks out the door. Arrangements for what? I wonder, passing through the lifeless dining room. I find Trev sitting tall in his wheelchair with his tray table in front of him. His color is back. His eyes are lively. He's wearing his checkered Vans.

"Check out the size of this chick's taco," he says, referring to the Travel Channel hostess, a lithe, trout-mouthed brunette splaying poolside at the Winn Casino in a skimpy yellow two-piece.

"Can you say she-male?"

When the TV goes to a commercial, he rears his torso back, gripping the remote Tyrannosaurus-style, and with a leaden thumb, flips to the Weather Channel. It's seventy-three degrees in Salt Lake City, with winds out the southwest at ten to fifteen miles per hour.

"He'll be back today," Trev says, irritably. "You watch."

"He left already."

He lolls his head in my direction. "How do you know?"

"I don't know. Just a hunch, I guess."

Rolling his shoulders and arching his spine, he flips back to the Travel Channel.

"What does he think?" says Trev. "He's going to buy my love with fried chicken?"

Sadly, it's almost true. But at least he's trying. "Ah, give him a break," I say.

Trev furrows his brow, and his face darkens. "He's had plenty of those."

Maybe he's right. Why am I so quick to forgive Bob? The guy's a loser. While his dogged endurance may be admirable, it's plain as day that he expects to fail at every turn. Sometimes it's not enough to try. Maybe Bob doesn't care enough to succeed. But I doubt it. As far as I'm concerned, the onus is still on Trev to be the bigger man. If he's big enough to accept the complete and senseless betrayal of his own body, surely he's big enough forgive his old man for being a well-intentioned deadbeat.

"He seems like an okay guy to me."

"You don't even know him."

"I think he means well. I really do. I think he realizes he fucked up. Maybe you should just give him a chance to —"

"You know what?" he says, glaring at the television screen. "Maybe you should just mind your own business, and show up on time."

He's right. I've crossed the line again, muddled the roles, brazenly defied the first fundamental of caregiving. I can feel myself blushing. Luckily, Trev's quick to forgive me.

"I don't either," he says.

"What?"

"Know the guy. Seriously, I've seen the guy like twenty times in my life that I can remember. Maybe thirty. What I do know about him is that he left."

He squints irritably at the television. I'm done pushing for today, I'm not crossing any more lines. I ought to know by now. Just as I'm about to duck into the kitchen and prepare his breakfast, Trev surprises me.

"I'm hard on him, I know," he says. "In a way, it's not fair. But whatever. He left me. And yeah, sometimes I am a little curious about him. Sometimes I even think he's not all that bad of a guy. Sometimes I think I should give him a break, get to know him. But I don't."

"Why not?"

"I don't know," he says. "I just don't."

no time

Bernard has me feeling pretty optimistic about the future by the time the kids pile back in the car. Maybe he'll actually pull the trigger on the Discovery Bay property. I love it out there. I could see myself in a skiff on weekends, drinking a few cold ones. I could see us all out there together, all summer long, without all the distractions. Bernard in his goofy hat, burning steaks, while I ice the cooler. The kids splashing about in the water. Ruth making jam. Janet asleep in a lawn chair. Who knows, maybe we will build something out there. The thought is almost enough to make me forget my headache.

"Where are we going now?" Piper demands.

"Shopping."

"You said we were going shopping at three o'clock."

"I was wrong."

"You lied."

"No, I didn't lie. I miscalculated."

"That's not our fault."

"Okay, fine. What about the duck pond?"

"No!" says Piper.

"C'mon. That's all over now."

"No! I won't go."

"Okay, okay. What about the park?"

She eyes me suspiciously. "Which park?"

"The waterfront park."

"That's not a park. There's only two swings."

"Then where?" I look to Jodi. "How about you, Jodi? Where to?"

"Squishity-squash-something-something," he says.

"There, it's settled," I say.

"You don't even know what he said!"

"What did he say?"

"He wants to see the octopus."

"Octopus?"

"At the Marine Science Center."

"Honey, there's not time for that. We need to be home by four to meet Mommy."

"Tell *him* that," she says.

"You tell him," I say.

She folds her arms and zips her lips up tight and looks out the side window.

I sigh. "Jodi, buddy, sorry, but there's not time for the octopus."

"Daddy says no," Piper adds.

First, Jodi wrinkles his little brow. Then he begins to kick his feet a little bit, with a whimper, a single whimper. Once the bottom lip juts out and commences to quiver, it's too late — time to put out or pull over.

The octopus is named Sam. I doubt anyone ever called him cute before Piper. He's in a glass holding pen about the size of three phone booths, where he lays around in a blob to no apparent purpose, oozing and contracting just enough so that you know he's still alive. There's a placard on his tank, which I don't read. Nothing against Sam, but I'm too busy watching hands — ever since Jodi got ahold of that sea cucumber back in February. Thank goodness it wasn't a hermit crab or some sort of electric eel. We were asked politely to leave when Jodi started pitching a fit. I don't think the lady at the reception desk recognized us when we came in this time, maybe because Jodi fell asleep in my arms before I could set him down, and now I'm stuck carrying him. He's a sweaty little guy, thirty-two pounds of dead sticky weight, clinging to me like hamburger.

"Mr. Caruthers showed us a video where an octopus kills a shark," says Piper, face pressed to the glass. "He says that the octopus might be the greatest predator in the whole ocean."

"You wouldn't know it looking at old Sam here," I say.

"That's because Sam knows he's locked up in a tank. But if he could ever get out, you'd see."

As if he were listening, Sam rolls over slowly, unfurls a huge tentacle, and peers at us with one of his big bulging eyes. He looks like he's about to comment. But he doesn't. He just rolls back over and oozes some more.

look at us now

Her choice of venue says it all. She has not selected the food court for its cornucopia of flavorful choices but for its singular lack of intimacy and plentiful escape routes. It's easy to see from the way she strides purposefully past Quiznos, clutching her purse and a manila folder, that she intends to make this a short meeting. Even her attire is businesslike, from her modest lavender blouse (the color of sexual frustration), to her gray pencil skirt, right down to her close-toed leather flats. Her expression is benign but determined, thin-lipped and straight, neither hard nor soft in announcing itself — the expression of a woman collecting sperm samples. Though she's walking straight for me, she does not invite eye contact but rather engages some fixed point behind me. Already, she is a stranger to me, yet achingly familiar.

Smoothing the back of her skirt, she sidles into the fixed metal stool across from me, heaving a sigh as she sets her purse and envelope on the tabletop.

"Tacoma was a mess, sorry," she says.

Her hair has grown out a shade darker than almond. Two years ago, she all but shaved her head completely. She looked like a Polish POW. Now her hair is lustrous and looks as if it smells good — like peach-scented wax. She parts it in the center, just as she did when I first met her, from which point it cascades evenly down both sides of her face, two inches below the jaw line.

"You look good," I say.

"I look old," she says. "I feel old."

Though I've dressed young myself, in jeans and Chucks and a Penguin shirt, I wonder if it doesn't have the opposite effect.

"I'm the one who's aged."

"You look fine," she says. "You look the same as you looked three years ago." She's managed to make it an insult.

She slides the envelope across the plastic table. "I brought you these in case you lost them."

"I've got the papers."

"Then you brought them?"

"I thought we were having lunch."

She tenses up and stares out across the food court toward Macy's, looking spent. She just drove 160-odd miles for this. I want to set my hand atop hers and give it a little squeeze, the squeeze I gave it a thousand times before the disaster — when they found the cyst, when her brother died, when Jodi had a staph infection, when Piper had the chicken pox, when it seemed at every turn that the winds of fate had blown our lives afoul, financially, emotionally, or idealistically. Look at all that we endured. Look at all we managed to light along our path through the long shadow of adversity. Look at the seemingly indestructible affiliation that was once us. And look at us now. She, pretending to be a stranger behind her cakey makeup and impenetrable eyes, and me, pining for access, knowing that if I dare reach out to her, she'll stand up and leave.

"Ben, please," she says, and sighs heavily.

Looking away, past the colonnade of potted palms toward Orange Julius, I can't help but think of Piper's favorite meal: french toast, shrimp cocktail, and Orange Julius (my version, anyway). I can't help but remember all the blessed disorder that was the four of us nightly around the dinner table, more often than not eating four completely different meals but eating them together, unquestionably, indivisibly together.

"Please," I hear her say again. I let it hang there, this desolate plea, realizing that it's probably the last of its kind, for every remaining shred of her patience seems to have gone into it.

"Do you remember when we went to the ghost town," I say. "When you were pregnant with Jo — "

"Of course, I remember," she says.

"Do you remember how, right before it happened, Piper got—"

"Yes," she says. "I remember."

"It wasn't so long ago," I say.

"It was six years ago, Ben—two lives ago."

The knot in my stomach tightens. "More like four lives ago."

"Speak for yourself," she says, rifling through her purse.

My God but she's grown hard. Somewhere the old Janet still lives inside of her, I've got to believe that. If only to reach her, if only for the briefest moment of contact. She needs me—now more than ever. Who but I could ever understand her devastation? Surely not Jim Sunderland.

"It could still work, you know."

She looks up from the purse. "I'm tired of feeling like a heartless bitch just because I need to move on."

"You mean Jim?"

I've caught her off guard. She searches my face. "What do you know about Jim?"

"I know all about Jim and his ugly kid."

"Oh, so now you're stalking me? What is wrong with you? Why are you doing this to me? Haven't you done enough already?"

I'm stunned by the cruelty of it. The slackening contours of her face say that she wishes she could take it back. But she will not allow herself to soften. She stiffens up again almost immediately.

"Leave Jim out of this. I want those papers, Ben. Don't make me get nasty."

"You mean this isn't nasty?"

"I gave you six months, I gave you a year. I did what you asked. Now it's time for you to hold up your end of the bargain."

"Do I hear wedding bells? Please tell me you're not marrying that clown. Whatever you do, don't breed with him—the ugly gene is dominant."

"You want ugly, Ben. Fine, you've got it." Calmly, she hefts her purse, and picks up the envelope. Rising to her feet, she smoothes out her skirt and stands tall, a portrait of self-possession. "But remember," she says. "You did this."

Before I can even think about defending myself — though let's be honest, I'm guilty as charged, and we both know it — Janet turns and strides away across the food court, past Quiznos, just as purposefully as when she arrived five minutes ago. She halts in front of Busby's long enough to ram the envelope into the heaping trash bin, brushes a stray hair from her face, and does not bother to look back as she pushes through the glass door and into the gray afternoon.

Do I go after her? Do I attempt to right this ship with one of the two thousand apologies I owe her? My feet say no. My heart says yes. I can only trust one of them. Outside, the low sky has begun to spit rain. I am not proud of who I've become.

As I'm rattling out of the parking lot in the Subaru, I spot Janet in her silver sedan. She is too consumed to notice me. She has not moved from her parking space. Her forehead is between her hands resting on the steering wheel, and it's obvious from the convulsions racking her slumped shoulders that she is crying. There is an opportunity here for some small redemption, if only I were man enough to seize it. With a mere signature, I could offer Janet comfort long enough to reach Jim Sunderland's arms. I could offer her the chance to take a small step forward and start forgetting our apocalypse, to walk away from the rubble of our lives once and for all and forge some new path for herself. I could care enough to save Janet. Instead, I roll by slowly, fixed on her wrecked figure slumped in the driver's seat, as though she were the scene of some grisly accident.

monday, monday

I've just set the kettle to boil and arrayed my coffee cone precariously on the rim of my oversized Les Schwab mug when a double rap rattles the compartment door. It's never good news at 7:40 a.m. Probably Madge in 212 again, come to berate me for feeding chocolate bars to her thirty-pound cat, an offense of which I am decidedly not guilty. Looking up, I'm startled by a clean-shaven male face, late twenties, pressed to the window, fighting the glare of the reflection with both hands and a legal-sized envelope as he peers into the compartment for signs of life. Instinctively, I dive for cover behind the kitchen counter. Seconds later, rising tentatively on my haunches, I extend my neck and prairie-dog over the countertop to find that he's still there. I pop back down, though probably not before he's spotted me. Glancing at my watch, I see that I'm going to be late for work again.

A tap on the window.

I don't budge.

Another tap.

Maybe he didn't see me, I reason, just as the kettle begins to moan. By the time I scurry crabwise across the linoleum to the stove, the damn thing is screeching like a rabid spider monkey. Groping blindly around the stovetop, a bolt of lightning shoots down my wrist to my elbow.

"Ah!" I call out, releasing the kettle with a metallic clatter on the range, where it continues to warble and wheeze.

The doorbell rings. Immediately, the neighbor's terrier starts going nuts. The kettle continues to squeal.

Thrusting my arm up again, I give the kettle a push until it clears the burner completely and begins to settle. Sidling over toward the sink, I slump against the cabinet. Janet wasn't bluffing this time. Nothing to do now but wait it out.

After two minutes, when the incessant tapping and dinging and yipping have finally subsided, I peep over the counter and see that my pursuer has apparently thrown in the towel. Forgoing my coffee, I rush madly about the apartment gathering my keys, my wallet, my crossword, and my sweatshirt. Poking my head out the apartment door, I scan the causeway in both directions, see that the coast is clear, and stride briskly down the corridor. I spot the courier below, leaning against the bike rack, tapping the envelope on his knee. If I can get to the stairs, I can sneak around back, run some interference if necessary, and circle the far side of the building to the Subaru.

No sooner have I passed 210 than Madge emerges from her apartment with folded arms, blocking my way like a sentry. She's wrapped in a tired blue terry-cloth bathrobe covered with cat hair. She's got curlers in her hair and a cigarette in her mouth. I glance at my watch, then over the rail, where I note that the courier has cut his losses and is crossing the lot toward a blue Bronco. I lean back out of sight.

"Stop stubbing your Winstons out in my planter box," Madge wheezes.

"I'm not."

"Don't get smart with me, mister. I've seen you."

"No you haven't."

"Are you calling me a liar?"

"I don't even smoke."

I attempt to sidestep her, but she blocks my way.

"Not so fast," she says. "Not until you pick every last one of those butts out of my gladiolus."

Eyeing the planter, I see that the gladiolus are nothing but withered husks. Indeed, a dozen or more crooked butts jut out of the soil like gravestones.

"They're not mine," I say.

"And I suppose you're not feeding Hershey bars to my Agnes?"

"That's right, I'm not."

As though on cue, Agnes emerges, slinking through the crack in the apartment door, and begins rubbing herself around my ankle.

"The heck you aren't," says Madge. "Now either you start fishing those butts out of my gladiolus, or I'm going to march right down to Chuck's apar—"

Before she can finish, I force my way through her blockade.

"Hey!" she yells. "You come back here!"

Over the rail, I see that her shouting has alerted the courier. He freezes. We lock eyes for an instant. *Gotcha*, he seems to say. We both break at once for the stairwell. Madge is calling after me.

"You asked for it!" she hollers. "I'm going straight to Chuck with this!"

I hit the top of the stairs at a sprint and don't slow for the corners. I beat him to the bottom, just barely.

"You! Benjamin Benjamin!" he calls. But I don't turn—to turn would be to admit that I'm Benjamin Benjamin. Instead, I jump the boxwood hedge, sidestep a silver Lumina, and dart straight for the Subaru at the far corner of the lot. I jump behind the wheel and hit the ignition, which doesn't catch the first time around. I can hear that little solenoid tapping away under the hood as I turn it over twice, three times, before it ignites on the fourth, and I whip the car in reverse. In the rearview, I see my pursuer turn halfway across the lot and run for his Bronco. He should have kept coming. Hemmed in by Emilio's gardening truck, I'm forced to back into a three-point turn, which turns into an eight-point turn. I hook Emilio's bumper on the final maneuver. The Subaru rears up on three wheels momentarily and crashes back down with a squawk from the rear suspension. No sooner am I free of Emilio's bumper than I stomp on the gas. The Subaru chokes on her own exuberance. I give her a few seconds to recover, then lay rubber pulling out. Squealing around the corner of unit B, I nearly collide with the blue Bronco as it noses around the edge of the building. We both lay on the brakes in the nick of time. The little cockroach is smiling behind the wheel. He thinks he's got me. We're still locking eyes as I shoot past him, up on the curb, side-swiping the juniper hedge and narrowly eluding an electrical box.

The back end squawks again as I regain four wheels and speed toward the exit. But the Bronco falls in right behind me. The kid is still smiling. He's right on my tail as I swing onto Madison, where immediately the Subaru stalls. Desperately, I turn the key over once, twice, three times, looking anxiously up at the mirror. The kid is actually laughing now. On the fourth try, the Subaru lurches back to life, and I sputter north toward the library, gaining speed steadily. At the roundabout, I catch my first break as two school buses pull in behind me. I squirt out the north exit just ahead of some middle-schoolers at the cross-walk, for whom the Bronco is forced to pause. By the fire station, I've got three blocks on him. When I catch the light at Highway 305, I leave him in the dust. But I know I haven't seen the last of him.

Arriving at work ten minutes late, I find Elsa waiting impatiently in the kitchen with her gear. I can tell she'd rather give me the silent treatment, but she can't help herself.

"You know," she says, hefting her tack bag. "I realize this job doesn't pay much. And I realize you have a life outside of work. But if this job is getting in the way of your life, maybe it's best for everybody if we have Social and Human Services assign a replacement. Frankly, I can't leave in September without knowing I can count on a provider to be here when we need him."

She looks tired. I can tell it takes something out of her to give it to me like this, and I feel terrible for putting her in such a position. "I'm sorry," I say. "It won't happen again. Really. You can count on me."

"This isn't personal," she says.

WHEN I GET home from work in the evening, I find a note from Chuck on the door.

We need to talk, it says.

So I march straight down to Chuck's apartment and knock on the door. He doesn't invite me in but steps grimly out under the causeway, scratching his neck. He's wearing slippers and a Ravens jersey, and he smells like weed. He'd rather have this conversation some other time, I think.

"Uh, look, Madge says you're trying to poison her cat," he says.

"She's nuts, Chuck. She thinks I'm siphoning her electricity, too."

"Yeah, well I don't know about that, but she also says you've been using her planter box as an ashtray."

"I don't even smoke."

"Well, what about Emilio's truck? He says you dented the front fender."

"I just clipped the bumper. I was late. He boxed me in, Chuck. I was in a hurry."

"Look, man," Chuck says. "I like you, I do. Until recently, you've been a decent tenant." He looks down at his slippers, and scratches his neck some more. "But . . ."

"But?"

"Look, I don't know what kind of stuff you're mixed up in, and to tell the truth I don't want to know. What I do know is that I looked out my window this morning and saw some guy chasing you through the parking lot."

"I can explain."

"Don't bother. Just do me a favor, okay? Just keep the shady stuff away from the complex, man. And quit feeding chocolate to Madge's cat."

"But Chuck —"

"Dude. I'm just doing my job."

Walking back to the compartment, I'm shell-shocked. How did I arrive here? At what point did my character become so suspect? When did I sink so low that I can hardly sustain a nine-dollar-an-hour job, that my car stalls at every intersection, that I can't hit a lousy .250 in slow-pitch softball?

green beans

J anet used to take long lunches on Fridays. When weather permitted, the kids and I would meet her by the duck pond at Battle Point. We would buy fresh artisan bread from the T&C deli at four and a half bucks a loaf. Janet would've killed me had she known. But Piper insisted that it wasn't fair that ducks should have to eat stale bread all the time.

"And not the white kind, either," she said. "Mommy says it's not good for you. So it must not be good for ducks."

Piper and I would pack a picnic, Jodi watching with dark placid eyes from his high chair as we assembled peanut butter sandwiches. Piper handled the peanut butter side, since I always made it lumpy, and we cut the sandwiches into tiny squares as per Piper's instructions.

We'd fill Ziploc bags with cold canned green beans. Jodi loved them, ate them like jelly beans while the rest of us endured them. For dessert, there was Yoplait yogurts. I once tried passing the healthy brand (alternately known as the lumpy brand) off as dessert, but it didn't fly. Piper ate it (and seemed to enjoy it, I might add) but only under strict protest. She also managed to finagle Scooby-Doo Push-Ups and a player to be named later out of the deal. We'd bring a gallon jug of apple juice to wash it all down. I let the kids drink all the apple juice they wanted on Friday afternoons, though Janet swore it would rot their teeth.

Picnic packed, we'd gather our raincoats, boots, and artisan bread and the umbrella we'd never use, and pour out into the driveway to the RAV4. The RAV4 was my choice. Janet wanted a minivan. She wanted an automatic. I told her no self-respecting dude drove a minivan. Or an automatic. I'm often reminded of this. What if we'd bought an automatic?

I'd buckle the kids in the backseat and hike up socks and boots. Sometimes when I was well rested, we'd sing on the drive to the park. Sometimes we'd talk about alligators. Or special schools people could attend to learn how to speak dog or other animal languages and how you could use it to explain to the coyotes why they should stay out of garbage cans so people wouldn't want to shoot them. Or you could warn mice about traps. Or teach raccoons to look both ways before crossing.

We were invariably at least five minutes late when Janet stepped out from beneath the gazebo to greet us. We'd trample out into the muddy parking lot and across the field to the pond, where honking ducks converged to greet us. Bread in hand, Piper would dash to the shoreline while Jodi faltered along in her wake, his little hands grasping at the air in front of him. Janet would begin setting the picnic out on the table, under the cover of a maple. Yum, she'd say, in reference to the canned green beans. She'd talk about work. A sixteen-year-old retriever riddled with lymphomas. A tabby with heartworm. She'd ask me about my day. I'd tell her about dirty dishes and the Wiggles and how Jeff fell asleep in the Big Red Car. Again. And if I seemed tired or grumpy or a little short on patience as I watched my kids like a hawk at the water's edge, it's not because I didn't live for those Friday afternoons, for muddy feet and dandelion bouquets, for grass-stained knees and half-eaten lunches. Friday afternoons were perfection, the sort of perfection childless people can't possibly understand. It wasn't an easy perfection, all of that wiping noses and scuttling around duck ponds. It tried my patience to the ragged edges. But today I would trade an afternoon of cold green beans and muddy feet for every tomorrow I have left. And if that's not a convincing argument for eating your green beans, I don't know what is.

postcards from the hinterlands

B ob has a new strategy. Either he's taken some vacation time, or he's logging heavy miles on the weekends. He's spending his money on postage in recent weeks. They arrive almost daily — postcards from the Utah hinterlands, from all corners of the Industry State; from Logan and Monticello, from Cedar City and Provo. The first card came about four days after his last visit. By now, a thin stack of them have accumulated on Trev's tray table amid the pill jars and pushpins: Hobbitville, the World's Largest Dog Head. Even the aforementioned Biggest Pit in the World.

While Trev is sleeping, I make it my business to thumb through the stack. Bob's roadside missives are invariably brief — a smart move, since Trev isn't a big reader. Like the rest of Bob, his handwriting is mild-mannered. A cursory knowledge of graphology yields little in the way of insight. No felons claws or big looping letters to suggest his character flaws, no heavy pressure applied, no distinctive slant, no wavy baseline. He writes like he dresses. He signs them all Bob, not Dad — another wise move.

OF THE BIGGEST Pit in the World, Bob has this to say: *You're right. Clifton is bigger.*

Of the Mormon Tabernacle, he says: *Q: Why do you take two Mormons fishing with you? A: If you bring one, he'll drink all your beer.*

Of the Two Story Outhouse near Moab, Bob offers this: *Unfortunately, no wheelchair access for the top one. But at least there's no line for the bottom one.*

Who is this guy? Al Gore was never this clever. I can't help but feel a little proud of Bob. He's making progress. He's thinking outside himself. He's giving himself a chance, albeit a slim one, to finally reach Trev.

Bob, on the Bonneville Salt Flats: *Just when you thought it couldn't get more exciting than a big hole in the ground.*

Bob, on the IRS Headquarters in Ogden: *Okay, the Salt Flats are starting to look fun now.*

Bob, on Monument Valley: *Meep meep.*

Maybe Bob's most brilliant tactic of all — if indeed it's a tactic — is the general tone he employs in these briefs, the dry postmodern distance from which he delivers his summations. From the languid to the downright bored, his tone seems to suggest that Trev's not really missing anything by sequestering himself in the living room all day long. What better way to arouse Trev's curiosity than by withholding one's own? What better way to entice his imagination than by forcing him to lean heavily upon it? What better measure to counter Trev's resistance to the extraordinary than by embracing the cause oneself?

Bob, on Bryce Canyon: *Six bucks for two triple-A batteries in the gift shop. Amazing.*

Trev never talks about the cards, never really lets on that he even reads them, but I can't help but notice that he stacks them scrupulously. This morning, drinking his Ensure, he says out of the blue, "The Mormons build some weird-looking shit." And after breakfast he says, apropos of nothing, "You don't really think about Utah being desert."

desperate measures

I've taken to parking the Subaru three blocks away on Hildebrand, so the Cockroach can't find it. Otherwise, he lies in wait behind the hedges clutching his legal envelope, and some form of foot race invariably ensues. I don't wear my Chucks anymore because they won't stick to the wet pavement. The Cockroach loves the chase. Whenever I look back, he's smiling. Though he's younger and faster than I, the Cockroach is easily outwitted. Wednesday I lost him by dodging around the northeast corner of unit A and quickly squatting between two Dumpsters, where I'm pretty sure Chuck saw me out his back window just as the Cockroach sprinted by. I waved sheepishly just in case, but Chuck didn't wave back.

Yesterday I was forced to shimmy out the bathroom window and drop eight feet onto the uneven knoll in order to elude not only the Cockroach, but Chuck, too, stationed outside my front door in his bathrobe, foot tapping. This morning, they've got me trapped in the kitchen again, pinned behind the counter. I scramble for my cell and frantically dial Janet from memory. She answers on the first ring.

"Call them off," I say.

"I want the papers, Ben."

"Look," I plead, sneaking a look around the corner of the counter, where I see Chuck's bushy mustache pressed to the window. "I'll sign the papers, I swear. But I want to do it in person."

"You had your chance at the mall."

"Okay, I blew it. But I want to do it right, I just need to say one thing first. That's all. And it probably won't change anything — and I know that. But I need to say it."

"So say it."

"In person, to your face."

Chuck and the Cockroach are tapping madly at the window pane. I think they can see my foot sticking out from behind the counter. I reel it in slowly.

"Ben, damnit, there's nothing to say."

"But there *is*!"

"What, Ben? What is there to say?"

Wedging the phone between shoulder and ear, I sidle crabwise across the linoleum toward the mouth of the hallway, where I plan on making a run for the bathroom. "What I've got to say, I want to say in person. I need you to hear it."

I'm only half lying. I *do* need her to hear it; I've never needed anything so badly in my life. I just have no idea *what* it is I need her to hear. What is there to say? What word or acknowledgment could possibly undo any of the damage? Why do I bother clinging so desperately to this crumbling hillside when I know in my heart of hearts that I'm destined to go over the edge?

The fact that Janet has given even the slightest of pauses to consider this proposition, especially after what I've put her through, is another testament to her weak will.

I'm on my knees now, readying myself to slink around the corner undetected. I can hear Chuck and the Cockroach conferring on my doorstep. I hear keys jingling. "I'll come to you this time," I say to Janet, darting down the hallway. "I'll bring the papers."

"Why should I believe that?"

"Because it doesn't cost you anything."

"So far it's cost me nearly two years of my life."

"So what's another week or two?" I can hear the doorknob rattling, as I wedge myself up through the bathroom window. "Hold on a sec," I say.

She takes in a long breath. If there's no hope for us, why is she on the verge of caving in? The thought that maybe, just maybe, there's more at work here than Janet's weak will has me smiling ear to ear as I shimmy out the window and drop once again onto the grassy knoll eight feet below, landing with a thud and rolling over onto my shoulder.

"You still there?"

"Yes," she says.

Yes! Like a welling of sunshine deep down in my belly, yes! Yes, she's still there — willing to jump out of windows with me, willing to sprint down Madison weaving between cars with me. Yes!

"Are you running?" she says.

"Just walking fast," I say, stealing a look over my shoulder.

"You sound strange. Like you're out of breath."

"I guess I'm walking pretty fast is all." Another glance over my shoulder tells me I'm probably free and clear. Still, I tear around the corner at Wallace, jump a weed whacker laying across the sidewalk, slalom between a team of Mexican landscapers clearing ivy along the edge, and immediately slacken my pace, doing my best to disguise the fact that I'm out of breath.

"Are you okay?" she says.

"I'm fine," I say. Especially fine considering the circumstances — and there really are so many to consider.

"You don't sound fine. You sound crazy."

"I'm just walking fast."

"Maybe you should slow down, then. Take a deep breath."

"Maybe if I wasn't being chased down the street by a . . . Oh, look, never mind. What about you? How are you? Are you okay?"

"I'm fine, Ben."

"Still working at the zoo?"

"Yes, Ben."

"That's good. You sound good."

I'm sitting on the curb in front of the Subaru now, fully intent on Janet on the other end of the phone, reminding myself not to rush intimacy, to disarm her first, to elicit casual conversation, rather than to leap headlong into full disclosure. The problem is, I can't think of anything to say. It seems that I'm only capable of full disclosure. With anybody. Maybe that's what happens to crazy people, they become too honest. They can't see anything but truth anymore, and they're compelled to share it, when they ought to shut up about it.

"Is it raining down there?" I say.

"I'm not by a window. But yes, it has been. You need to pull yourself together, Ben," she says. "Start thinking about the future."

I should probably take offense, even if it's true. But along the hoarse edges of her exasperation, I hear strains of genuine concern.

"I'm trying," I say. "It may not seem like it, but I am."

"I believe you."

"Then call them off."

"I've gotta go, Ben."

"Call them off."

"Ben, I'm at work. I've gotta go."

"Please."

"Don't do this to me. You always do this."

"I'm not trying to do anything, look, I just . . . For everything . . . I'm . . ."

I'm too late. She's already hung up. Still, I can't help but feel strangely hopeful as I climb behind the wheel of the Subaru. My optimism is rewarded immediately. The car fires up on the first turn. She doesn't stall when I put her in gear. Rolling by the apartment on Madison, I spot Chuck and the Cockroach in the parking lot, conferring once again. Chuck is slightly hunched, breathing heavily, with his arms akimbo. The Cockroach is shaking his head side to side and looking at his wristwatch. He isn't smiling. I can see Madge on the balcony, smoking a cigarette, while the cat circles her ankle. I honk as I drive past.

accidents

Optimism does not prevent me from arriving ten minutes late for work again. This time, Elsa is not waiting in the kitchen with her tack bag or in the foyer tapping her foot but in the living room, where she's seated in my spot on the couch with her hands in her lap like she doesn't know what to do with them. Otherwise, she's calm like a cobra.

"Sit down," she says.

I sit in the chair along the near wall. The first thing I notice is that the map is gone. There's a giant white rectangle running the length of the far wall. Faintly, you can see hundreds of tiny pinholes in the sheetrock, more or less evenly spread. The second thing I notice is that Elsa's not dressed for work. She's in a yellow sweater and man's corduroys and rubber gardening clogs.

"There's been an accident," she says.

Suddenly I can hear the blood surging behind my eardrums. My voice comes to me as though from a distance. "Is he okay?"

"It's Bob."

A silence sets in as I grope for an appropriate response to this news.

"He was on his way to see the Biggest Watermelon in the World," Elsa explains.

I knew all along Bob was destined for something like this. Sooner or later, his Magoo-like inattention to the ever-lurking potential for disaster was bound to betray him.

"He was driving through the desert," Elsa explains. "He fell asleep at the wheel."

"And he hit a watermelon?"

"A billboard. The only one within miles."

"Jesus. Is he —"

"He's okay, stable. Pretty banged up, though. A broken leg, three broken ribs."

It's comforting to know that Bob's probably taking it like a champ. Making lemonade. Stroking his baby blanket.

"Thank God, he's all right," I say.

She searches my face, briefly but critically. I'm not sure what she's looking for, but my sympathy for Bob must be written there.

"You know," she says, "Bob hasn't always tried this hard."

"I know. I got the impression. Trev's told me as much."

"Yes, I'll bet he has," she says, as though it were an accusation. "Bob likes to do things on his terms. Bob is conditional. He likes to show up with gifts and pretend he never went away. He thinks fried chicken is the cure to everybody's problems."

Not anymore he doesn't. I could tell her that. But I've learned my lesson about defending Bob.

"Everybody lets Bob off the hook. Everybody is so quick to forgive Bob. And do you know why? Because he's basically an infant."

I wonder if she knows about the blanket. She must.

She glances at the bare wall for diversion. I watch as her gray eyes make a sweeping survey of the faint pinholes, just as mine did. Her face slackens ever so slightly. She looks sad and overwrought beneath her hard veneer. When she catches me staring at her, she looks back at me intently for what feels like a long time. So long that I begin to feel transparent.

"He trusts you," she says.

"Bob?"

"Trevor. And that scares me."

"Scares you?"

"Trevor needs continuity. Nobody's doing him any favors by not sticking around. It does more damage than it does good."

"I'm not going anywhere."

"Don't make promises you can't keep."

"Where am I going? I have no family. I have no job opportunities. I have no life."

She leans forward on the sofa and looks me right in the eye. It's like looking straight at the sun. I stare shiftily back at the bridge of her nose.

"It's not about you this time," she says. She releases my eyes, and they dart straight for the window. I can feel myself blanching as she leans back in her seat.

"This time it's about somebody else."

I have no clue where she's going with any of this, but wherever it is, I'd rather not go there. Suddenly, I feel as though I'm on trial along-side Bob.

"I'm not sure what I think of you," she says. "But Trevor likes you, he trusts you, and that's all I need to know to be scared of you. And that may sound ungrateful."

"I think I understand."

She pins my eyes in place once more. "Do you? Then maybe you could clear something up for me. Because this was never supposed to be personal. So I'm a little confused about how we got here."

"I'm sorry," I say, though I'm not sure why I'm apologizing. I'm even less sure what any of this has to do with Bob's misfortune.

"So how did we get here?" Elsa wants to know. "Tell me."

"Get where? Where are we? I don't understand."

"I was required to get a license, you know?" she says, by way of explanation. "Just like you. I took all the same classes as you. I have to do ten hours of continuing coursework every year just like you. I remember all the checks and balances, all the idiot-proof diagrams, and those silly mnemonics. But what I don't remember is the part about creating unreasonable expectations and dispensing unsolicited advice."

"What are we talking about?"

"For starters, I'd like to know how he got it in his head to take this road trip?"

"You mean the map? The map was just an exercise. Nobody ever said we were actually going to do it. Did he say that?"

"He's got it in his head that the two of you are driving the van to Utah."

"For real?"

"To see Bob."

"I — but I had no idea."

She looks at me doubtfully. "His pulmonary is weak, his breathing is shallow. The last virus could have killed him. He needs access to medical facilities at all times. The next bug could be too much for him. What on earth were you thinking?"

The answer, of course, is that I wasn't. All of this is Trev's doing — everything short of Bob's accident. And I'm only beginning to see the elegance of Trev's design. This is an invitation. Or maybe a challenge. Trev is counting on me to answer this call. But why? For what? Could it be that by putting the onus on *me*, by making this visit to Bob *my* idea, Trev is protecting his mother? Is it for Elsa that Trev has fought the Battle of Bob all these years; beaten back his father's flagging offensives, rejected his peace offerings like Trojan Horses? Is Trev — Would-You-Give-Her-Moroccan-Meatball Trev — really so expansive that he would go to such ends on his mother's behalf? Could it be that by allowing her to protect him — from Bob, from the world at large, from all things uncertain — Trev is actually trying to protect her? Suddenly Trev seems like a stranger, his inner workings invisible to me, like he's been somebody else all along. And yet I've never felt closer to him.

"Tell me, then," says Elsa. "What you were thinking when you cooked up this trip? And just when were you planning to tell me about it? Or were you just planning on leaving while I was in Bend and not telling me at all?"

"I guess I was thinking it's something he needs to do," I lie.

Elsa clamps her eyes shut and breathes deeply. Calmly, she proceeds. "What gives you the right to decide what my son needs? I don't remember any of this in the service plan. Are you a psychologist? A physician?"

"I'm the best friend he's got."

Now she stares me down more intently than ever. This time I meet her eyes unflinchingly. But truth be told, I'm only reflecting her glare, shining it back on her in hopes of blinding her to my own weakness. I'm not sure how long I can hold it. We both know she's stronger. We both know that I'm ultimately unreliable, that even my best intentions are suspect, and that in my own way I'm every bit as crippled as her son. But somehow I manage to outlast her, and she looks out the window.

"You're fired," she says.

mr. goodbar

Consider my selfishness. Consider that in the seven minutes I've been parked in front of the Chevron Mini-Mart, staring stupidly at the dash console, feeling sorry for myself as I ponder my invisible future, I've yet to reflect upon Trev's fate in all of this. He's the real victim here, right? He's the one being denied a friend, an ally, or at the very least, a bathroom attendant. But maybe I'm still giving myself too much credit. Maybe this is what Trev wanted. Maybe we weren't conspirators, after all. Isn't it more likely that Trev put me in the hot seat because it was the closest one to the door? Isn't it more likely that I pushed him one too many times?

I'm feeling reckless. It's ten in the morning. But nothing short of a twelve-pack will do. And some chips. And a gigantic Mr. Goodbar. Failure makes me hungry. It's a wonder I'm not three hundred pounds. In thirty-odd visits to the Chevron Mini-Mart, the counter guy — and it's always the same guy: midfifties, big belly, narrow shoulders, tattooed hand, one bad tooth — has never spoken to me beyond the obligatory "Is that it?" or "That'll be ten eighty-six." But of all days, today he's suddenly Chatty Cathy.

"Mornin', boss," he says, as I heft my twelver onto the counter.

I nod, just barely. Among the riot of moods and impulses presently elbowing for room at the forefront of my emotional queue, chattiness is somewhere near the back.

"Thirsty today, huh? You want some bacon and eggs with that, boss?"

"Good one."

"Thanks." He glances at the clock above his head as he's bagging the beer. "Good day to drink," he observes.

"It's for tonight," I explain.

His neck gets fatter when he smiles. "Oh right, tonight," he says, with a little wink. "Gotcha."

"Look, how much?"

"Fifteen thirty-six," he says, dropping the giant Mr. Goodbar in the bag. "Hope you're not diabetic, boss."

"Just give me my fucking change, please."

"You ever tried the sour cream and onion?"

"No."

"You should."

"You know what?" I say. "I don't need this. Stop. Please. Just give me my change, and let me get on with my life."

"Suit yourself, boss."

On the drive home, my thoughts turn to Bob. I imagine him in traction, encased in some kind of body cast with his legs hoisted up, doing his best to be cheerful in a world where billboards and giant watermelons conspire to annihilate you, smiling sheepishly, almost apologetically up at a squat gray nurse with skin tags on her arms who ministers to his exposed areas with a wet towel. You can't fault him for being cheerful. Who knows, maybe he planned all of this. Maybe in spite of all his broken bones and dashed desires, in spite of the complete and unmitigated fiasco he's made of his life with his clownish bungling, Bob has reason to hope. I almost envy him. He's still got something at stake.

I park on Wallace and approach the apartment from the back. Skirting the laurel hedge along the north side, I peek around the corner. No sign of the blue Blazer. Venturing out a few tentative steps, I crane my neck and confirm that Chuck's blinds are closed. Easing into the corridor, I sniff the air for Madge's cigarette smoke. I crane my neck once more and make a sweep of the laundry room. All clear. I scurry up the steps with my bag of beer and duck under Madge's window when I pass. As I'm fidgeting with my keys, I hear footsteps on the stairs and begin to fumble in earnest, cursing myself for carrying around a bunch of keys that no longer unlock anything, since everything they ever protected has vanished, fled, or been liquidated.

Lighting upon the proper key just as the steps reach the landing, I slip into the apartment and close the door stealthily behind me. I stand with my back pressed to the door, breathing quietly lest I betray my presence as the footfalls round the corner and proceed with purpose in my direction. They stop in front of my door. I feel the percussion of the knocks on my back. After three fruitless attempts, I hear a shuffling of feet, and soon a shadow descends on the living room through the window. It's only a blob, further obscured by the Levolors, so I can't tell whether it's Chuck or the Cockroach, or Donald Rumsfeld for that matter. I don't even know who the enemy is anymore. My twelve-pack is getting warm. I want to cry. I want to be left alone, to lick my wounds and drink my beer and eat my Mr. Goodbar. But no. My wrist is beginning to cramp from the weight of the beer. Just when I'm sure I can't hold out any longer, the shadow recedes, and finally, the footsteps retreat slowly from whence they came.

I lock the door, and close the blinds, and feel my every muscle slacken as darkness envelops the room. A relative calm washes over me. Retiring to the sofa, I crack a beer, and stare dully straight ahead at the luminous clock face. It's 10:31 a.m. I think I can smell the bottom from here.

manning up

Arapping, brisk and staccato, upsets the darkness. The clock reads 4:37 — I'm guessing p.m., though I could be wrong. I'm clutching a warm beer, a little less than half empty. There's spittle on my chin. Outside the door, voices confer. They've come for me. It's time to man up. To meet my punishment standing tall. Or just beg for mercy. I take a long pull of warm beer just as another sequence of knocks rattles the hinges, these duller and wetter, as though delivered with a canned ham.

"Pinche guero pendejo," says a voice.

"Let me handles this," says another.

"Somebody handle it," wheezes a third voice.

I can hear the faint humming of an air compressor, which I soon deduce to be the purring of a certain morbidly obese feline.

"We know you're in there!" says Chuck.

"Fucking *puto.*"

"You git now, Agnes. Go on. It's not safe here."

A fourth voice joins the fray. "What's the problem? Is something wrong?"

"Who are you?" says Chuck.

"I'm here for Ben."

"Take a number," wheezes Madge. "What'd he do to *you*?"

"He's my friend," says Forest.

"He's a *stupido,*" says Emilio. "He hit my truck with his *pinche* Subaru."

Now Forest thumps on the door, wiggles the doorknob. "Yo, Benji, open up!"

When I open the door a swath of dusty light illuminates the darkness, and they all file in like tomb raiders as I shield my eyes from the daylight. Forest raises the blinds without further ceremony.

"What a dump," says Madge, ashing her menthol on the carpet. The cat has followed her in and is currently milling around the coffee table.

Squinting, I note that at long last the compartment looks lived in. I backpedal to the sofa and resume my seat. They form a phalanx about me. Emilio's got a black eye. The brim of his dirty Dodgers cap is pulled down even lower than usual. Chuck is wearing blue fuzzy slippers and his Ravens jersey. As usual, he smells strongly of weed. Forest keeps sniffing the air around him. Forest is still in his work clothes. I'm guessing it was casual Friday, because his white dress shirt is tucked into jeans, and he's wearing running shoes.

"Why haven't you been returning my calls?" he demands. "It's dart night."

"I've been busy," I say.

"Look, we need to talk," says Chuck, stepping to the forefront. "To begin with, I can't have high-speed chases going on in the middle of—"

"What about my truck?" Emilio interjects.

Madge puffs her menthol, then shakes it at me. "What about my Agnes?" she turns to Forest. "The sonofabitch is still trying to poison my cat."

Emilio thumps his chest. "My truck is my work, you understand? My business!"

"Whoa, whoa," says Forest. "Everybody hold up. What's going on here?"

"He hit my truck!"

Forest appeals to me with a questioning look.

"Just barely," I say.

He frowns.

Madge jabs the air in front of her with her menthol pointer. "He's been feeding chocolate to my cat!"

Forest looks to me again.

"It's not true!" I say.

"He's lying!" she says.

"I'm not!"

"Well, what about *that*?" she says, pointing at the coffee table, where Agnes is still nosing around.

"What?"

"*That!*"

The coffee table is strewn with beer bottles and gutted potato chip bags. "You want some chips, Madge?"

"No, *that!*"

Then I see it: partially obscured by the surrounding chaos, its foil wrapper peeled back in preparation, my gigantic Mr. Goodbar.

Forest shakes his head disappointedly.

"That's for *me!*" I say.

But nobody believes me. A pall settles over the room. Cat poisoner.

"I didn't do it!" I plead. "I swear to God!"

"Like you didn't do my truck, eh, *pendejo*?"

"Look, I'm warning you," says Chuck. "The next complaint I get — whether it's from Madge, or Emilio, or Darlene in 316 — "

"What'd I do to her?"

"I'm just saying. The next complaint I get, I'm gonna have to shut you down, Benjamin."

"You pay for my truck!" says Emilio, thumping his chest again. "Or I be your next complaint."

"And I want your guarantee," says Chuck, "that I won't have anymore bounty hunters running around my parking lot."

"He's a courier!"

"Whatever you want to call him, I don't want anybody running around here."

"No running."

"And no more reckless driving."

"Got it. Are we done here?"

"No," says Forest. "I think you owe Madge an apology."

Chuck and Emilio nod in agreement. Madge gathers her bathrobe in front and straightens her posture.

"But . . ."

Forest shakes his head woefully and crosses his arms.

I have but one choice: swim with the current. "I'm sorry, Madge," I announce. "It was an accident. I didn't know that chocolate was . . . you know, not good for cats or whatever. I should've told you."

Madge undresses me with her eyes through a blue cloud of menthol smoke. I can't help but wonder if she was happy once. Or even young. She straightens her hair, and raises her chin up and sucks her cheeks in haughtily.

"Apology accepted," she says.

"SO WAIT," FOREST says, a half hour later at the Grill, where I'm abstaining in spite of happy hour. "You were lying that you *didn't* poison the cat? Or lying that you *did* poison the cat? Or lying that it was an accident?"

"Forest, I've never touched her cat. Or siphoned her electricity or ashed in her gladiolus or pissed in her agapanthus, or anything else. She's crazy."

"And what's all this about bounty hunters?"

"Nothing. Collections. An old phone bill."

"You need a loan?"

"No."

"You're sure?"

"Positive."

Forest sips his beer and looks around the bar, nodding to someone in back. "So, how's work?" he says.

"Good."

"That's good."

I'm not sure why I always lie to Forest, whether I don't wish to burden him with my never-ending difficulties or because I'm afraid of disappointing him. After a long moment of uneasy silence, it's clear to me that something is weighing on Forest.

"I fucked up, Benji," he says, at last. "I fucked up bad."

"What do you mean?"

He bows his head a little and stares down at the tabletop and shakes his head slowly.

"What is it?"

He lifts his head and looks me steadily in the eye, and I see that his eyes are moist.

"I cheated on Melissa," he says.

I'm breathless. "What are you saying?"

"I'm saying I fucked up big-time, Benji. And I hate myself for it. God, I hate myself." He slumps at the shoulders and looks back down at the table top, where he spins his glass slowly counterclockwise.

"With who?"

"Gina at work. Big Gina."

"You had sex with her at work?"

"We didn't have sex. I just kissed her."

"Just once?"

"Yeah. But it's the principle, Ben. Kissing her, sleeping with her, having a crush on her, talking to her about Melissa — it's all the same."

"Have you told Melissa?"

"No."

"Are you gonna tell her?"

"I have to."

"You don't, Forest. Really, listen to me, you don't."

"I do. I owe it to her."

"You do fucking not!" I say, loud enough to arouse the attention of the adjacent table.

Forest is confused by my tone.

"You'll only make things worse," I explain. "Trust me. You're not going to do it again, are you?"

"Of course not."

"Then let it lie, Forest. Anything you tell her about what happened, you're telling her for your own sake. Because you're not doing her any favors. You're not doing anyone any favors. This I fucking know."

"She deserves to know, Ben."

"That what? That you're full of remorse?"

"That I broke our trust."

"Don't be stupid."

"How is that stupid?"

"Suppose I hadn't told Janet the truth: that I wasn't really sure what happened, whether I left the car in neutral or whether it popped out of gear. Suppose I had just kept my mouth fucking shut on that count?"

I've managed to arouse the discomfort of the party next to us again. I subdue myself momentarily, avoiding eye contact, scratching at the cardboard surface of Forest's castoff coaster.

"Suppose this," I resume calmly. "Suppose I just told Janet the car popped out of gear, that it was a freak accident? How did my telling her I wasn't sure change anything for the better?"

Forest doesn't have a ready answer. He just keeps spinning his glass counterclockwise as though he wishes it were a clock.

"Do you suppose it was comforting for Janet to know that it might have been my fault, Forest, that I might have caused it? That by trusting me with her children, she caused it? Did it help her to push away the one fucking person in the world who could ever possibly understand her loss?"

Sad-eyed, Forest looks up from his imaginary clock. "I'm sorry, Ben. I mean, that everything worked out the way it did. But this is different. That was an accident."

"Of course it was. And Big Gina was an accident."

"Big Gina was a mistake."

"And you paid for it. You're paying right now. You're living with it. Why make Melissa live with it?"

Forest stops spinning his glass long enough to take a pull off it and shake his head in disappointment.

"Sometimes you lie, Forest. Sometimes it's the right thing to do."

"I don't believe that, Ben."

"And why is that?"

"It always catches up with you."

"It doesn't, not always."

"It does."

"Bullshit."

"It's the truth, Ben."

"No, Forest, it's another kind of lie. If Lizzie draws you a picture of a catfish and it looks like a big hairy turd, what do you tell her? That it looks like shit? That you could draw a better fucking catfish with a crayon up your asshole? No, Forest, you tell her it's the most beautiful catfish you ever saw, don't you? Of course you do. Truth's a slippery slope sometimes."

Forest stops his spinning at last and fingers his mustache, looking at once thoughtful and mildly amused as he stares at the table-top. "You have a strange way of putting it, but thanks, Benji boy." He reaches across the table and pats my shoulder, then takes a healthy swig of beer and sets his empty glass back down on the table.

Knowing that I've influenced Forest in some small way is almost enough to make me feel like I'm more than a shadow.

"Well, I better be getting home," he says.

"But it's dart night."

"I'm just not feelin' it tonight, Benji." He pats me on the shoulder again as he gets up to leave. I wish I could go with him.

meet the replacement

I've been thinking about all the things I might have done differently. All the choices I didn't make. All the decisions that made and unmade me, all the actions and inactions I did or didn't take. With the shades drawn and the garbage overflowing, I've been thinking about all the bold steps I never took, all the gut instincts I didn't listen to, all the people I let down. I've been thinking about the cruel mathematics of my life, looking at my sums and wishing I'd shown my work. From my station on the sofa, surrounded by pizza boxes, I've been thinking about all of it, and I've come to some conclusions: I hate this sofa. I hate this apartment. I hate Pizza Factory. And more than anything, I hate the options available to me.

Yesterday afternoon, the phone rings. It's Trev.

"What's up?" he says.

"Not a whole lot."

An awkward silence ensues, during which I can hear the drone of the television in the background.

"You mad at me?" he says, finally.

"Nah."

"That's cool," he says. "Sorry. I mean, you know, for the way it worked out."

"Not your fault," I say. "She's just looking out for you."

"Yeah, I guess."

Another silence takes hold. The television drones on. I hear the click of the joystick, as he repositions his chair.

"So, what are you up to?" he says.

"Just playing catch-up," I say. "Getting résumés together, that kind of thing."

"Oh," he says, and I can hear his disappointment clearly. But unlike the sort of disappointment I usually inspire, it occurs to me for once that I might actually control the outcome somehow, what however else I may have depleted, exhausted, or reduced my life to a heap of smoldering rubble, I still have the power not to disappoint.

When I arrive at Trev's house, my replacement greets me at the front door. She has the look of a disgruntled gingerbread man — short-armed, about five feet tall and three feet wide, with thick cropped hair and wire-rimmed glasses. Her bruised-purple hospital scrubs fail to strike a festive chord. She's clutching Trev's urine jug in one hand and a straw in the other. Clearly, someone wasn't paying attention in class. Blinking twice in lieu of a greeting, she extends a stubby arm (the one holding the straw) to mark my passage, following on my heels through the gloomy dining room.

Trev awaits me in the living room, smiling behind his tray table. "Thanks, Jackie," he says. "I'm good for now."

Jackie blinks, sets the straw on the tray table, and stands at attention holding the urine receptacle.

I take a seat on the sofa, across from Trev. Almost immediately, the cat springs onto the couch and readies himself to curl up in my lap.

"Uh, I'm good for now, Jackie," says Trev. "You can go read your magazine or whatever."

To which Jackie blinks but makes no move.

Trev draws a slow breath and closes his eyes. "Good-bye, Jackie."

Finally, Jackie retires to the dining room, receding into the shadows beyond the threshold, where she sits in the half darkness. As soon as she's out of sight, Trev fashions his gnarled hand into something resembling a pistol, hoists it to shoulder level, and lowers his head slightly until the barrel is six inches from the side of his head. Clumsily, he pulls the trigger.

"That bad, huh?" I say softly.

"Worse than you can imagine." He leans in closer. "Scalp-eater," he whispers.

"What?"

"Yeah, I'm pretty sure she's retarded."

"What do you mean 'scalp-eater'?"

"Twice yesterday I caught her scratching her head — really going at it, I mean, pinching and digging like she was after something — and then, swear to God . . ."

"No."

"Yes. Like a chimp."

I wince. "Damn. And that's the best they could do down at DSHS? What about the fat lady in sweats?"

"Unavailable."

"The spiderweb dude?"

"Booked solid — that guy has like eight clients now."

I whistle. "Wow." Through the window I see Elsa crossing the front lawn.

"Look," says Trev. "About the whole you-getting-fired thing. All I said was that we talked about it — not that we actually talked about it. Going to Utah, I mean. She just assumed the whole thing was your idea. Technically, she can't fire you. I'm an adult and everything, so it's supposed to be my call. But . . . I mean, the thing is . . ."

"Don't worry, I'm not here to get my job back."

He casts his eyes away toward the window. "Just so you know, she doesn't have anything against you. It's not personal."

"Don't worry about it."

On cue, Elsa clomps up the ramp into the foyer, where she drops her tack bag on the linoleum and kicks her boots off. Releasing her hair from its bun and shaking it out, she crosses through the dining room, where Jackie is reading a magazine in the dim light.

"I'm home for the rest of the afternoon," she says.

Jackie looks up from her magazine, blinking slowly twice.

"You're free to go, Jackie."

Absorbing this information, Jackie blinks once more, then begins gathering her things without a word.

"Don't worry," says Trev to Elsa, as she enters the living room. "He doesn't want his job back."

"Oh?" Elsa sits in the high-backed chair.

"I've got a proposition," I say.

"And what are you proposing?"

"That Trev and I take the van to Salt Lake City."

Her face darkens. She stands up.

"Hear me out," I say. "Please."

"C'mon, Mom, let him talk."

Elsa warily resumes her seat, just as Jackie crests the driveway in a plum-colored Astro van.

"You're in Bend the first week of September," I say. "So either you'll be arranging live-in care for Trev from, oh let's say, Jackie."

"Scalp-eater," says Trev.

"Or," I proceed, "you're taking Trev with you to the show. But how are you going to tow the trailer with the van? Because the truck isn't accessible. Unless Trev is going to travel in the horse trailer. And who's going to help Trev while you're working the show? This solves everything — why not let us take the van to Salt Lake?"

"I've already made arrangements," she says flatly. *"Yes,* with Jackie. Look, Ben, there are a lot of things that you haven't taken into consideration. Traveling with Trevor is a lot more complicated than you think."

"He knows," says Trev.

"I've Googled virtually every medical facility from here to Salt Lake City," I say. "Pharmacies. Emergency care. Hotels with access. Red Lobsters. I've got it all printed out — directions, maps, rates. I've taken everything I can think of into consideration. And if you have more considerations, just tell me what they are, and I'll prepare for those, too."

Elsa bites her lower lip. For the first time, she seems to be listening. "And who pays for this trip?" she says.

"We pay our own ways."

"You don't have a job," she says.

"Exactly. But I've got a credit card."

She's still biting her lip. "Why are you doing this?" she says.

"It's personal," I say.

She looks me hard in the face, then turns to Trev, who bobbles his head back and rolls his shoulders slightly.

"If anybody should be scared, it's me," he says.

I can actually see the tension slacken in Elsa's shoulders as she gives into us. "Does Bob know?"

"Not yet," I say.

"Well, check with Bob first. And I'm not making any promises, here. I'm going to have to really think hard about this. But if I do decide it's a go, understand there will be guidelines. You'll do it my way."

"Of course."

"And you'll make all your reservations in advance. And I'll expect phone calls."

"Of course."

"One week," she says.

"One week."

Trev smiles uneasily.

As I'm leaving, Elsa stops me in the foyer. "Ben," she says, locking my eyes in place. "If anything happens to my child, I — "

But she stops herself when she remembers who she's talking to.

liftoff

Seven thirty-five a.m. on departure day, and it's shaping up to be a stunner. Already the autumnal chill is burning off, as the sun clears the tree line beyond the pasture with nothing but blue sky in its path. Ideal travel conditions. Under the watchful gaze of Trev from the window, with Elsa beside him gnawing a cuticle, I load the freshly serviced handi-van in preparation for our departure, fastidiously checking each item off the master list — flares, cook stove, cooler, flashlights, baby wipes, straws, moisturizer, Enalapril, Digitek, Protandim, respirator, memory foam, deodorant, Advil, jock-itch cream, Q-tips, acne pads, electric razor, wool socks, aqua socks, windbreaker, ski jacket, swim trunks, Sorrels, flip-flops, bottled water, insurance cards, medical files.

Oh yes, we are prepared — Shackleton and Scott should've been as prepared. And yet I know we're not going anywhere. Elsa will change her mind for the tenth time. She's been waffling all morning. Trev will lose his nerve. Something will stop us. The gods will intervene — some unforeseen, unaccounted for detail will act as our foil come launch time, I'm sure of it. It's simply impossible to imagine Trev and me side by side on the edge of the salt flats, or even strolling the dusty halls of the Idaho Potato Museum.

But by 8:07 a.m. Trev is strapped in beside me, looking a little pale, while Elsa is stationed outside the open passenger's window of the idling van. We linger there, inviting delay, postponing the inconceivable.

"Are you sure about this?" she says.

"Not exactly," says Trev.

"It's not too late to make arrangements. I could call Jackie, or we could always just — "

"See you later, Mom."

Elsa forces a smile as we pull clear of the carport. In the rearview mirror, I see her waving as we crest the driveway. I wonder if amidst all her doubt and concern, there isn't the tiniest bit of relief in watching Trev go.

Trev sits rigid and upright in his wheelchair, staring straight ahead at the double yellow line, as we wind down Little Valley Road toward the highway.

"Did you bring the files?" he says.

"Got 'em."

"And the insurance cards?"

"Yep."

"Both of them?"

"Yep. In with the files."

"They won't fall out?"

"They're in an envelope, paper-clipped to the files."

"What about the Tums?"

"In the side pocket of your black bag."

"Where's that?"

"In the very back, next to my backpack, under the sleeping bags and the foam and a bunch of other stuff."

Trev retreats into silence until we reach the stop sign at Bond, where I can see that his uneasiness persists.

"What is it?" I say.

"Sorry, dude."

"For what?"

"I think I'm gonna need those Tums."

east of the mountains

We motor east on I-90, through the broad-shouldered green foothills and into the steep-faced swells of Snoqualmie Pass. We travel mostly in silence. Trev takes in the scenery with what appears to be only mild interest, but it's not that he isn't interested. He's just anxious; I can tell by the way he leans forward slightly, his elbows on the armrests, his knotted hands dangling inches above his lap. We've already made bathroom stops in Factoria, Issaquah, and Fall City. Trev would like nothing more than to avoid the indignity of another service station bathroom with no stall and yours truly standing by at a distance of three feet. But he'll have to settle for even less. When nature calls again at the Snoqualmie summit, we've no choice but to pull over at the rest area, where the only facilities are glorified honey buckets. Further complicating matters, the structures are not in compliance. No ramp, no bar, no room to maneuver. The entire ordeal is awkward in every way.

Emerging with Trev in my arms, and setting him in his chair, I see we're being watched by a teenage girl in fingerless gloves and a tartan skirt, sitting on the curb in the shadow of the van, smoking a cigarette. Trev blushes when he notices her, no doubt embarrassed by his predicament. She wears her hair cropped short and bleached blond, except for her long black bangs. Her nose is pierced. She watches us with the expert dispassion of a teenage misfit, picking absently at the skin of her wrist and spitting on the sidewalk, as Trev pilots his chair onto the ramp, and I begin raising it with an electric whir. Cute kid, when you get beyond the fashion statement. About sixteen or seventeen, I'd guess. If she's not a runaway, she could play one on TV. Somewhere nearby, a car honks, and abruptly the girl tosses her cigarette aside, stands up, and dashes into the tree line separating the autos from the trucks.

"Something we said?" says Trev.

"Or maybe something she ate."

I joke, but the truth is, I can scarcely lay eyes on a teenage girl without wondering what kind of teenager Piper might've been. I picture her like the smoking girl, except happier and not smoking and not biting her cuticles or running away from anything.

As we roll down the leeward side of the Cascades through the basin and into the high desert, the dense fir and cedar give way to sparse pine woods and channeled scablands riddled with boulders and basalt. Soon Trev is asleep in his wheelchair, still leaning slightly forward, and I'm alone with my thoughts and two hundred miles of desert.

I can't help but think of that family trip in '05 through the Southwest, all the cracker crumbs and hokey fanfare — miracle ponds and painted rocks — all the sticky vinyl seat backs and starchy hotel linens and gas-inducing roadside victuals. Sort of an exhausting nightmare, really, what with Janet seven months pregnant and the hundred-degree heat and the broken air conditioner. I can see Piper, as though in a photograph, on the south rim of the Grand Canyon, the bright red halo of a cherry slushy ringing her mouth. I can see her holding hands with a venerable Indian in full-feathered regalia at the Jackrabbit Trading Post. Beaming in pigtails at the Amboy Crater. Wild-eyed at the Rattlesnake Museum. None of the photographic evidence suggests what was nearly lost that afternoon at the ghost town.

Trev awakens about ten miles west of Vantage, where the high desert begins its gradual descent into the gorge. His spirits have improved considerably. His whole comportment is more at ease, and he leans back, his arms stretched out at forty-degree angles (which is as far as they can stretch), looking out the side window at some distant point.

"What'd I miss?" he says.

"Oodles. There were some cows about sixty miles back. And something that looked like a tree."

"Damn."

"Oh, and a hitchhiker — I think it might've been Moses."

Trev breaks into a grin — not his signature evil genius grin or the uncomfortable tacked-on grin with which he so often greets adversity great or small but a genuine, lighthearted, devil-may-care grin. And something about it makes me want to cry.

george, washington

The town of George, Washington (population 528), just east of the gorge, is the first lunch stop on our seven-day itinerary. We are an hour and thirty-seven minutes behind schedule as we pull off on exit 149 in the blistering heat of midafternoon. Had we arrived in 1983, we might have been treated to a slice of the World's Biggest Cherry Pie (subsequently dethroned in Traverse City, Michigan in 1987, and again in Oliver, British Columbia, in 1990). However, those golden days of seventeen-thousand-pound pies have flown. As it stands, visitors are forced to settle for a six-story water tower emblazoned with our founding father's silhouette, which looks more like the silhouette of an infant with Paget's disease and a cauliflower ear.

The chamber of commerce really dropped the ball in George. Talk about missed opportunities! No gift shop. No powdered wigs, no wooden dentures, no coin-fed lie detector, no nothing. Okay, there's a bronzed bust of General Washington outside a filling station on the near edge of town. Otherwise, a tour of George, Washington, might include the sheriff substation, a squat green portable surrounded by scorched lawn and a couple of parched-looking trees. Fire District No. 3, an equally squat gray edifice of the sort of cinder block construction one might expect to see in an outbuilding at Stalag Luft. The George Community Hall, the very nerve center of public life in George, a blotchy and windowless structure possessing all the architectural allure of a two-car garage. And no tour would be complete without a drive past aluminum-sided city hall, which with a few more windows might make a nice retail outlet for ball bearings. I can only hope that the town of Joe, Montana, has more to offer.

After a brief stopover at the foot of the water tower, during which

Trev and I scrutinize President Washington's silhouette in the manner of a Rorschach test, we lunch at a dubious Mexican restaurant on the edge of town, a dicey proposition given the recent state of Trev's digestive tract. But Trev is in high spirits at last and insists on a fiesta. The place is called La Paloma or La Palamino or Los Pintos, but the pretense ends there. The interior could just as well be any truck-stop diner from Cle Elum to Bismarck. They're playing newfangled country over the sound system — Clint somebody or Toby what's-his-name or maybe that Kenny guy. The waitress is rail thin in that chronic smoker kind of way. If she had a name tag it might say Lana Sue. She looks about thirty-five long years old.

Trev orders the fish tacos in spite of my nonverbal exhortations — a prominent two-handed yield gesture, accompanied by an emphatic shaking of the head. The scablands of eastern Washington are not generally noted for their seafood.

Trev winks at me as Lana Sue takes leave. "What can I say? I'm feeling reckless."

Our food arrives much too quickly. My beef chimichanga is the size of a yule log, slathered in an improbable gray-brown gravylike substance.

"Yikes," says Trev, inspecting his entrée. "Blue tacos? Uh, how did that happen?"

Maybe it's just the afternoon light filtered through tinted windows, but the fish does seem be a bit on the blue side. "Looks like you got the Smurf tacos," I say.

Trev smiles warily, picking around the edges of his blue tacos with a fork, wondering perhaps whether he should attempt to pick one up or abort the whole ungodly mess. In the end, he decides to abandon the tacos in favor of his side of beans and rice. Meanwhile, I begin poking my way tentatively around the edges of the yule log, which has begun to sag beneath its own weight and seems to be breathing. The more I poke at the behemoth, the more it lets off steam and slumps in its gravy wallow, until I've exhausted the thing and it lies breathless, flat on its belly. I keep waiting for it to groan.

"How's the beans?" I inquire.

"Not bad. How's your, uh . . . how's that thing?"

"Dead, I think."

Near the end of the meal, by which point in time I've devoured roughly 20 percent of my burrito, my cell phone rings. The caller ID is unknown, though I'm fully expecting a check-in call from Elsa anytime now.

"Okay, Ben. This is it, do you hear me? I'm dead serious this time." It's Janet. She's trying to sound tough, but I know she's exhausted; I can hear it in her voice.

"Relax. I'm coming down there to finalize everything," I assure her. "I swear. Everything's ready to go."

She knows I'm lying. "Oh, cut the crap, Ben. I'm coming up there the minute I get off of work, and you're going to sign those papers, and this time I'm not going to leave without them."

"You can't do that."

"Watch me."

"It won't do any good — I'm not there."

"Then where are you?"

"I'm on my way to Utah."

She's greets this news with a silence so cold and dense it has a vacuum effect.

"For work," I say.

I can feel her gritting her teeth on the other end of the line. "What kind of stunt is this, Ben? *Exactly* where are you?"

"Look, I swear, this isn't a stunt, I'm not running. I thought we agreed that — "

"Where are you right now?"

"On the road."

"Tell me where you are."

"East of the mountains."

"Okay, Ben, fine. That was your last chance. I'm officially done."

"No, wait, listen."

"I'm done listening. This time I'm not letting you talk me out of anything."

"Please, wait. Just — "

But before I can finish, she hangs up on me.

Trev looks uncomfortable as he watches the hope drain from my face; a forkful of beans is poised halfway between his plate and his open mouth. In an attempt at levity, he tacks a frozen half smile on his face.

"You want a Smurf taco?" he says.

skylark

I know it sounds silly. Paranoid even. But I swear we're being followed. The shit brown Skylark with the crooked plate started tailing us around Moses Lake. How on earth Janet pulled this off, I have no idea. Is this guy gonna serve me? For twenty miles, I've been stealing covert glances in the rearview mirror, careful not to alert Trev to our pursuer, whoever it may be. Granted, it's not a busy stretch of highway — two lanes through a moonscape and hardly any exits between Moses Lake and Ritzville. But most drivers would've passed me miles ago. In fact, no less than a half-dozen cars have passed the Skylark and the handi-van in tandem. But the Skylark sticks, keeps a measured distance. It slows when I slow, speeds up when I speed up.

At Shrag, I signal as if to exit. The Skylark doesn't bite. That just tells me he's no dummy. Whoever this guy is — and I'm assuming it's a guy — he's done this before. At Odessa, I don't signal but veer toward the exit lane at the last instant. Immediately, the Skylark drifts toward the exit. When I pop back out into the right lane, the Skylark drifts back.

"What're you doing?" says Trev.

"I was gonna piss, but it doesn't look like there's any services."

"I've gotta piss, too."

It's settled. At exit 220, I pull off at Ritzville. The Skylark follows suit but slows considerably on the exit ramp, so that even while I linger at the stop sign it doesn't pull close enough for me to get a look at the driver. Finally, I swing a left and cross I-90 on the overpass. Checking the rearview mirror, I'm relieved to see the Skylark hang a right toward Pasco. Okay, I'm paranoid. What was I thinking? By the time I pull into the service station, the whole idea seems laughable.

The filling station is all but deserted, except for the girl in the fingerless gloves, who has apparently managed to pass us during our lunch hour — one can only assume using her thumb — as there are no vehicles out front. She's leaning against a newspaper dispenser, alternately gnawing on her cuticles and smoking a cigarette, glaring straight ahead from behind her black bangs, as though daring somebody to look at her. Where the hell is her father that she's out here hitchhiking through the desert? The thought of it pisses me off more than it ought to — I'm pissed at her parents, more than I have a right to be, pissed at whatever circumstances have compelled this girl to be out here to the middle of nowhere, whatever impulses have prompted her to take flight in the first place. But who knows, maybe it's her own fault, maybe she's not running from anything but boredom and stability and her own teenage angst. Maybe her mom's a nurse and her dad's a fireman and her big brother's pulling straight A's at the U. Maybe she's still got a bunch of teddy bears lined shoulder to shoulder on her windowsill. Maybe she used to play the clarinet, and her parents and her teachers can't figure out why she quit. Maybe her folks are at home pulling their hair out right this minute. Should I alert the authorities? Maybe I should offer the kid a ride. Instead, I just keep sneaking glances at her as we approach. I've little doubt that she can feel my eyes on her, though she continues to glare straight ahead. Not only is her nose pierced, but she's got a tiny hoop through her eyebrow. She's doing everything she can to make herself ugly, and it's still not working.

I'm not the only one attentive to the smoking girl. Trev is doing his damnedest not to stare at her, and if I'm not mistaken, the effort is even causing him to blush as he wheels off the ramp. The hot wind is kicking up desert grit and swirling it about the parking lot in dust devils. An empty wrapper skitters across the pavement. Out beyond the frontage road, big dust clouds are gathering in the parched fields, obscuring the distant hills in a haze.

The smoking girl gives us a sidelong glance as we pass. "Cool shoes," she intones, with all the enthusiasm of a tollbooth operator.

Trev looks down at his gold Chucks, and his eyes stick there. "Thanks," he says, his voice threatening to crack.

Pushing the double-glass doors open to let Trev pass through, I resolve myself to offer the girl a lift on the way out. Maybe I can talk some sense into her, convince her to go back to her teddy bears and her clarinet, to quit vandalizing her body, and start carving out a future. At the very least, I can get her safely to point B.

Trev and I discuss the matter as I zip his fly down in the bathroom.

"Whaddaya think? Do we give her a ride?"

"Hell yes," he says, dribbling into his plastic vessel.

But by the time I've fastened Trev's fly; rinsed his vessel; wrapped it in its plastic bag; replaced it in his storage pouch; taken my own leak; zipped my own fly; washed my hands; prepaid for the gas; bought a Powerade, some pork rinds, and some baby wipes, there's no sign of the girl.

"You see what happened to that girl that was out front?" I say to the clerk.

"Beats me," he says, bagging my pork rinds.

Once again, I'm left holding the groceries.

"Damn," says Trev, wheeling across the dusty lot. "I was gonna hit that shit."

I lower the ramp, and Trev rolls on, squinting against the gritty wind. Once aboard, I buckle him in, circle the car, and unscrew the gas cap, gazing off toward the blurry horizon while I fill up.

It's 4:36 p.m. as we ease back onto the interstate. We're two and a half hours behind schedule now, but I'm not worried. As it stands, we ought to make Wallace by 7:00 p.m., check into our motel, and grab some dinner. Maybe I'll pick up a few beers for the motel, and we'll pore over tomorrow's itinerary, which includes the Oasis Bordello Tour, an old mining shaft (provided they offer wheelchair access). Sunday, it's on through the panhandle to Montana, where we'll wend our way north to Polson, for the Miracle of America Museum. There, among other attractions, a two-headed calf awaits us.

But for the crunch of pork rinds, and the hum of the tires, the desert landscape unfolds in silence. Thoughts of my old life threaten to linger, but I turn on the radio and scare them off like so many pigeons. Clint what's-his-name. Something about bad good-byes. Within twenty minutes, Trev dozes off again with his mouth open, his big head lolling to one side. I'm having trouble keeping my own eyes open. I crack the window to fight the drowsiness.

Suddenly, about a mile after the Harrington exit, I glance in the rearview mirror and receive a jolt. The Skylark is on our tail again.

fingers

Yes, she's demanding, capricious, at times exhausting, but my Piper will break your heart with her new gap-toothed smile, and her flapper haircut, and her tiny bitten fingernails. When you see my Piper in front of the Toasted Oats, spindly-legged in her rubber boots and cape, her brow crinkled in concentration as she runs her nimble fingers up and down the grocery list, you will want to gather her up in your arms. You will marvel at the care and attention with which she guides Jodi hand in hand down the supermarket aisle, past the Grape Nuts and the Lucky Charms. She will shame you with her patience as she bends down in the shadow of Tony the Tiger and endeavors for two minutes to interpret her baby brother's earnest garblings while Daddy waves her on impatiently from the head of the aisle. And when she succeeds in understanding baby brother, and you see his little face light up in recognition, you will understand why he clings to her so.

When you see her coercing me in the checkout line, clutching a Heath bar as she tugs at my shirttail and begs me politely to make an exception to the not-before-dinner rule, you will pity me for having to say no. And when you see us pushing our cart across the parking lot toward the RAV4 and see that she is eating the Heath bar, you might think I'm a bad parent.

"DADDY, JODI HAS a snot," Piper chimes from the backseat, where she insists on sitting beside him for the drive home from Central Market. The rain has let up and the clouds are hurrying east, and the weak sunlight fights its way through the treetops intermittently.

"Wipe it, then, honey." Our eyes lock briefly in the rearview mirror, long enough for Piper to roll hers. She sighs at my inability to grasp the obvious — a habit she recently picked up from her mother.

"But I don't *have* anything," she explains.

"Then just leave it for now," I tell her, turning my attention back to the road. "We'll get a Kleenex when we get home." *Fuck. I knew I forgot something.*

"Eww," Piper says.

Glancing back, I see she's defied me, she's gone ahead and wiped Jodi's nose. Corkscrewing her face, she now holds a glistening index finger at arms length.

I knit my brow into the mirror. "Don't you dare wipe that on the seat, young lady."

She knits her brow right back at me, makes sure I'm paying attention, then wipes her finger on the back of the driver's seat.

"Damnit, Piper! What did I just say?"

She's smiles devilishly at the *D* word and ribs Jodi, who is smiling, too. He garbles something unintelligible, unable to control his mirth.

"It's not funny!"

They laugh at my ire. Daddy is a joke, a reliable source of amusement. Daddy is to be teased and taunted like a terrier. Above all, Daddy is to be tested.

"Damnit, it's not funny!"

Piper eggs Jodi's laughter on still further, poking his distended belly and pointing at the back of the seat, until the boy begins kicking his feet deliriously.

Just as I let up on the accelerator, swing my head around, and begin easing onto the muddy shoulder for a time-out, Piper thrusts her still glistening finger over my right shoulder, so that I might inspect the punch line inches from my face.

"I wiped the other one, silly."

Jodi dispenses a snotty laugh and kicks his legs some more.

Daddy is a sucker. Daddy takes the bait every time. What choice does Daddy have, even in his edgy state of nerve-worn fatigue, but to laugh at himself?

When Piper sees that I'm in on the joke, she gives me the smile, the new one, the one where she jams her tongue through the gap in her front teeth.

take no chances

We've just passed through Spokane, and we're funneling out the east end of the valley around Otis Orchards, when Trev awakens.

"What'd I miss this time?" he says groggily.

"Just a Klan rally."

I sneak a glance in the rearview mirror.

"Nice music," he says.

It's the Toby guy, I think — the fat one, the Democrat. Something about "pickin' 'em up, and layin' 'em down." This newfangled country is starting to grow on me, the adult despair of it all. Stuff I can relate to: lost loves, lost houses, lost dogs. Besides, it soothes my nerves. The Skylark is still tailing us, though its driver is exercising an additional degree of finesse now, keeping one or two cars between us at all times, even as I try to elude him, weaving in and out of traffic.

Trev catches me monitoring the rearview compulsively.

"Cop on our ass?"

"Thought so for a minute. Just a roof rack."

I don't want to worry him. He doesn't need to know about the Skylark. He doesn't need to know about the check-engine light that came on around Medical Lake, either — it's just a dummy light, anyway. But a mile west of the first Coeur d'Alene exit, Trev catches me monitoring the light obsessively between checks of the mirror. He leans his chair back with an electric whir, and cranes his neck toward the driver's side dash.

"What's that red light?"

"It's just a dummy light."

"What does it say?"

"Check oil," I say. "Er, engine. Check engine."

Trev's face darkens in annoyance. "Well?"

"It's just a dummy light."

He looks straight ahead, darkly.

"It'll probably go off in a minute, trust me. It's just a scam so you'll have to go into the dealership or whatever."

He's getting moodier by the second. "You should've said something. You should've woken me up."

"It's just a dummy light."

"You should've stopped in Spokane."

"For a dummy light?"

His eyes are just slits, his greasy forehead is wrinkled. I've crossed the line with my negligence. "Get off at the next exit," he says, shaking his head grimly. "You should've stopped when it came on."

He's right, of course. I ought to know better than to take chances. I ought to know better than to ignore warning signals. How many dummy lights did I ignore before my life exploded? How many have I ignored since? Above all, I ought to know better than to try and hide anything from Trev.

After a chilly two miles of silence, I pull off on exit 15 while Trev still fumes on the passenger side. I keep praying for the dummy light to go off and redeem me. But the damn things seems to be burning brighter than ever. My flagging spirits are buoyed, if only briefly, when I see the Skylark whiz past us on the interstate.

By the time we've checked into our motor court motel on the scrubby outskirts of Coeur d'Alene, Trev has forgiven me.

"You're probably right," he says, piloting a tight semicircle between the twin beds. "It's probably just a dummy light."

The room is decorated in early fleabag. Swampy green carpet, jaundiced yellow drapes. Everywhere the residue of twenty-year-old smoke. Dust particles the size of gnats swarm in the lamplight. The alarm clock is bolted to the nightstand. On the wall behind the twin headboards is a most curious work of art—I guess you'd call it a painting: a violent mess of blue oils on canvas, with a big bloody swirl in the center, partially obscured by the hodgepodge of blue, all of it executed in brush strokes suggestive of some psychomotor disturbance. The workings of a dark imagination — something Richard Ramírez might have conceived with a bad case of hiccups. I can't tell whether it's thunderheads blotting out the sun or an alpine sunset reflected in the surface of Lake Coeur d'Alene. Whatever it is, I find it unsettling.

"Shall I call room service and have some Grey Poupon sent up?" Trev says.

"Shit, I forgot to tip the porter," I say.

But at least the place has free wi-fi. Some Googling soon yields a Pontiac dealership across town, but the service department is closed on weekends. We've little choice but to wait until Monday. Further Googling yields a Red Lobster four miles away, but Trev doesn't want to risk driving until the dummy light has been resolved, marooning us in the outskirts for the foreseeable future. The adjoining motel restaurant, pretty scary-looking by any measure, is closed, forcing us to dine on mini-mart fare. We cross the court and the main drag to the 24/7 Chevron, where we procure corn dogs and some jojos that look like they've been sitting under the heat lamp since the dawn of the Pleistocene era. I can't help but think of the four trips to the bathroom I'll be making with Trev in the middle of the night.

Back at the room, I set up Trev's tray table and recline on the bed, snapping off a bite of corn dog. Now that we're settled, there's the question of Elsa. Do we risk worrying her with this detour, or do we save her the trouble? Wouldn't it be best to wait and see — after all, it is a dummy light, right?

"I don't think we should tell my mom about the van," he says, reading my mind. "She'll overreact, probably." He's got mustard on his chin. He waves at it with a swipe of his napkined hand but misses.

"Good call," I say. "Why worry her?"

"We should still call her, though. Tell her everything is going as planned."

"Totally."

"It's probably just a dummy light," he says.

I make the call to Elsa around 7:00 p.m. Trev watches nervously as I pace the tiny room.

"Oh yeah, smooth sailing," I tell her. "Yep, Wallace . . . at the Stardust . . . How is it? It's . . . Trev, how would say the Stardust is?"

"Like a motel," he says.

"It's average," I say. "Basic motel setup. Parking. That kind of thing . . ."

Trev and I exchange nervous glances.

"Oh, great, yeah," I say jauntily into the phone. "Mm-hmm, like a top . . . Yeah . . . Totally . . ."

Trev winces and smiles at once.

"Oh yeah, I will," I assure Elsa with regard to checking the fluids. "He sure is, hold on a sec . . ."

I flip the phone open to speaker and perch it on Trev's armrest.

"Hi, honey," she says.

"What's up?" he says.

"Are you having fun? It's not too much, is it? How's your breathing?"

"Fine," he says.

"Honey, I can't hear you."

"Fine," he says, louder. "What about you?" he says, diverting her. "You ready for the show?"

"I've still got some braiding to do. I'll be ready by morning, though. You remembered your Enalapril after dinner, right?"

"Yeah."

"Was that a *yes*?"

"Yeah," says Trev louder still, hunching down toward the phone. "I gotta go, Mom. I'm getting tired."

And just like that, he's off the hot seat.

"Okay, I love you," says Elsa. "Let me talk to Ben again."

I snatch up the phone.

"You bet . . . uh-huh . . . I won't . . . Sure will . . . Talk to you soon."

I set the phone on the now cluttered nightstand.

"That was easy," says Trev.

Late that night, after we've cemented our status as conspirators, after we've given up our channel surfing, set the remote aside, and I've put Trev to rest with a pillow between his knobby knees, I lie awake on my back in the weak light spilling in from the motor court, listening to the plumbing through the walls and the occasional rasp of Trev's breathing as though it's a million miles away and savoring that sense of remoteness that only cheap motels in unfamiliar towns seem to inspire.

here and abroad

I've covered the Ramírez painting with a pillow case. The curtains are drawn to ward off the sunlight. On the nightstand, beside my castaway corn dog stick, a couple of jojos repose in a grease-stained paperboard boat. In spite of our unfamiliar surroundings, our morning, which begins shortly before noon, adheres mostly to Trev's routine. Enalapril, Digitek, a morning piss. Khaki cargoes and a black T-shirt. Everything but the waffles. It's sixty-nine degrees in Charleston, seventy-three in Baton Rouge. On the Travel Channel, we spelunk the caverns of Callao, explore the garish catacombs of the Great Barrier Reef, learn about the medicinal benefits of turmeric.

Sometime in the early afternoon, my cell rings. It's Forest.

"It's me," he says.

"Hey."

"Ben, I need a place to crash."

"What are you talking about?"

"It's nothing, it's just — can I stay at your place? While you're gone, I mean?"

"What happened?"

Silence.

"Well? What is it? What happened?"

"I told Mel," he says. "About Gina."

I groan. "You didn't."

"I had to, Ben."

He really believes it, the big dummy. He still doesn't know any better. A long silence ensues, as I consider a prudent course of action. "Okay, look," I say. "Damage control. How did all this play out? Did she kick you out, was she furious, was she crying?"

"I offered."

"You what?"

"I thought she might need a little space to . . ."

"To what, Forest?"

"Well, you know, get used to the idea, I guess."

I groan again. "Why? Why on earth should she get *used* to the idea? Is it going to happen again? Are you *trying* to destroy a perfectly good marriage? Are you in love with Big Gina, or something?"

"Of course not."

"Then why?"

"I guess because, well —" Here, his voice falters and nearly gives out. "Christ, Ben, I don't know. I said I was sorry, but that just didn't seem to be enough, you know?"

I wish I could give the big lug a pat on the back, or even a hug. "This is gonna blow over, buddy. You just stay at my place for a few days. Chuck's got an extra key — tell him I said it's all right. He can call me if he needs to. Just hang tight, pal. Mel will come around."

"Thanks, Ben."

"Forget it, man. Just lay low for a couple of days. Call me if you want. Whatever you need."

"You're the best," he says.

"Not by a long shot," I say.

I know the impulse is misguided. I know it's meddling. But I dial Mel, certain I can help in some way. She picks up on the second ring.

"Forest isn't here."

"I know. He told me."

A cool silence. I wonder if it's because he confided in me, because I've known all along, or if it's because of Gina. Maybe Mel holds me responsible, and who could blame her? All those nights I kept him away from his family.

"You were right," she said. "He shouldn't have told me. But he did."

"And?"

"And what do you think, Ben? I'm hurt. I'm confused. I don't know what any of it means."

"It means he fucked up — just for a second."

"Just for a second what? He forgot? He was weak? He wasn't even drinking. What was he thinking?"

"Maybe he wasn't."

Mel sighs. "I dunno, Ben. Something like this makes me feel like I don't even know him."

"You do. C'mon, Mel, this is Forest we're talking about. The Grape Smuggler. Mr. Clutch. Best Dad in the West. Most Devoted Husband. Look — his bachelor party. Okay, bachelor party — strip clubs, right? Drunken debauchery. Closing the book on bachelordom with a bang. What did Forest wanna do? Did he wanna go to Vegas? Did he wanna go to Toy's Topless? No, he wanted to go fishing. Just he and Max and me. And for two days, up and down the Dungeness, wading in the riffle, drinking by the fire, all he wanted to talk about was his future with you. To the point where it got annoying, okay?"

"How do I know he won't lapse again?" she says.

"Have you ever seen Big Gina?"

"Oh, stop it, Ben. How do I know?"

I wish I had another answer rather than the obvious one. "You don't, Mel, not really. He's a good bet, though."

More silence but not as chilly. I get the feeling she's already forgiven him. Hard not to forgive a guy like Forest.

"Did he put you up to this?" says Mel.

"No, not at all. The poor guy's a wreck. Look, Mel, honestly, the thought of my best friend staying in that crummy compartment of mine, eating fish sticks and drinking flat root beer, watching *Law and Order* repeats, not shaving, not answering the phone — basically living *my* life, even for a few days, is too pathetic to ponder. Call him, Mel, please. Make him come home."

"Did you ever cheat on me?" she says, catching me off guard.

"What, like in college?"

"When we went out."

"That's going back a ways, Mel. I honestly couldn't tell you. But I'm not Forest — I'm a lot needier than he ever was. So I'm guessing I probably tried."

"Forest says you've been writing poetry again."

I feel myself blanching. "Nah. Nothing like that. I'm about as poetic as a forklift these days. I tried writing a girl a note a while back, and, well . . . Anyway, stupid idea."

"How are you *doing,* Ben? Are you holding up?"

"Look, I gotta go, Mel. I'm on the road. Just promise me you'll call him."

"I will. And thanks, Ben. Take care of yourself, okay?"

"Okay."

dot

Sunday morning, Trev and I brave the nameless motel restaurant, which we soon decide should be called Crazy Willard's. The dining room, awash in a suffocating array of miscellany, from muskets to animal pelts, is as dark and filmy as any antiques mall. The decor adheres to no theme whatsoever. Pirate hats. Mustache combs. Victorian lace. Here a framed photo of Lana Turner. There, a three-masted schooner in an ancient bottle. The place smells of corned beef and cat litter. Mr. Willard himself, a scarecrow of a man in a moth-eaten flannel shirt, who also happens to be the motel clerk, leads us to a booth by the window and presents us with a pair of greasy menus. I immediately feel ill at ease in the booth, as though I'm being watched. Turning, I discover the source of my discomfiture, perched like a raven on the bench back above my right shoulder: a stuffed marmot who looks as though he's been caught in the act of rear-entry coitus — either the shoddy work of an amateur or a taxidermist with an adolescent sense of humor.

"That's Jessie," explains Old Willard. "Pert' near the fattest damn whistle pig I ever did see in these parts. Stuffed him myself."

"Oh."

"Wow," says Trev.

"Shot me a twelve-pound yellow belly over in Post Falls back in 1967. Biggest rockchuck I ever bagged in Kootenai County. Squealed like a teakettle from hell. 'Course they got even bigger over in Shoshone."

It is now apparent that Old Willard has no intention of leaving us to our menus.

"You boys fish?"

"Once," I say.

"No limit on bass up at Bonner Lake — they got largemouth and small. Used to have a cabin up that way, 'fore them Nazi kids burned it down. You kids aren't Nazis are you? I don't serve Nazis. Did two tours in WW2. Hell if I'm gonna feed 'em."

"We're not Nazis," I say.

"Good. I've had it up to here with Nazis. Used to be we was known for our spuds and our fishin'. Now it's neo-Nazis. Ask me, it ought to be open season on Nazis. I'll tell you what: the next snot-encrusted little Nazi punk who crosses my path has got another thing comin'. I'll slit his belly, pry him open, scrape out his guts, and stuff him like a twelve-point buck. Biscuits and gravy's good."

"I'll have the waffles," says Trev.

Old Willard furrows his brow at this selection.

I'm not prepared to take any chances with the old spark plug, so I order the biscuits and gravy, a choice which seems to please Old Willard, who dons a yellow porcelain smile as he scratches out my order.

"Them's good."

"Should I be scared?" I say, as he disappears into the kitchen.

"Holy crap," says Trev, looking wide-eyed out the window. "Check it out."

Leaning against the burned-out COZY 8 sign in the motor court, with a dirty gray backpack at her feet, is the girl with the fingerless gloves. She's smoking as usual. Today she's wearing a denim miniskirt (too short) and a skimpy sleeveless T-shirt (not warm enough), which says something on it that I can't see, though I assume it's offensive.

"Damn, she's hot," says Trev. "Don't you think?"

"Way too young for me. But she's cute, yeah. Even though she's doing her best not to be."

"What do you mean?"

"I don't know, she's just a kid dressed up like a . . . strumpet."

"*Strumpet*? Dude, how old *are* you? What the heck is a strumpet?"

"A prostitute."

"I don't think she looks like a prostitute. I think she looks rad."

Old Willard is back, proffering a yellow smile which looks half apologetic and half triumphant. "We outta waffles," he says. "How 'bout biscuits and gravy?"

"Perfect," says Trev.

We both turn our attention back to the window. The sky is growing darker by the minute. A stiff wind out of the west pelts the window with desert grit. A sudden gust sends a brown paper bag billowing across the court. Smoking Girl sits down on the pavement and pulls her knees in close. She ought have a coat on and some jeans. When she catches Trev and me staring at her, she gives us the finger.

"I wonder what the deal is with her," Trev wonders aloud.

"Looks like one of them little Nazi tarts," says Willard, arriving with two steaming platters. "Don't be shy now," he says.

"What are those lumps?" Trev inquires.

"Them's mushrooms."

"I'm gonna let mine cool," I say, an answer that apparently displeases Old Willard, whose yellow smile withers.

"Suit yourself," he says, and walks away.

I sneak a glance at Smoking Girl, who has turned her back on us. It flusters and embarrasses me that she should think I'm a dirty old man. Maybe her old man's a pervert. Maybe he can't keep his hands off her. Maybe that's why she's out in the middle of nowhere with a dirty backpack. Maybe that's why she dresses the way she does, because she feels cheap.

Sand pelts the window furiously, and in an instant the sky ominously darkens. Smoking Girl looks up and tosses her cigarette aside. She crosses her arms and regains her feet, turning around just in time to see a rippling curtain of black wash out the horizon. It advances with terrifying speed out of the west, like a tidal wave, swallowing everything in its path. Within twenty seconds it's on the very edge of the motor court. Smoking Girl snatches her backpack off the ground, and I lose sight of her.

"What the hell?" says Trev.

"What is it?" I say. "Is it rain?"

"I think it's sand."

Whatever it is, it's fully upon us now, blotting out the sky, howling like the mother of all banshees as it washes over us. Old Willard pokes his head out of the kitchen and whistles like he might whistle at a thirty-pound bass. Even Jessie the Marmot looks incredulous as the overhead lights begin to flicker and the entire restaurant shudders, setting knickknacks and silverware to rattling. I can't see two feet out the window. The motor court is awash in a churning miasma of dust. Smoking Girl is at large somewhere in the thick of it — I've got to find her. Instinctively, I jump to my feet and stride down the aisle, arriving at the entrance just as she bursts through the glass door with a gasp. She drops her bag on the floor, coughs twice, and leans forward with her hand on her knees to catch her breath. When she straightens up, she's looking me right in the chest. I can see now that her shirt says THE CRAMPS, in warbly lettering. BAD MUSIC FOR BAD PEOPLE.

"What are *you* looking at?" she says.

"I was just going out to make sure you were okay."

"How sweet," she says, with mock sincerity. "I need a cup of coffee."

All at once light floods back into the restaurant, and just as suddenly as it began the storm is over. For us, anyway.

Smoking Girl walks right past me, muttering about the sand in her shoes, and sits down in the booth on the far side of Trev.

"Hey," she says flatly.

"What's up?" he says.

"Right, you're the guy with the shoes," she says.

Smoking Girl runs her hand through her cropped bleached hair, then sifts some sand out of her black bangs. "What's that?" she says, grimacing at his biscuits and gravy, which has ceased its steaming and oozing and developed a skin.

"The house specialty," he says.

"It looks disgusting."

I resume my seat. "You hungry?" I say.

She ignores me. "So, what's your name, anyway?" she says to Trev.

"Trevor. What about you?"

"Dot."

"Dot?"

"Do I look like a Dorothy to you?"

"I guess not," he says.

"And this ain't Kansas, either," I say, to which she rolls her eyes and glances vaguely out the window.

"Yeah? Well, it may as well be."

Old Willard returns to check on our progress. "There a problem here?"

"No, everything's great," I say.

"You ain't touched it."

"We got sidetracked."

"Hey, Gramps," says Dot. "Who do I gotta blow to get a cup of coffee around here?"

I don't know who's more shocked, me or Old Willard, whose brow furrows as blood suffuses his face.

"Cream and sugar," she says. "And can I see a menu? This old perv wants to buy me breakfast."

Old Willard is visibly at a loss. He's seen a few things in his day: kamikaze fighters, mutant rockchucks, some awfully big bass — but never this. He retreats in search of a menu, shaking his hoary old head and grumbling.

"So, where are you guys headed?"

"Salt Lake City," says Trev.

"Why? You Mormons?"

"Nah. My dad lives there."

"Poor him."

She turns her attention to her backpack, rifling through the front pocket and producing a compact, which she holds in front of her face as she wipes her mascara off with the tail of her Cramps shirt.

"What about you?" I say. "Where are you going?"

"Denver."

"What's in Denver?"

"Not much," she says, snapping her compact shut. "My stepdad."

"Where are you coming from?"

"Tacoma," she says.

Old Willard won't even look at her as he flips her cup over and fills it with coffee. He drops the menu on the table and turns, then thinks twice, and turns back.

"You ain't one of them little Nazi tarts are you?"

"Do I look like a Nazi to you?"

"Okay, then," he mutters, walking off.

"I'll have waffles," she calls after him.

"We're out," he says gruffly, without turning around.

"Out of batter?"

Now he swings around, holding the coffeepot. "That's right. Out of batter."

"So, there's no more made? Is that it?"

"That's it."

"But you've got more in a box somewhere, right? Probably the same box you use to make those biscuits, I'll bet. Bisquick or whatever, right?"

"Could be."

"Could be, huh?"

They lock eyes. In the brittle silence, neither one of them flinches, though Old Willard's chin begins to quiver slightly under the strain. Dot's pale little face is screwed up in a portrait of defiance. Old Willard glowers back at her like she's Heinrich Himmler as Trev and I exchange expectant glances.

Then, very slowly, very decisively, Dot looks from empty table to empty table, then looks back at Old Willard and hoists an eyebrow at him. "Looks like you could use the business," she says.

I can see the air go right out of the old guy. He turns, he slumps, he mutters. And ten minutes later, he returns with waffles.

"See, Gramps?" she says. "That wasn't so bad now, was it?"

terrible things to say

I planned that summer vacation in '05 a year in advance. I was dead set on taking the family road trip that my family never took. The one where everyone piles into the station wagon. Route 66. The Grand Canyon. The stuff of American myth. Never mind the 150 miles of scorched earth between Barstow and Needles. Never mind the hundred-degree heat. Never mind that Janet was seven months pregnant with Jodi.

Unlike the vacation, Jodi was not planned.

"Do you think I wanted to get pregnant, Ben — *now*? Right when things are coming together for me? For us?"

We're in a dirt parking lot outside Kingman, Arizona, in the paltry shade of a lone pine off the interstate. We've just gassed up. Janet and I are stretching our legs. Piper sleeps in the backseat, her hair pasted in strands to her forehead, the skin of her arm stuck to the vinyl. It's been a long stretch between Needles and Kingman. Not the stuff of American Myth. Janet is blotchy. She has sweat rings at the armpits.

"What about me?" I say, kicking up a cloud of dust. "Do you think I wanted you to get pregnant? I finally get a chance to have a life again, and now I'll be back to square one — stuck at home, drowning in shit-smeared onesies, tiptoeing around the house at all hours. I swear if I'm forced to watch *Clifford the Big Red Dog* once more, I'll hang myself. Do you have any idea what this means for me? You get to see people every day, Janet — adults. You get to eat lunch wherever you want. I eat french toast, shrimp cocktail, and Orange Julius. Do you think this is what I had planned for myself — this is what I wanted to do when I grew up?"

She mops her sweaty forehead with the sleeve of her blouse. "What *did* you want, Ben?"

"What do you mean by that?"

"Did you want to be a parade float painter? A poet? That's lucrative! Or did you want to keep selling scones your whole life? It's never too late to get your real-estate license, you know."

"We can't all play *animal proctologist to the rich,* Janet."

"Well, good thing some of us can, because the last time I checked you couldn't raise a family on free verse and scones — you can't even pay for child care with that."

"Got *one* of us through grad school, though, didn't it? I don't remember your student loans paying for that apartment on Roosevelt. Or all those free cups of coffee."

"Well, I'd say that I've more than evened the score on that count, though I'd like to point out that we've moved up in the world somewhat from that studio with the leaky ceiling and the rusty bathtub ring."

I'm out of comebacks. Moreover, I'm out of fight. She's right, anyway — what have I ever done with my life? Without Janet, I'd probably still be living in that leaky studio, stacking scones, writing self-conscious poetry.

Janet sees me pouting. Suddenly she laughs, and it's not bitter or pointed. "Remember the guy upstairs?" she says.

"What, the drummer?"

"No. Him, too. But the crazy guy. The guy who always accused you of 'zapping' him with your 'faggot secret.'"

"Felix."

"Yes! He was convinced everybody was gay."

"Everybody but him. Poor Felix. Remember the Vietnamese place downstairs? I think it was Vietnamese."

"Yeah."

"Do you remember the name of it?"

"It was something funny. You used to always joke about it."

"It was called Don Pae."

She smiles. "Right. You used to say it was an invitation to dine and ditch." She looks off at the dusty horizon, until her smile fades, then she turns back to me. "I'm sorry, Ben."

Suddenly I feel like a heel. I've driven her to the edge of despair with this trip. How could I not know better? She's been a trouper through it all — fun, adventurous, patient. Despite an aching back and swollen ankles. Here she is, seven months pregnant. It's ninety-eight degrees, in a dirt parking lot in Arizona. We've just driven two hundred miles. Of course she's distraught.

"No, I'm sorry," I say. "I should've called off this trip."

"I'm glad we didn't," she says. And she steps toward me and hugs me, and I can feel her sweat-glistening forehead against my cheek.

the story with dot

Yeah, he's okay," Dot says. "Kind of a dork but stable, you know? Even after my mom died — especially then, I guess."

Dot blows into her coffee, and a little steam curls up around her pierced nose and past her pierced eyebrow. "He pretends like it didn't really affect him. But it's all an act. He's just trying to make me feel safe or whatever. He talks to me different now — like I'm all fragile, or superdepressed, or I'm gonna swallow a bottle of pills the first time he turns his head." She sets her coffee down, but immediately her hands seek occupation. She picks up her fork and draws syrup squiggles on her plate.

"Yeah, I know it's a big deal. She was my mom. Hello, I get it. And it seems unfair. But it happened, you know? Now I wish everybody would just leave me alone about it. Especially Ron. It's not like the whole freaking world telling me how sorry they are is helping. It's not like all of a sudden I'm some little lost lamb or whatever. Like I can't take care of myself or like make my own decisions. It doesn't mean Ron's gotta like try to be my mom *and* my dad."

Looking at her with her waiflike attire, her dirty backpack, and her pale delicate finger tracing circles around her empty coffee cup, her innocent little face molded into something worldly, it's hard to blame Ron or anyone else for trying to protect her.

"It's like the whole thing with Kirk," she says. "Kirk was like the only person who understood me. He was the only person who didn't keep saying he was sorry or like try to get me to talk about it or cry on his shoulder. He treated me like a person, not some helpless baby. When my mom was alive, Ron wouldn't have said anything about Kirk. He might have thought stuff, but he wouldn't have done anything about it — like refuse to let me hang out with him or whatever, just because he's older and he's got a little ink and he likes to hang out downtown. It's like all of a sudden Ron was trying to protect me from Kirk, and Kirk was like the only good thing about Denver. Everyone just thinks because Kirk looked the way he did, he was like some sort of bad influence. Kirk had his shit together more than anyone wanted to give him credit for. It's not his fault the whole freaking world was like . . . *against* him."

"Where is he?"

"Jail — but he didn't actually do anything. His stupid roommates were dealing. He didn't even know about it."

Poor Dot. So young, so loyal, so misguided. And what about Kirk? Does Kirk, in the fog of his adolescent self-absorption, realize the value of a lover willing to forgive him anything? I doubt it. And Dot can see me doubting.

"See what I mean? You're just like Ron and the rest of them. You just jump to conclusions, make up your mind about stuff before you even know about it. But whatever, I guess I can't blame you, you're just male."

She lays her fork aside and picks up her coffee cup again, then sets it down and begins fiddling with the saltshaker.

"Anyway, after Kirk's whole deal, it didn't make sense to hang around Denver for another summer. So I left."

"To live with your real dad?"

"Hmph," she says. "Real dad. Yeah, I guess you'd call him that. Except that he thinks he's like fifteen years old or whatever — even though he's like forty. I always thought he was cool when I was younger, even though he didn't hang around and my mom always called him a deadbeat. He'd send me cool presents from Thailand and Australia and places. Like one time he sent me one of those didgeridoos. And once he sent me a really rad turquoise bracelet, which I still have." She reaches down and fishes around in the front pocket of her ragged backpack, until she finds the bracelet. She spins it around in her hand, so we can see it from all angles. It's a chunky silver thing, inlaid willy-nilly with dozens of tiny turquoise chips.

"That's totally rad," says Trev.

"Yeah, I know, huh?"

Instead of returning the bracelet to her pack, she slides it over her thin wrist just above her fingerless glove and spins it around absently a few times as she looks out the window.

"I always thought my mom was jealous of my dad," she says. "For leaving, I mean. Because she was like stuck in Denver. And even though he left, I always kinda thought it was her choice not to be with him, and she was dumb not to. Now that I'm older it's like, I don't know, he just seems immature. It's kinda hard to believe he's my dad. Or anyone's dad."

"Are you mad that he left?" says Trev.

She spins her bracelet some more, inspects it vaguely. "Nah. Denver sucks. I just think he needs to grow up. For a while, he was acting like an adult, sort of. He was wearing Dockers, working for some company that distributed investment videos or something like that. But then he quit, and then his car got repossessed and he never really got another job. Now he drives around in a total bomb, and he built like a skateboard ramp in the driveway. Can you believe that? A skateboard ramp? At his age? He wears baggy shorts and Mossimo shirts and says 'bro' all the time. He wants to act like we're friends or whatever instead of being my dad."

Dot shakes her head, and waves it off, as though she's weary of the whole subject. She looks out the window again, where a thin layer of dust covers the pavement. "I don't know," she says. "It's weird. My dad's weird. Tacoma sucked, anyway."

Shortly before noon, the rain, like the dust before it, blows in suddenly and furiously from the west. No warning from the Weather Channel. I think it's the weather that has inspired Dot to forsake her thumb and cast her lot with us, at least as far as Butte. The three of us loaf in the darkened motel room through the remainder of the morning, with the TV on mute. By two, the wind has died down somewhat, but the rain continues in fat droplets, battering the ceiling and running down the window in sheets. Come late afternoon, I order Domino's, wondering why I didn't think of it before.

When the delivery kid raps, I open the door to find that he's not a kid at all but a skinny guy about my age, whose Domino's hat looks new compared the the rest of his wardrobe. He's got a tattoo peeking out from beneath his shirt collar — something faded with talons. He wears the brim of his cap low and avoids eye contact throughout the transaction. I tip him, he nods once, hops back in his idling Festiva, spins a semicircle, and speeds off.

I linger in the open doorway listening to the hiss of the rain, which seems to go on forever. The sky is oppressive: slate gray and inching eastward. Not a sky for dreamers. A sky for people just trying to get by. It could be dawn, or dusk, or three in the afternoon. This could be Medford or Wenatchee or Bismarck. I can still smell the cool dust rising off the pavement, even through the pungent warmth of the steaming pizzas. Across the courtyard, the motel office is darkened, the red neon vacancy sign reads ANCY. The little restaurant is deserted but for Old Willard standing at the window like an apparition. A lake has formed in the center of the court, barren except for the van. Then I see it, and my scalp tightens, and that welcome sense of anonymity drains right out of me. Across the way, gassing up at the Chevron, is the brown Skylark.

"Fuck me," I say, scurrying for cover. I close the door behind me, plop the pizzas down, and draw the heavy curtains closed. Immediately, I peer through the crack, and out the blurry window.

"What's the deal?" says Trev.

"I think Janet is having me followed."

"For real?"

"Who's Janet?" says Dot, leaning up in the far bed.

"His ex-wife."

"Wife," I say.

"Did you do something wrong?"

"It's a long story."

I can't quite make out the guy at the pump — his back is to me — but it's a guy, that much is clear from the broad shoulders and the baseball cap.

"Dude's been on our ass for two hundred miles."

"For real? So what do we do?" says Trev. "It's not like we can leave."

"I don't know, I don't really get it. If he was gonna serve me, he would've done it before we ever left the state, right?"

"You mean that brown car?" says Dot.

"You saw it?"

"You're just paranoid," she says.

I probably am just paranoid, I tell myself. The fact is, Janet couldn't possibly have gotten somebody on me that quick. We picked this guy up around Moses Lake. Janet didn't even know I was on the road until George, and I didn't tell her exactly where I was. This is a coincidence. It's the interstate — there are only so many exits. The guy's probably selling dog brushes out of his trunk, probably living on jojos and pizzas and motel beds like us, stopping at the same mini-marts as us.

"Let's eat some pizza," I say, and begin rolling out Trev's tray table.

Halfway through my second slice, I can't stand it anymore. Peering through the crack again, I scope the vicinity from the southern horizon to the Chevron station. A red pickup swishes past on the main drag. A police cruiser pulls into the Chevron and parks in front. Panning back in the other direction, I catch Old Willard out of the corner of my eye, still standing at the window scanning the area for Nazis.

After three hours of incessant window checking and no further sign of the Skylark, I finally relax as evening falls, assuring myself that if our pursuer should reappear (though he won't, because he's not really pursuing us), I will take the offensive. I will not be hunted. Fishing my Bob Frost out of my backpack, I sink into my creaky roll-away in the corner near the bathroom, beneath the dangling coat hangers. I prop myself up on a folded pillow, and futilely scan the pages for a few minutes, half listening to Trev and Dot converse in the glow of the muted television.

"So why'd you change your mind about visiting your dad?" she asks.

"I'm just excited to see him in a wheelchair."

"That's sick."

"Thanks," he says.

Dot is flipping through the road atlas. I hear the pages turning. "Hey, so what about the Germs?" she says.

"Never heard of them."

She stops flipping pages. "You've never heard of the Germs?"

They go on and on like this, talking about punk bands and movies I've never heard of and things that get on their nerves and the various indignities of youth. All the while, the fat heavy rain drones on, washing away the dust. A dull, delicious ache sinks into my bones.

When I awaken, I find Dot asleep on her bed atop the covers, her bare legs pulled up under one of Trev's sweatshirts. Trev is still awake, leaning back slightly in his wheelchair, clutching the remote weakly in his lap.

"How you doin'?" I whisper, approaching him in the half-light.

"Not bad," he says. Then he smiles a thousand-watter, nods his head, and smiles some more. I couldn't be more giddy if it were my own smile.

"You ready?"

"Yeah."

"Gotta piss?"

"Nah."

"Wanna brush your teeth?"

"I'm good."

Leaning in, I get ahold of him under the knees, and drape his stiff arm over my shoulder, readying myself to scoop him up. I feel the heat of his wasted body, feel the stubble of his cheek against my forehead, smell the grease of his scalp and the sour sweat rising up from beneath his shirt collar, tinged with Speed Stick, and none of it is unpleasant. "So, you're not bummed we missed the bordello tour?"

"What do you think?"

"Yeah," I whisper back. "Me neither."

Hoisting him, I prop him on my knee, wiggle his shoes off, and unfasten his cargoes, working them down past his boxers, over his white bulbous knees. Once I've situated him in bed, on his side, with a pillow tucked snugly between his knees, I plug in his chair to charge for the night.

"Good night," I whisper.

"Good night."

Pausing at the foot of Dot's bed, I can't resist one more look at her curled up atop the covers. She stirs but does not awaken. She doesn't look so tough with her delicate features in repose, her little lips parted slightly. Hard to look tough with drool on your pillow. Resisting the urge to tuck her in, I snap off the TV and climb back into my creaky roll-away.

Lying on my back, I can still feel Trev smiling in the darkness, and I can't help but smile back.

the dealership

O h that," says the mechanic, a heavyset bald guy with a maple bar in one hand and a powdered donut perched on the rim of his coffee cup in the other hand. "That's just a dummy light. But I'll check it out. You kids help yourself to a donut."

He walks off gingerly, balancing his donut. We kids retire to the waiting area, a windowless den lined with folding chairs in the rear of the dealership, where we help ourselves to a donut.

"These are stale," says Dot.

"I'll bet if we rubbed two of them together, we could start a fire," says Trev.

But for a sport fishing calendar on the wall, which is current (September features a bearded dude in yellow waders, dangling a trophy trout), the waiting room is a time warp; 1970s faux wood, balding gray carpet. Thumbing an issue of *Hot Rod* from 1997, it occurs to me that we could be waiting a long time.

But within five minutes, the mechanic is back, still clutching a maple bar. "Gas cap," he says, over the rim of his coffee cup.

"Excuse me?"

"Your gas cap was screwed on crooked. Sends a message to the dealy-bob."

Trev and I exchange glances.

"See, between you and me," he says, and here he lowers his voice, "damn near everything sends a message to the dealy-bob. It's like the brain of the whole car. But the thing is — and don't say I told you so — the dealy-bob, it ain't so smart. Fact is, my dog's smarter. Now and then, it'll be a vacuum leak or a hose, and once in a while it'll be a thermostat. But often as not, it's the gas cap. You kids get a donut?"

We're two days and five hundred miles behind schedule as we ease east onto I-90, with the fuel topped off and the gas cap properly secured. If all goes according to plan, we'll cover half that distance today, skipping Wallace, along with our scheduled detour to Polson, and aim for Butte by nightfall. We'll lunch along the way and make a brief stop at Big Stack in late afternoon if time allows. I'm willing to grant Dot two cigarette stops, which makes me an enabler, I guess. But the fact is, I don't want to lose her. From Butte, she insists she'll make her own way, and I'm afraid there's nothing I can do to convince her otherwise, though I hope I can at least persuade her to bunk with us again tonight and wait until morning before lighting out by thumb. If nothing else, maybe she'll let me buy her a bus ticket. But I doubt it.

The rain clouds scattered sometime during the night. Travel conditions are ideal for making up time: dry pavement, clear skies, and no Winnebagos glutting the flow of traffic. With Couer d'Alene in the rearview mirror, we begin steadily gaining elevation and winding our way through the heart of the panhandle toward the divide, where hulking green ranges, rock-ribbed and dark, close in on us from either side, until the sky is just a pale blue ribbon. The effect of this landscape is at once cozy and oppressive. I'd hate to spend a winter in one of these narrow valleys, socked in a haze of chimney smoke. This was silver country back in the day, and gold and quartz, too, if memory serves. At one point, the Idaho panhandle nearly became the state of Lincoln, something I recall from Piper's second-grade state report. She chose Idaho because it was "skinny on top and fat on the bottom," and because potatoes were her "sixth-favorite food." But I'm determined not to think about Piper or Jodi or Janet today, so I turn the newfangled country on low, low enough that Trev and Dot don't notice, so low I can barely hear it myself. Somehow it's enough to know it's there, that somebody's telling it like it is, even if the music sucks.

Trev and Dot have taken up where they left off last night, passing the miles in what is for the most part easy conversation, though Dot, like me, has a tendency to push. I'm perfectly content to be invisible in the driver's seat, listening to Dot lead this dance from the backseat, where she's stretched out lengthwise with her head on the armrest, tracking Trev's eyes in the rearview mirror. She does not pity him as far as I can tell, nor does she go easy on him, as do most people.

"So, do you get sick of people staring at you?" she says.

"It's worse when they talk to me like I'm retarded."

"That sucks."

"What about you?" he says. "People must stare at you."

"Old pervs and religious people, but that's about it."

"I'm not religious," he says.

"I guess that makes you an old perv."

"But I'm not old."

"Older than me, anyway. So, then, can you have sex? I mean like everything works or whatever?"

Blushing to the roots of his hair, Trev looks straight ahead at the road and shifts uncomfortably in his chair.

When, after a long moment, he fails to reply, Dot pushes him. "So is that a yes or a no?"

Poor Trev is caught in the headlights.

But Dot refuses to veer. "I guess I'll take that as a no."

"Yes," he says, at last, with an edge of impatience. "Everything works."

"You don't sound too happy about it."

"Should I be?"

"Uh. Yeah? Duh." And with that, she finally lets the subject drop, and we hum along in silence for a few miles until she trains her cross-hairs on me. "So, how old are you, anyway? Are you like my dad's age?"

"Yes. I'm old enough to be your father. But don't worry, I don't want to be."

"Got any kids?"

Trev casts an uneasy sidelong glance at me.

"Nope," I say.

"Why not?"

"Long story."

"Well, it's not like we don't have time to kill, right?"

"Trust me, it's not a good story. You won't like the ending."

"What, you just never wanted any? Or you just never found the right person or what?"

"Like I said," and this time I say it more firmly: "Long story."

"What, are you gay?" she says. "Because I've got no problem with gay people."

"I'm not gay."

"So, you just didn't want any or what? Because I can see not wanting to have any."

I grip the wheel tighter and stare straight ahead.

"He doesn't like to talk about it," says Trev.

His defense, though welcome, catches me by surprise — it's the first indication I've had that he knows anything about Piper and Jodi. I could hug him for never bringing it up.

Dot heaves a theatrical sigh. "What is it with guys? They never want to talk about anything."

almost home

We're halfway down Agatewood now — right before the dogleg west of Dolphin Lane, coasting through that familiar sun-checkered corridor beneath the tall firs. My window is down. I can smell the trade winds blowing through Agate Pass. Piper is growing impatient in the backseat, Jodi's snot still clinging to her index finger.

"It's starting to dry," she complains.

"Well, put it in your mouth, then."

"Eww," she says. "Daddy, you're grotie."

"Thanks," I say.

"Daddy grotie," mimics Jodi, clearly enough that I can understand him.

"He says you're grotie."

"I heard."

"Grotie," says Jodi once more. "Squishity-squish-squash grotie."

What will that speech pathologist cost? What if Piper needs orthodontia? Whatever any of it costs, Janet can afford it. And should we ever run into trouble financially, Bernard and Ruth will always be there. I hope Bern pulls the trigger on that Discovery Bay lot. The kids would love it.

"Squish-squishy-bah-buh-squishity-squish, Daddy." Where does he get the saliva, I wonder?

"He wants to see the octopus," Piper says.

"We already saw the octopus."

"*We* saw the octopus. *He* was asleep."

"Jodi, buddy. Octopus go night-night. We'll go visit the octopus another time, okay?"

Checking the rearview mirror, I expect to see pouting lips, a quivering chin. But he surprises me, and I love him for it.

"Kaykay," he says.

the box

Weary of Dot's hounding, and harassed by my thoughts, I'm gripping the wheel a little tighter than usual as we wind our way up through the rugged Bitterroots toward the Montana border. Trev has fallen asleep in his wheelchair, his mouth wide open. He's scruffy. He's got bed head. He's going to need a shower. Stretched out in back, Dot has resorted to headphones. Her green Chucks tap out a rhythm against the elbow rest. Her sweet lips mouth angry words. Occasionally she blows her bangs out of her eyes or contemplates her fingernails, looking bored but comfortable.

At Lookout Pass, without warning or expectation, without so much as a cloud visible for the past thirty miles, we round a wide bend not unlike thirty bends before it, when suddenly it starts hailing stones the size of marbles. They're beating hard on the roof. The din is such that Dot removes her headphones, and sits up. The racket wakens Trev, who rolls his shoulders and straightens his head. "Holy crap, now what?"

"Look at the freakin' size of it," says Dot.

Pellets begin collecting on the wipers and under the lip of the hood, pounding the glass like gravel, hammering the roof. The clatter is so loud that Trev is forced to raise his voice to be heard.

"No way," he says. "This is insane."

On the roadway, hailstones shimmy like oil on a hot skillet. You can hear them bouncing up against the floor of the car, rattling under the grille. They quickly begin to accumulate along the fog lines. Just ahead, a pair of trucks have pulled over and are huddled on the shoulder against the onslaught, their red lights flashing dully through the haze. I slow to thirty as we pass. I ought to pull over, too, and I'm almost certain Trev is about to suggest as much when abruptly the hammering ice gives way to the muted patter of rain, and suddenly the world seems quieter than ever.

"Damn," says Trev.

"That was intense," says Dot. She's left her seat and is on her knees now, just behind Trev and me, leaning in close, her gloveless right hand clutching the armrest of Trev's wheelchair.

"Totally intense," says Trev.

Then we all lapse into a reflective silence, the kind you savor after big events. About a half mile past Henderson, I spot through the haze a shit-can Isuzu pulled over on the left shoulder with its hazards on. A figure hunches in the rain before the rear wheel, clutching a tire iron. Slowing as I pass, I see that it's a very pregnant woman. Drenched, she is apparently having a tough time removing the flat. There's a dude smoking a cigarette in the passenger's seat who appears to be barking instructions out the open window. Without consulting Trev, I pull off on the left and back slowly down the shoulder until I'm fifty feet or so in front of them, where I throw the van in park and leave it idling.

"I'm gonna see if they need a hand," I say, hopping out of the van into the downpour.

The Isuzu is at least four different colors, if you include bondo gray. Really, it's several cars fashioned into one. The hood is blue. The front left side panel is yellow. The doors are green. Cars are speeding by at seventy miles per hour, trailing sheets of gritty road water. When the girl turns on her haunches to greet me, her enormous belly pressed tight against a cheap cotton dress, she's smiling. You can tell she smiles a lot. She's young, maybe three years older than Dot. Her heart-shaped face is wide open and freckled, framed by straight, wet, dirty blond hair to the shoulders. Her hazel eyes seem to hide nothing. She's lovely in the most wholesome of ways. Even extremely pregnant, squatting in a nasty rain squall on a muddy shoulder, with a tire iron in her hand, and a fuck-stick of a boyfriend hollering instructions at her, she's got that unsullied youthful glow about her, the same one that Dot tries so hard to hide.

"The thingy just snapped right off," she explains. "And the lower thingies won't budge."

"Lug nuts," says her skinny companion impatiently, through the open window. "They're called lug nuts!"

"You guys want me to call a tow truck?"

"Ain't got no money for a tow truck," he says, spitting out the window.

"We've got Triple A," I offer.

"Never mind that," he says. "I've got business in Missoula. Then we gotta make Jackson 'fore she busts. Ain't got time to deal with this rice burner. Damn cylinder block's made out of aluminum cans, anyway. Probably wouldn't make St. Regis, even if it *did* have four wheels."

With that, he climbs out of the car with a cigarette dangling from his mouth.

"I'm Peaches," says the girl, standing upright. "And that's Elton."

Elton looks like a skinned weasel — weak chin, beady eyes, long body. He's wearing a dirty Copenhagen cap, with the brim pulled down low, and a flannel shirt that looks like it may have survived a house fire.

"Elton's got a lousy back," she explains. "That's why I'm changin' the tire."

"Fishin' injury," he explains.

Something about Elton doesn't inspire confidence. Could it be the fact that he'd let his pregnant girlfriend change a tire on the shoulder of an interstate in the rain? Or maybe it's just those beady eyes. He doesn't seem dangerous, exactly, or even malignant, just sort of shifty.

"So, you goin' as far as Missoula, hoss?"

"Let me talk to my friend," I say. "He's in charge."

Elton nods doubtfully and spits on the ground. "All right, then."

I stride back to the van and station myself by the passenger's window, signaling to Dot to roll it down as an eighteen-wheeler speeds past, spraying me with a light mist.

"These guys need a ride to Missoula," I explain.

"I dunno," says Trev. "Dude looks sketchy to me."

"The girl's nice," I say. "And she's pregnant — really pregnant."

"What do you think?" Trev asks Dot, over his shoulder. "It'd be crowded back there."

"Fine," she says. "But I wanna smoke first."

Dot crawls around the driver's seat to smoke on the shoulder in the rain, as I give Elton and Peaches the thumbs-up. Peaches soon hefts two huge suitcases out of the rear hatch and begins conveying them toward the van with tiny, hard-won steps.

"Don't let that right one drag," says Elton from behind her. "It's gettin' muddy!"

Ten minutes later, Elton, Peaches, and Dot are all crowded into the backseat, and we're driving along in silence.

"So, business in Missoula," I say, by way of making conversation.

"That's right," says Elton.

"What kind of business you in?" I inquire.

"None of yours," he says.

"Elton's gonna make us rich," says Peaches. "He invented a —"

"Shush up," says Elton.

"Well, you said that —"

"I said it ain't patented yet. Don't go runnin' your mouth."

"Your secret is safe with us," I say.

Elton meets my gaze with narrowed eyes in the rearview mirror. "Well, I ain't takin' that chance, hoss. Not until I got my patent. And not until I got all my ducks in line so far as investors and such."

"Oh, c'mon," says Dot. "Just tell us."

"Hell no. I ain't tellin'. Ain't nobody gonna steal my idea."

"Well," I say. "At any rate, sounds like you've dotted your i's on this thing."

"Hell yes, I did. I got a whole business plan wrote up. I even sent it to myself to get it postmarked — see, then I kept the whole plan sealed up in the envelope. That's to protect the idea until the patent comes through. In some cases it's admissible in a court of law. Long as it's postmarked and sealed up tight. I got 'er in a safe deposit box."

"Boy, you've really covered your bases," I say.

"Hell yes. Fella don't just squat on top of a gold mine with no protection and no plan. You gotta keep a lookout. And you gotta know how to mine that gold. Idea's only as good as its execution."

"You've got that right."

"Hell yes, I do."

"Must be a hell of an idea."

"Hell yes, it is."

"I don't blame you for keeping the lid on it. Probably smart. The suspense is killing me, though. Must be a good one."

Flush with excitement, Elton leans forward, and speaks in low earnest tones. "Fine then, I'll talk around the edges a little bit, but I'm not tellin' my actual idea. Just the edges."

"Fair enough."

"And this don't go no further than this van, you hear? I'm dead serious about that." Like a leery weasel, Elton frisks us with beady eyes. "You got that?"

"Got it," we say.

"Well then, first, let's talk about basic business principles and whatnot. For starters, you gotta consider — even before you consider the capitalizin' part — whether or not there's a market for your idea. And there's a market for mine. Trust me, I worked in the industry. Matter of fact, there's a bunch of products already on the market tryin' to do roughly what my product does, but none of them work for diddly."

"Like what?" says Dot.

"Well, for starters, you know them fake electronic dog boxes they sell to keep burglars away? Them ones that's motion-activated, so that it sounds like you got a watchdog?"

"Yeah."

"Well, they don't fool nobody, and they sure as shit don't scare nobody. Fact is, they got a zero point zero percent success rate at burglar deterrin'."

"You researched it?" says Trev.

"How d'ya s'pose I ended up in the joint in the first place? By burglin' houses, that's how. And who d'ya suppose oughta know more about deterrin' burglars than a burglar? You want a game warden, hire a poacher. So, yeah, I researched it plenty. Eighteen months on the inside gave me plenty of time to think about this — really wrap my brain around it. Idea like this don't just come to a guy like a flash of lightnin'. Takes concentration — a whole mess of considerin'. Like

I say, you gotta ask yourself all the right business questions: Who's gonna capitalize it? Who's gonna handle the manufacturin'? You gotta ask yourself, is my idea executable?"

"So what's your idea?" I say.

Again, his beady eyes meet mine in the mirror, squinting fiercely. "Nice try, hoss."

"Right, the edges, sorry. Well, what about the capital, where does that come from?" I say.

"He's got a plan for that, too," says Peaches brightly.

"And what's that?" I say.

"He won't tell me. He has 'vestors lined up, though."

Determined to be mum on the subject, Elton's thin lips are set, his eyes evasive.

"Oh, just tell us your idea," says Dot.

"Yeah, c'mon," says Trev. "How good could it be?"

This one gets Elton's attention, he locks eyes on the back of Trev's head.

"Tell 'em, honey," says Peaches.

"Look at it this way," I say. "You're a guy who likes to dot his i's. We could be like your focus group. Help you iron out any wrinkles in the plan. You know, head off any questions your investors might have. That's how your corporate think tanks do it."

Elton considers, scratching his weak chin a few times and looking out the side window at the Montana landscape. "S'pose there's some-thin' to all that," he says.

"And besides," says Trev. "You've already applied for the patent, right? So it's probably processing as we speak. Plus, you've got the sealed envelope. By the time anyone tried to steal your idea and get a patent, you'd already have the patent."

"True," he says. "You gotta point there, hoss."

"So just sketch it out for us," I say. "Give us the general idea. With-out the schematics."

Elton gives me a final snake-eyed once-over before making the leap. "Okay. I'll give you the gist of it. But just the edges." He leans forward in his seat. "See, it's kinda like one of them boxes with the fake dog barks I was on about, except that this is even better 'cause it makes a burglar think there's a human bein' inside. Human bein' is gonna deter a burglar better than any dog. Only takes a porterhouse and a tranq to disarm a damn dog, no matter what he is. Believe me, I know."

"So like your box is a person talking?" says Dot.

"Better," says Elton. "Burglar's gonna get wise when he hears every house on the block has the same voice talkin'. And then you gotta have two voices, 'cause who sits and talks to themselves on and on? I s'pose you could have different voice selections or different models, but that's just making things too complex. The most successful business ideas are simple."

"So what is it?"

Elton folds his arms, and leans back on the bench seat, his weasel eyes smiling for the first time. A quick mirror-check of Peaches confirms that her eyes are smiling too.

"My box," says Elton triumphantly, "is a TV."

"A TV."

"Right."

"I don't follow."

"You know, like instead of a dog barking, my box — and it's got a name, but I ain't tellin' it — has a recordin' of somebody watchin' TV."

A short dull silence settles in along with Elton's revelation. I hesitate to comment. Who am I to shit on Elton's dreams? But I just can't help myself.

"Why not just use a real TV?" I say.

"Because this is smaller. Who wants a big TV sittin' in their entryway?"

"Right," I say. "But who keeps a TV right by the door? "

"You don't, dummy. You keep the box by the door. That's the whole point."

"Okay. But what I'm getting at is, your idea — the box — is supposed to make burglars think that somebody's inside watching TV, right? So they won't break in."

"Now you're getting' it, hoss."

"Right. Okay. I mean, yeah, I can see why a dog would be right by the door, because he knows somebody is out there. But who keeps their TV right by the door?"

"Hoss, you ain't the sharpest tool in the shed, are you? You don't have to keep your TV right by the door. That's why I invented the box."

"No, I mean, like why the box in the first place? Wouldn't it just be better to use a regular TV? I mean, since the sound would be coming from where people normally keep their TVs — instead of coming from right behind the front door? Wouldn't it be more realistic?"

If not stunned by this line of questioning, Elton appears at least a little confused, as though he's just found himself in the ring with a southpaw. For a brief moment the implications appear to trouble him, and he's back on his heels, circling, figuring, looking for an opening. But soon his eyes light up again, and with a wink in the mirror, he goes in for the kill.

"Well then, hoss. In that case, you just keep the box by the TV."

grand canyon

Not until the AC goes tits up east of Seligman do I really begin to fathom what a terrible idea this southwest vacation was. What was I thinking? Arizona in August. Wife seven months pregnant. I must be an idiot. By late afternoon, Janet is so sweaty and blotchy she looks as though she might faint at any moment. Piper slumps in the backseat, her fair skin burned lobster red. The car is a blast furnace with the windows open wide.

"How much farther?" says Piper.

"Almost there, honey," Janet moans.

The truth is, we're still sixty-odd miles shy of the south rim.

"Maybe we should just stop in Williams," I say. "Bag the Grand Canyon for today. Get a motel and rest up — maybe take a swim."

"No!" says Piper.

"Mommy doesn't feel good," I say. "She needs rest."

"No, no. I'm fine," Janet says, her eyes closed. She pats me on the thigh and smiles weakly. "It'll be fun."

"But I just think —"

"Really, I'm fine," she says. "I think it's starting to cool off."

"Ha!" says Piper. "Cool off? It must be a gazillion degrees. How many more miles to go?"

"Not many," I say.

"*How* many?"

"About sixty."

"Oh brother," says Piper. "Why did they have to put the Grand Canyon way out in the middle of nowhere in the first place? Why couldn't they put it where we live?"

Janet smiles weakly once more with her eyes closed. "Be patient, sweetie," she says. "It'll be worth the drive."

"How do you know?" she says.

"I just know," says Janet, who leans over and rests her sticky head on my shoulder. Laying a hand atop her swollen belly, she opens her eyes briefly and looks up into my face.

"How about you, handsome?" she says to me. "You doing okay?"

"Tip-top," I say.

"You're sure?"

"I'm sure."

Within minutes, they're both asleep, and I'm wending my way north through the scrubby pinewood toward the south rim, all alone. But nowhere near alone. Because I can feel the weight of Janet's head on my shoulder, and her cool breath on my neck, and I know for certain that she will always be there beside me. And in the rearview mirror, I can see Piper, her determined chin pressed fast against her sunburned sternum, her little mouth twitching in sleep, and I know with equal certainty that she will always be my little girl, no matter how big she gets. And next to that, what's the Grand Canyon?

the story with peaches

By Alberton, the rain has let up, though Montana's signature big sky remains hidden behind a low sheet of gray muslin stretching from horizon to horizon. In the past hour or so, the cramped mountain landscape has gradually unfolded into a sprawl of green grazing lands, peppered with poplar-ringed farmhouses and grain silos, broken on all sides by a relief of knobs and rolling green hills. The interior of the van is at once stuffy and moist. I can smell the cigarette smoke clinging to Elton's ragged flannel. Something smells like wet dog.

Trev is asleep again, mouth open, chair tilted back at a twenty-degree angle, his hands stuffed in the pockets of his big blue hoodie. I'm proud of him, and a little shocked. He's been a great traveler despite the absence of routine. Never have I known him to be so flexible, and I can't help but think Dot has everything to do with it.

Dot has resumed wearing headphones, face pressed to the fogged-up window, looking sleepy-eyed out across the landscape. Peaches sits in the middle, with Elton slumped beside her, his weak chin resting on her shoulder, snoring intermittently. Peaches has slipped on some jeans in lieu of her cotton dress and borrowed one of my sweatshirts, a faded black pullover. Her big stomach rests on her knees, out in front of her, where she lays a protective hand on it. Though her grammar may suffer, her voice is melodious. What is almost drawlish coming from Elton sounds like gentle strains from the mouth of Peaches. One projects laziness, the other ease.

"Actually, it don't matter much that Leon kicked us out," she says. "We was plannin' on deliverin' the baby in Jackson all along. My mama's there. And my insurance coverage is there. Elton got the minimum nine months' parole since he copped, so we ain't gotta be in Montana but another week, anyhow. Says he don't need to worry as long as he keeps his nose clean for seven days."

"Things have a way of working out," I observe.

"We got it all planned out already. We'll wait till next spring to get married. Elton's gettin' what he calls start-up money from his 'vestors. That'll get us settled. Overhead, he calls it. He says it ain't good to be overly optimistic, on account of it bein' bad business. Says a lot of good ideas fail on account of too much optimism. So he says he might have to sub-size our income for a while. He did some cookin' back in Henderson."

Mental note to self: Don't eat in Henderson on the way back.

"Do you know if it's a boy or a girl?"

"He's a boy." Here, she lowers her voice. "Elton wants to call him Elton. But I like Daniel, after my granddad."

"Daniel's a nice name," I say. "So, Peaches is your real name?"

"Yeah, I know, funny name, huh?"

"You're asking a guy name Benjamin Benjamin?"

"But I'm used to it. Peaches, I mean. Folks in Henderson say it suits me."

Indeed, she's just a sweet kid, any way you slice her. Rosy-cheeked, genuine, forthcoming. How long before the optimism runs out? How long before Elton runs out on her or gets jugged again? How long before she's buying formula with food coupons? How long before the cumulative effect of all that disappointment exacts its toll, and Peaches starts holding her cards close, and those cheeks start going sallow, and she looks more like a Madge than a Peaches?

"So when's your due date?"

"Not for three weeks," she says, as though three weeks were an eternity.

"You excited?" It's a question I need not ask, because even in a dirty sweatshirt, with her wet hair hanging in straggles, and Elton snoring fitfully into the nape of her neck, she glows.

"I can't wait to get my hands on my little bubba. My mama already made up the sewing room into a nursery—made it into a circus theme."

"What about Elton?"

"Oh, he's excited in his way. He just don't show it much. Sometimes he acts scared about it. But last week up in Helena, I caught him pricin' teddy bears when we was at Target."

"That's a good sign."

"We wasn't there on account of the baby, though. We was there pricin' various antitheft alarms and thingamajigs. Market research, Elton calls it."

"That Elton's on the ball."

She lowers her voice again. "Well, by God, he's tryin', he really is. Better than I can say for most. Better than that no good brother of his." She glances sidelong at Elton to make sure he's sleeping before taking her voice down another notch. "His daddy beat him up pretty regular. Beat him up bad. It was no secret in Henderson. Never laid a hand on that brother. It got so poor Elton lived in a friend's garage senior year, on account he was afraid he might start fightin' back. Elton ain't ever laid a hand on me."

"That's good."

"So far, he's always done right by me. So I got no choice but to believe in him."

Just as Missoula appears on the horizon, Elton wakes up, as though to testify on his own behalf. "Hot damn," he says, snapping his fingers. "I been thinkin' in my sleep again, and I think I saw what you was drivin' at regardin' my box. You was trying to say, '*Well, why not use your real TV, 'cause it'd be more realistic,*' am I right?"

"Exactly."

"It came to me that you was right. It *would* be more realistic. Not because what you said about keepin' it away from the door, though, but because of somethin' else even more realistic." Here Elton leans in conspiratorially and rests a hand on my shoulder. "I don't know how I didn't see it before. The lights! Don'tcha see? My box has gotta have flashin' lights, so it'll look like a TV—you know, bouncin' off the curtains and the walls and whatnot!"

"But . . ."

Elton bowls right over me. " 'Course, it'll cost a little more to pro-duce. But then we'll make that up on the other end, so margins reckon out roughly the same, maybe better, since it's fancier. Now, with the lights, we can call it an antitheft *system*, see? 'Cause it's got more than one part."

"But Elton, if . . ."

"Hell, colored LED lights oughta do the trick. Can't be that expen-sive. Makes the whole system more, I don't know, ingenious, I guess."

Once I'm sure Elton is going to pause, I fill the breach. "But Elton, if it looks and sounds like a TV, and you're gonna set it by the TV, to act like the TV, well then, I guess what I'm trying to say is, why not . . ." But I just don't have the heart and wave it off at the last second. "You know, I think you're right, the lights really take it up a notch. I think people will feel safer."

"They will be safer," he says with conviction.

Peaches gives his leg a proud little squeeze and keeps smiling. She believes in him, with all her heart she believes, and nobody's going to talk her out of it. For that, I love her. Suddenly she grabs Elton's wrist excitedly and sets his hand on her belly.

"He's kickin'," she says. "Feel it? You feel it, hon?"

Elton's face lights up in recognition. "Well, I'll be damned. The hell if he ain't!"

Peaches is all aglow, and I think: He's a lucky sonofabitch, that Elton.

That's when I spot the Skylark in the rearview mirror, hovering just above Peaches's right shoulder, and my blood begins to boil.

and many more

What's the big rush, anyway? Jim Sunderland's not going anywhere, the little prick. Anyone who listens to that much NPR can't be in a hurry. If Janet thinks she can bully me into her stupid divorce, if she thinks she can hunt me down and physically coerce me into signing those papers, she's sorely mistaken. It's gonna take a lot more than some guy in a shit brown Skylark to persuade me.

It's three in the afternoon. We're on mountain time now. Neither Trev nor I are in a hurry to lose Peaches and Dot, even if it means waiting for Elton in front of every bar in Missoula. Presently, we're parked in front of Red's, where Elton has convinced us to make a business stop before final drop-off. He's been in there for twenty minutes already while Trev, Peaches, and I wait in the van. Dot's at the curb, smoking her second cigarette.

The Skylark is parked down the block on the opposite side of the street. I've been monitoring it in the side mirror, quietly seething. I still don't know how Janet managed this. How dare she try to force my hand. How dare she leave me holding the groceries and walk away. She owes me all the time I need, the way I see it. To send some loser in a Skylark all over the western United States to do her dirty work for her — that's weak. What barrel did she dredge to find that guy?

Miraculously, even as my bitterness is rising to a slow boil, a text arrives from Janet: "Met with my lawyer today . . . We need to talk . . ."

By the time I make my move, I can feel the certainty of violence welling up in me.

"I'm gonna get some air," I say, at last.

Gritting my teeth, I march straight down the middle of the street.

Halfway there, I angle toward the Skylark at the opposite curb, heart thumping, fists clenched. I can make out the driver at the wheel with his baseball cap, one tan arm dangling out the window, clutching a Mountain Dew. I can feel the bile rising in my throat. My anger is way out of proportion — I'm aware of that. I can smell it like an electrical fire raging inside my skull. I'm dangerously close to careening out of control. And you know what? Let the careening begin! I'm gonna throttle this guy. I'm gonna send Janet a message, and I couldn't give two shits about the consequences.

Skylark sees me coming now and drops his Mountain Dew. I'm only about a hundred feet away, when the car suddenly revs to life with a squealing fan belt and a cloud of exhaust. Before I know it, I'm charging the car at a dead sprint, with no idea what I'm going to do, whether I'm going to beat the car back with my bare fists or pull this guy out of the driver's seat and pulverize him in the street. I'm close enough to see real panic in his eyes as he screeches away from the curb and speeds straight for me. I stop in my tracks and square off like a matador as the hurtling Skylark bears down on me. I can see the driver clearly, now, but I can't tell how big he is. He looks about my age, tan with some gray stubble, and a loose-fitting shirt. Ruggedly handsome, in an aging beach bum kind of way. Or that's just my impression as he speeds straight for me at twenty miles per hour. The panic in his eyes turns to unmitigated terror the instant he realizes that I have no intention of moving. He's saucer-eyed as he swerves to elude me, mouth wide open.

My attempt to tackle the car, while bold and completely unexpected, is by no means effective. After a knee-crushing impact, I manage for a fleeting interval to ride the hood, arms and legs splayed, face pressed to the glass. But the Skylark bucks me, the antenna snaps off in my hand, and I roll off the side. I scramble to my feet in time to pound the hood of the trunk as he speeds past. I'm still clutching the antenna as I sprint down Ryman after him. He's got too much steam. No way I'm catching him. I pull up short and wing the antenna after the retreating Skylark just as the glass door to Red's flies open, and out comes Elton, reeling backward, tripping over his own feet and landing on his ass. He's quickly followed by a huge bearded dude in a flannel shirt even dirtier than Elton's. He must be three hundred pounds, with a big shock of kinky hair. This guy is a Yeti. He descends on Elton, who tries to sidle away like a hermit crab. But the Yeti snatches him up by the shirt with one hand, yanks him up, spins him, and slams him against the brick wall of Red's.

"You're either brave or stupid to show your face around here," says the Yeti, upon delivering a crushing blow to the chest.

Elton doubles over and covers his head. Suddenly I'm sprinting again, my heart beating triplets, adrenals pounding, my field of vision a washed-out blur. Before I know it, I'm climbing the Yeti, literally climbing the guy. I'm halfway up his back, scrambling higher, as I clutch him with both arms around the neck from behind. Elton is back on his heels. He looks like he wants to run. But the Yeti catches him with a right cross, and Elton is on his ass again as I try to get a better purchase on the Yeti.

"Always knew you was a snitch, Elton," he says, trying to shake me off his back.

Peaches is out of the car in a flash, charging the Yeti with her swollen belly out in front of her. She lands on him with a flurry of fists, which he fends off with a forearm as he simultaneously tries to extract me with the other arm. I've got a fistful of beard when he finally manages to shake me off. I'm momentarily weightless until I hit the pavement with a flash of lightning. The wind rushes out of me in an instant. But I'm still rabid. Foaming at the mouth, I scrabble forward on my elbows and clutch the Yeti desperately by the leg of his jeans with both arms. He struggles to tear himself free, but I've all but wound myself around his leg. Peaches is still assaulting him like a cloud of insects as Elton straightens up and looses a haymaker, which grazes the Yeti's massive shoulder.

The last thing I remember before coming totally unglued is the smell of burned circuitry and a throbbing behind my eyeballs. The next thing I know the Yeti is howling like a jackal with a fire poker up his ass. Wrapped around his right leg with a death clutch, I've forced his pant leg up past his boot top and sunk my teeth deep into the fat of his calf. I'm locked on him like a bull terrier, my mouth's filling with blood, maybe his, maybe my own, as he kicks me repeatedly in the ribs with his other foot, screaming horrifically. But I just keep biting like it's the last thing I'll ever do, until everything is a wash of hot crimson. All I remember after that is I came out the other side feeling great.

But for the mustache, the county sheriff looks like he could be Elton's father — same weak chin, same skinned weasel composure. He wears his wide-brimmed sheriff hat low over his beady eyes. He likes his job, but he doesn't want you to know it. He's not a talker. His name tag says SCRUGGS. He's got a chubby older wife somewhere, in a manufactured home. Her name is Bev. She can shoot skeet. She can bowl the lights out. They have a fifth wheel they take up to Flathead Lake on weekends. Bev makes a great Waldorf salad. They have matching green vests and an overweight corgi. Strangely, these are the thoughts, calm and bemused, which presently occupy my mind, even as a medic tends earnestly to the Yeti's calf, and I see the fear written plainly on Peaches's face as she watches Elton being escorted to one of the three cruisers. As Scruggs cuffs me, I wink at the Yeti, who is quickly restrained by two EMTs and a cop. Then two cops. Soon a third cop is forced to join the scrum. They might need an elephant gun to get him down. Everywhere lights flash. There's a small crowd gathered on the sidewalk outside of Red's. Trev is among them, with Dot close beside him. She's got her hand resting on the back of his chair. They both look stunned and disappointed.

"No worries," I tell them as Scruggs shepherds me past. "It's all good."

I wonder if Scruggs and his wife still have sex. I'll bet they do on their anniversary, when Bev is a little flush with wine.

"Keep movin'," he says, pushing me forward.

"Fucking cannibal," somebody mutters from the crowd.

As Scruggs pushes me the last stretch to the cruiser, I feel strangely euphoric, awash in the pulsing lights. I nod to Peaches as I'm ducking into the car, just to let her know that everything is going to be okay.

Because suddenly I've come to see that, indeed, no matter what shit storm blows in my face, everything really is going to be okay.

And as Scruggs pilots us at a crawl past the scene of the crime, I find myself smiling stupidly out the window.

"Thanks for the lift," I say.

Scruggs just grunts, checks me in the mirror, and shakes his head, frowning.

"This thing is quiet," I venture, about two blocks down Ryman. "Is this real leather?"

But the art of conversation continues to elude Scruggs, who doesn't say a word until we've rolled into the sally port, where he opens my door and stands at his post like a disgruntled chauffeur.

"Up," he says.

The fluorescent light of the corridor only enhances my sense of well-being, though my reception is not quite all that I hoped for. Only one clerk looks up from his work as Scruggs conducts me across the office to his desk.

"Sit," he says.

I sit.

Scruggs is living in the Bronze Age. His work station is hopelessly outdated. The guy's got a typewriter. A Rolodex. An actual telephone. He has not one but two bottles of Liquid Paper. I scan the desktop for the flint scraper, the copper ingot. The desk is cluttered but orderly, like Bernard's workbench. The lone personal touch is a framed photograph of his daughter on horseback, decked out in jodhpurs, helmet, chaps, and a really tight sweater. She's maybe thirty years old, dark-eyed, luxurious, and stacked to the nines. She's clutching a leather crop in one hand suggestively — to me, anyway.

"Your daughter?" I say, though my last five attempts at small talk have met with stony silence.

"Wife," he says, without looking up from the typewriter. "Last name?"

"Benjamin."

"First name?"

"Benjamin."

Scruggs looks up at me doubtfully, two fingers poised above the keys. "Middle name?"

"None."

He shakes his head woefully. "Date of birth?"

"Nine nine sixty-nine."

Squinting, Scruggs enters the numbers with opposing fingers, slowly, powerfully — he types like a blacksmith.

"Happy birthday," he grumbles.

before agatewood

Before the Agatewood house, before we had any equity, back when I was painting parade floats in Kingston, and Janet worked as a vet tech at the Animal Wellness Center, we lived in a little rental cabin on the bay in Lemolo. The place was all of about six hundred square feet. Charming. Rickety. Cold as hell in winter — but cheap. None of the window frames matched. The front door creaked on its hinges. The oil stove didn't vent well or even heat, for that matter. The kitchen sink was too small, the toilet ran, there was no bathtub, and for a few months we had a rodent problem. But we loved that place. We had barbecues in spring, planted a vegetable garden, played badminton naked. And ultimately, we grew up in that cabin.

We lived in Lemolo when Piper was born. We stayed at home the night of our anniversary. I made enchiladas. We ate side by side on the sofa. Piper slept right under our noses, swaddled in the pink and yellow quilt that Ruth knit. I remember looking down into that bassinet and being both profoundly enamored and completely terrified of the pinched little face sleeping there.

I remember Janet saying that she felt ugly, and I remember telling her she was more beautiful than ever.

"You're just saying that," she said.

"But I'm not." And I wasn't.

We said a lot of nice things back then.

I remember us saying that we liked small houses, that proximity engendered closeness in a family. That nobody should be an only child. That nobody should be raised by a nanny or in day care. I remember us saying that time, not money, was the greatest resource. That everything would be all right. That the universe would provide. That belief was a force more powerful than gravity itself.

a year and a day

Sprung on a $762 bond, I'm free by 6:00 p.m. (at least until my court appearance next month). Elton, however, is not so fortunate. In violation of his parole, he's being held without bond, awaiting extradition to Mineral County, where according to Scruggs, he'll get a year and a day, if he's lucky. Getting that much information out of Scruggs wasn't easy.

Poor Peaches is beside herself with grief and worry. I've assured her that everything is going to be okay. I've promised her a ride to her mother's in Jackson, a detour that Trev has approved. All things considered — the fact that she's currently beholden to the kindness of strangers, one of whom has recently exhibited cannibalistic tendencies, while her fiancé, whose child she's due to deliver in three weeks, is at large in the Montana penal system — Peaches is taking it like a champ and doing her best to smile.

We've squeezed into a booth in the rear of Pita Pit, where I'm buying everybody dinner to commemorate my birthday. My optimism is seemingly boundless in this dark hour.

"Don't you see?" I tell Peaches. "You're going to be a mother — a *mother*. It's going to be the single most profound thing that ever happened to you. Seriously, everything will fall into place."

While arguably not the most comforting advice from a forty-year-old soon-to-be divorcé with no job and a nearly maxed-out credit card, Peaches leans into my assurances from across the table.

Dot sits close to Trev at the end of the bench near the head of the table. She buckled him in on the way here. She jockeyed chairs around to accommodate his passage when we arrived. Together, they flip through pictures on Dot's phone while Dot offers personal commentary at every turn. Trev is as giddy as I am. He still needs a shower, but he's looking good. His hair is falling just right.

I'm feeling extravagant in spite of my financial woes, triumphant in spite of my aching ribs. And why not? Today I climbed a man. Today I've known the glory of battle. I've tasted human flesh. And tonight I gather my ragged tribe around me for a celebration: gyros, club wraps, how about some hummus? Supersize that Coke! And how about a veggie platter, no, two veggie platters, and throw in four of those Otis Spunkmeyers! Tonight my appetites are huge. My senses are heightened. The whole world pulses with the heartbeat of possibility. Every thought is a revelation. Around every corner is a reason to hope. I am expansive. I am inexorable. I am loquacious. If I didn't know better, I'd think I was high on something.

Peaches, I say, take heart, my mountain wildflower! There is life beyond Henderson! There are pleasures and mysteries unfathomable to your young heart! Do not measure out your life with coffee spoons nor lay waste your powers — live, I say! Invent yourself! Let your reach exceed your grasp! And pass the hummus while you're at it!

When there's nothing left of the feast but the crinkled paper ravages, we pile into the handi-van in search of lodging. Downtown Missoula yields an array of inexpensive vacancies, promising value and comfort and savings. But tonight, I'm in the mood for something grander. Tonight, we will have luxury, tonight, we will have opulence — wooden hangers and a minifridge!

After an hour and fifteen minutes of searching, the C'mon Inn out on Expo Parkway looks like Xanadu with its tropical courtyard. The night clerk is wearing a blazer. He eyes us doubtfully one by one as we filter into the lobby through the double-glass doors. Indeed, we are a ragtag cabal. Without hesitation, I produce my wallet and attempt to book a two-room suite with on-demand cable and complimentary breakfast, fairly confident my card will not be declined. I paid the minimum two days before we left, which should leave $480 — give or take — after the cash advance for the bond (the bulk of the money that was supposed to finance my end of the trip). But I'm only reckoning to pass the time, financial trifles cannot touch me tonight, nothing can disrupt the smooth surface of my stability.

"You okay?" Trev inquires as the clerk runs my card. "You look a little sweaty."

"Must be the tropical air in here."

"Your current address is at 1599 Madison, sir?" says the clerk.

"That's the one."

He punches keys like an automaton. "Sir, do you have a current driver's license?"

"Of course."

"One I could see?"

"Ah." I fish my wallet out again, and surrender my license.

He glances at the license, punches another flurry of keys. Then another. I breathe deeply of the tropical air, admire the sturdy construction of the cedar mezzanine, cross my fingers in my pants pocket. The clerk punches and punches to the content of his bloodless little heart.

"You sure you're okay?" says Trev.

"Tip-top."

"You wanna sit down?"

"I'm great."

The clerk stops punching, looks momentarily puzzled, then starts punching again.

"How's the ribs?" says Trev.

"I can hardly feel them."

"Sure you don't wanna go to the doctor?"

"Oh no."

Punch-punch-*punch*-punch-*punch*-punch-*punch* goes the clerk.

"Is there a problem?" I say.

"Mm," he says.

"Mm?"

"Mm."

Abruptly, he stops punching. He shakes his head solemnly and right clicks his mouse. Spinning slowly on his heels, he gingerly removes a sheet from the printer, holding it at some distance from his body, before surrendering it over the counter.

"Okay," he says. "You're all set. Elevator's down the hall to the right."

The accommodations are a considerable step up from Old Willard's motor court. The master suite smells of fresh linens and window cleaner. The coat hangers, if not wood, are passable replicas of wood. The art on the cream-colored walls does not offend: resplendent fruit bowls and women with parasols. The dramatic center of the master suite is neither the quilted king mattress nor the dramatic floor-to-ceiling view of the rear parking lot but a pair of brown faux-leather La-Z-Boy recliners situated like rooks facing the flat-screen TV.

Dot steps around me, trailing the fruity scent of perfume, and immediately plops her bag down in the center of the floor and flops into one of the recliners. Trev buzzes straight for the remote on the nightstand.

"Hey, the lamps aren't bolted down," he says.

Peaches isn't exactly sure how to proceed. She lingers in the doorway, holding one of her gigantic suitcases.

"There's two queens in the other room," I say. "Dot, you take the other one. Trev, you're good with sharing, right?"

"That's cool."

"I can sleep on the floor," Peaches says. "I don't mind."

I swing open the door to the adjoining room. "Nope. You and Little Elton are in here."

Peaches waddles through, one hand clutching her belly and the other dragging her klunky suitcase. Poor kid. She must be exhausted.

"Do you want your sweatshirt back?" she says.

"You can give it back when we get to your mom's."

"You don't mind if I go to sleep, do you? It's just been such a . . . and I'm so . . ."

"Of course not."

She's still clutching the suitcase like she's afraid to let go of it. I'm surprised she's not carrying Elton's, too.

I step in and pry the bag from her clutches, swinging it up onto the dresser.

"You get some sleep," I say. "I'll tell 'em to keep the television down."

"I can sleep through anything," she says.

"Of course, you can."

"Good night," she says, sweetly. "Happy birthday."

"Good night," I say, closing the door behind me.

the calm

With Peaches sound asleep, and Trev and Dot hypnotized by the big screen, I don my Speedo in the bathroom, snatch a towel off the rack, fish my cell phone out of my pants pocket, and retire alone to the chlorinated air of the atrium. The Jacuzzi is empty, as is the adjoining exercise room. Sinking neck deep into the warm effervescence, a calm envelops me. I should know better than to trust it. My ribs should be reminder enough, if not my current financial and legal status, or the fact that I'm harboring a teenage runaway, a very pregnant unwed mother, and a kid whose heart could give out any minute. I know I've lost my mind. But I'm not concerned, because it's the first thing I've lost in a long time that actually feels good.

When it seems that nothing can touch me, that nothing can disturb the imperturbable calm, twin headlights slice through the atrium. Through the window I see the Skylark swinging a wide arc in the parking lot. And just like that, the putrid stink of crossed wires smolders deep in my sinuses, and the electrical fire is raging in my skull again. I'm out of the water before I even know it. I'm dashing barefoot through the atrium, clutching my cell phone like a grenade. Bursting out the side door with a metallic clatter, I charge madly across the parking lot in my Speedo with murder in my heart. I've got an insatiable hunger for flesh. I'll devour this guy. I'll chew him up and spit him out in Janet's face. This time I don't charge straight at him, but cut a tight angle along the side of the building to head him off at the exit, sprinting right past the lobby. I jump a small hedge, nearly slip on the grassy divider, break stride with an awkward lurch, but manage to keep my feet long enough for something to pop near the base of my neck. I careen forward, go briefly airborne, hit the sidewalk, and skid to a stop on my knees and palms, just as the Skylark swings onto the thoroughfare.

Peeling myself from the pavement, I stagger to my feet, fighting for breath. My palms are hamburger, embedded with gravel. My knees are bleeding. I can hardly move my neck. Standing at the curb beneath the glare of the streetlight, my naked body steams in the night air, as the Skylark's taillights recede.

I fall to my knees. Sobbing, I dial Janet.

She answers on the second ring.

"Call him off, please," I say. "It's over. You win."

"What are you talking about? Who?"

"Please, Janet. I give up. I can't take it anymore."

"What happened? You sound like a crazy person. Are you crying?"

I try to pinch off the grief in my throat, but I can't, and it only makes me angry. "Goddamnit, none of this is my fault, Janet!"

"Ben, I'm hanging up."

"Where were you that day at the duck pond, Janet? Where were you for the bumps and bruises?"

The air goes out of her like a ruptured balloon, and there follows a stunned silence. I huddle on the curb and grab my knees for warmth, teeth clacking, as I press the phone to my ear in the terrible silence and wish that my heart would stop beating. Faintly, I can hear Janet whimpering on the other end. They are the whimpers of a dying animal, slow and agonizing, the whimpers of something begging to be put out of its misery.

Cars hurtle by on Expo Parkway, a blur of lights and a steady thrum. I don't know what day it is. I clench my eyes and stare at the back of the lids; the hum of the traffic washes over me, and I hope that when I open my eyes I will be somewhere else. Someone honks as they speed past.

"Pervert!" they holler.

confusion

The last time I took the kids to see the ducks at Battle Point, Janet wasn't with us. It was late in spring, and the clinic was busy as usual. For the third week in a row, Janet didn't take her long lunch that Friday. She had a one o'clock with a rich lady's terrier. Or a tabby with a tapeworm. Or maybe it was a mixup in billing.

The treetops are swaying in a stiff breeze. The sky is mottled, as low clouds hurry east. Jodi is asleep in his car seat on the lawn beside me as Piper wades in the reedy shallows to the top of her red rubber boots. Before I can scold her for standing in the water (she knows the rules), she backpedals onto the shore.

"Something's wrong," she proclaims, pointing across the water, where she's intent on a lone duck drifting along the far bank. The hen is brown and gray but for a brilliant blue blaze on each wing. One of her wings is disfigured, bowed unnaturally above the radius. She flops the appendage uselessly, batting the water, as she drifts toward the rest of the clutch, grouped like an armada on north edge of the pond.

"Can we help him, Daddy?" she says.

"It's a her."

"Can we bring her to Mommy to fix?"

"Mommy only works on pets, honey."

"What if we keep her as a pet?"

"It's not that simple, sweetie."

"Why not?"

But before I can address the complexities further, a riot of furious squawking erupts from the far bank. Suddenly, a swarm of four or five drakes rise from the clutch in a blur, descending upon the injured hen. They begin nagging and pecking at her.

"Daddy, what are they doing?"

"I can't tell."

"They're hurting her!"

The green-headed mob drives the hen to the shallows, where they begin stomping her in concert with their webbed feet, forcing her head beneath the water time and again. In all my duck-watching days, I've never seen such a thing.

"Make then stop, Daddy! Daddy, make them stop!"

I jump into action. "Keep an eye on your brother," I say. "Don't you budge."

I circle the area madly, looking for something to hurl, a rock, a stick, anything to run interference. And when I can't find anything, I sprint down the asphalt walkway, around the bend toward the far bank.

"Watch your brother!" I shout over my shoulder. "Don't move!"

My sudden arrival on the scene, chest heaving, arms waving madly, triggers a winged explosion, as the drakes scatter in the air all at once, disrupting the surface of the entire pond. Squishing my way through the swampy shallows toward the injured hen, I find that I'm too late. She floats in the shallows at the edge of the reeds, ringed by a garland of gray feathers, her lifeless body bobbing slightly on the choppy surface. Piper is knee deep in the water on the other side, slump-shouldered, head hanging. Behind her, swept up in the wind, I can hear Jodi wailing in his car seat.

On the drive home, Piper presses her face to the side window, gazing dully at the trees through tear-streaked eyes. I reckon aloud in an attempt to soothe her. I reckon that the hen must have been very old and very sick and very injured, which is no comfort at all. I reckon that her suffering is over, though I cannot justify the existence of the suffering in the first place. I reckon that there's a logic to the brutality of the universe, but I can't account for that, either. Nobody can. All I can do is buy Piper an ice-cream cone on the way home.

the daze

I'm only dimly aware of the desk clerk gaping at me from behind his computer terminal as dazedly I trudge across the tropical courtyard toward the elevator in my Speedo. But for an icy sting burning distantly in either palm, and the fact that I can't move my neck, I am only marginally aware of my body. Mechanically, I summon the elevator, rocking slightly on my heels as I wait. Only one way to go from here. When the doors lurch open, the cleaning woman pushes a linen hamper out of the elevator, lowering her eyes as she passes me.

The elevator is restful in the way of a tomb. Gazing at the mirrored sidewall, a face looks back at me, slack, colorless, eyes open like a dead man. The inside of my head hums with the trilling of heat-dazed crickets. Arriving at the second floor, I step out into the foyer, ponder left or right, choose left, and plod down the carpeted corridor past rooms 214 and 212 to room 210. Clutching my cell phone, I am without card key and without towel, but when I knock on the door Dot opens it.

"Whoa, what happened to you?"

"I fell."

She takes me by the wrist and coaxes me into the room, where she seats me on the edge of the bed.

"Dude," says Trev, muting the TV. He buzzes toward me around the foot of the bed.

Dot promptly proceeds to the bathroom, returns momentarily with a wet washcloth, and begins dabbing my knees.

"There's a first-aid kit in the big black bag," instructs Trev. "Dude, what the hell? You're a mess."

"It's nothing."

"No, really. You're a mess."

Dot rummages around in the black bag. "What does it look like? I can't find it."

"Left side pocket," I intone.

Awakened no doubt by my entrance, Peaches emerges from the adjoining room, sleepy-eyed, wrapped in a blanket.

"What's wrong?"

"He fell," Trev and Dot say in unison.

"Oh no. Poor thing." Peaches lets her blanket drop to the floor and kneels at the foot of the bed in men's boxer shorts and a T-shirt, both of which look too clean to have ever belonged to Elton. Prying my clenched hands open, she inspects my shredded palms.

Dot returns with the first-aid kit. "Ouch," she says of my palms.

"Are there tweezers in there?" says Peaches.

Dot spreads the kit open on his lap and Trev begins clumsily picking through its contents for tweezers. When he locates them, he fishes them out on the third attempt and dangles them over his lap for Peaches, who begins cutting away the ravaged skin of my palms, blotting the scraped portions with hydrogen peroxide and a washcloth, wincing herself as though she can feel the sting. Then, mindfully, she applies ointment, dresses my palms in gauze, and wraps them with athletic tape.

Dot begins cleaning up my bloody knees, plucking out the gravel.

"Stay still," she says. "This may hurt."

It doesn't hurt. Not like I want it to. I wish it would. I deserve to hurt. But all I can do is sit on the edge of the bed, my damp Speedo soaking the duvet, gazing numbly at the big screen, where the Weather Channel plays silently. It's sixty-one degrees in Albuquerque, fifty-seven in Lincoln. I make no move to answer my buzzing cell phone. After a moment, it goes silent. Almost immediately, Trev's phone begins ringing. He arches his back and hoists his arm, then lowers his hand like a scoop into his side pouch. By the fourth ring, the device is in his clutches, and he raises it unsteadily to his ear.

"Oh hey, Mom," he says, cautioning the girls to keep quiet with a finger to his lips. "Great . . . Yeah, Butte was great . . . No, we didn't have time . . . "

Trev wheels toward the bathroom and stops beneath the threshold, where he winks at me.

"Oh, he's in the shower," he says. "Yeah, uh huh . . . I did . . . Yeah, I'm about to . . . "

I have to admit, he makes a pretty convincing liar. Calm. Collected. Cool as a ticket taker. His performance is almost enough to make me smile. But then I imagine Janet, slumping on the edge of a bed somewhere in Portland as she wonders whether she failed her children. And for once I hope Jim Sunderland is there beside her.

the long haul

Eight bucks buys a decent breakfast in Missoula. Twelve buys a thick foam cervical collar at the Missoula Rite-Aid.

"You want a helmet with that?" says the girl at the register.

"Very funny."

"You look like the Michelin Man," says Trev upon my return to the van.

Just east of Missoula, the valley tapers abruptly like a funnel, and the mountains close in around us, broad-faced and sudden, just as the interstate begins its dogleg to the south through Bonner, then Turah, then Clinton. Now and again a slice of the Blackfoot River shimmers along the roadside, cut crosswise with a rusting train trestle. Here a fat kid in a skiff. Some guy in a broken down truck. A barking dog lashed to a tree. A waft of steel guitar in the air.

The weather continues to baffle. It is eighty-one degrees at 9:30 a.m. I'm driving with the window down, my neck sweating profusely beneath my neck brace. The itching is unbearable. My rib cage aches. My mangled hands and knees, freshly dressed by the girls before breakfast, are mummified in athletic tape, so that I've little choice but to grip the wheel cautiously, as though it's hot. We have a gruesome day of travel in front of us if we intend to make West Yellowstone by evening.

Dot is cheerful between over-the-shoulder glances out the rear window. She has yet to utter a word about dropping her off in Butte. I wonder if Trev knows something I don't. The Skylark, which picked us up not two blocks from the C'mon Inn and has abandoned all stealth and pretense, now pursues us boldly like a starving wolf. The driver is of little concern to me, whoever he is. I have nothing left to fear. Any harm the stranger may wish to visit upon me would be welcomed at this point.

We cleave our way through the mountains until the interstate dips into a wide basin brimming with blue sky, broken by dusty roads and rocky saddles strung out along the southern horizon. This is our first real glimpse of the famous big-sky country to come, and I couldn't care less. For all its grandeur, the landscape does not move me. And why should it? The sky may be big, it may be blue and limitless and full of promise, but it's also far away. Really, it's just an illusion. I've been wasting my time. We've all been wasting our time. What good is all this grandeur if it's impermanent, what good all of this promise if it's only fleeting? Who wants to live in a world where suffering is the only thing that lasts, a place where every single thing that ever meant the world to you can be stripped away in an instant? And it *will* be stripped away, so don't fool yourself. If you're lucky, your life will erode slowly with the ruinous effects of time or recede like the glaciers that carved this land, and you will be left alone to sift through the detritus. If you are unlucky, your world will be snatched out from beneath you like a rug, and you'll be left with nowhere to stand and nothing to stand on. Either way, you're screwed. So why bother? Why grunt and sweat and weep your way through the myriad obstacles, why love, dream, care, when you're only inviting disaster? I'm done answering the call of whippoorwills, the call of smiling faces and fireplaces and cozy rooms. You won't find me building any more nests among the rose blooms. Too many thorns.

Beavertail, Bearmouth, Gold Creek, Phosphate, the signposts ebb, the landscape whizzes by, a blur of scrub grass and crumbling hillsides. Somewhere around Deer Lodge, we begin to discern the infamous Big Stack in the flats to the southeast, a gray monolith rising at a gentle taper to a height of nearly six hundred feet from atop a bald hill. The stack draws us like a beacon but seems to recede as we draw closer. For something so blunt, Big Stack is elusive. This industrial relic, all that's left of the massive smelter that once belched arsenic into the surrounding valley, represents a milestone in our journey, as it will be the first stop since George, Washington, that is actually on our itinerary. Exiting at Highway 1, we work our way south through the knobby foothills of Anaconda huddled in the shadow of the Rockies. Big Stack continues to elude us, now and again flashing its gray tip around corners, then disappearing around bends. Somewhere along our circuitous path we've managed to lose the Skylark, or it's just dropped back.

Cresting the final rise, Big Stack reveals itself in full, gray and lonesome atop the bald hilltop, stretching stupidly halfway to the sky, like some towering landlocked lighthouse. The perimeter is fenced off with chain link, circling a wide buffer of dead soil, maybe a hundred yards in diameter. They cordoned off the area in the 1980s because the stack was still bleeding trace amounts of arsenic. Back in the day, the smelter was the engine of Great Falls. Now it's the world's tallest tombstone.

Dot unbuckles Trev as I ready the lift. Trev rolls out of the van, and the girls duck out after him. The wind sweeps in hot gusts across the barren hilltop as we cross the vacant lot toward the interpretive area. At the fence, we diverge. Trev and Dot gravitate to the east in tandem, their voices trailing in the wind behind them. Peaches drifts to the west, where she stands with her back to the fence, hands on her swollen belly, and looks not at Big Stack but out across the foothills toward the interstate in the distance, running like a zipper down the center of the valley. I wonder what possibilities she sees down there, what future she envisions for herself and little Elton, as the shadow of a lone cumulus engulfs the valley. I wonder what Trev and Dot are talking about twenty miles from Butte. I can see by Dot's frenetic movements and Trev's bobbling head, that they are jovial. And though I know their merriment is perishable, that it cannot survive a thousand realities, I can't help but wish them a lifetime of it.

As I'm watching them, Dot breaks away from Trev and begins ambling slowly in my direction, pausing several times along her way to make cursory appraisals of Big Stack. Finally, she stations herself right beside me at the fence, where she remains silent for ten or fifteen seconds, as a warm gust of wind rockets past our ears.

"So I was thinking," she says, at last. "Even though it looks kind of stupid and touristy in the postcards, I wouldn't mind seeing Yellowstone." She fishes her cigarettes out of her jean vest, lights one up, hooks one hand through the chain-link fence, and exhales a plume of smoke straight at Big Stack. "I mean, you know, since you guys are driving through it or whatever. I've got money."

"Did you ask Trev?"

She turns her attention to Trev, who sits perfectly still at the fence about fifty yards downwind of us, straight-backed, still-headed, staring through the chain-link hexagons across the dusty expanse at the moldering brick remains of a boomtown. I don't know what Dot sees, but to me there's something achingly desolate about the scene, as though the whole world were dying before my eyes.

"I'm asking you," she says.

ghost town

Though we're still twenty miles shy of Yermo, already this excursion to Calico promises to be the shriveled cherry atop this melted sundae of a vacation — the one I've been force-feeding my family for six days. If the Benjamins were so red-eyed and road weary as to be underwhelmed by the Grand Canyon — if say, the unfathomable sun-striped revelation looked to certain Benjamins like a collapsed wedding cake moldering under a heat lamp — well, then, we are officially beleaguered two days later, as we start backtracking east on I-15 toward Calico. It's ninety-two degrees. Piper's peeling sunburn has exposed a fresh canvas for the searing heat. In the passenger's seat, Janet is no longer blotchy — just solid red and sweat-soaked. The air conditioner is still kaput. The baby is dancing the Nutcracker in Janet's womb. Nowhere, but nowhere, in this vast moonscape surrounding us is there even a hint of shade.

The nineteenth-century silver boomtown of Calico (that is, its reconstructed facsimile), squats in the dust at the foot of King Mountain. Upon approach, I'm thinking the place is sure to be a bust — just as sure as there's nothing even remotely regal about King Mountain, which looks to me like any one of a dozen piebald nubbins in the vicinity. Even as I'm paying the fifteen-buck admission, I'm visualizing another sticky fiasco in which I'm forced to ply Piper into submission with cotton candy and overpriced sarsaparillas. Janet will need to rest her swollen ankles. Some old lady will probably drop dead of a heat stroke at our feet while we're waiting in line for the Mystery Shack.

And yet . . . and yet . . . Calico surprises, even dazzles, in its hokey fashion! The whole town is air-conditioned. There's a whorehouse. An apothecary. A jail. You get to chuff around the perimeter in a little train. You get to pan for gold. Even King Mountain seems to loom larger, a little more stately, against a blue sky.

"They should've had this at the Grand Canyon," says Piper, sipping her butterscotch milkshake at the Miner's Cafe (six bucks!), where Janet is elevating her ankles, and I'm watching the clock — I don't want to miss the Wild West Show. I know that the main event will be a hopelessly lame reenactment, a clinic on bumbling theatrics. I know that the sheriff will have a big mustache and a name like Bart, that the villain will be a hyena with bad teeth (presumably Mexican). Somebody will fall out of a saloon window. Old Doc will pronounce him gut shot. A histrionic woman of questionable repute will be dragged kicking from his prone body. I know the whole thing will end with a standoff at high noon in the middle of Main Street. And I know that Bart will be the last man standing. But somehow I can't help myself. I'm giddy like a kid.

"See, I told you this place would be worth the detour," I say.

"Yeah, but you said the Grand Canyon would be worth it," she says.

"Your mom said that, not me."

"Same difference," she says, slurping at the dregs of her shake. "Can I get another?"

"Absolutely not," says Janet.

"Please."

"No," I say.

"What if I don't finish this one? Then can I try chocolate?"

"No," Janet says.

"Besides," I say. "You already finished that one."

"Nuh-uh! Look!" she thrusts the nearly empty glass at me. "And lots of it is still stuck in the straw."

"I'm sorry, Piper, but the answer is still no."

"Fine," she says, folding her arms. "Then I quit this dumb vacation." I can't help but laugh.

"It's not funny," she says. "I quit it. It's the dumbest vacation ever."

Again, I can't suppress my amusement. Poor kid. She's been a trouper. Look at her: a road-weary waif worthy of Dickens, greasy-haired and slump-shouldered, her ravaged forehead flaking like onion skin. By God, the kid has earned another milkshake. I might consider letting her have it, even if meant going to bat against Janet, were it not for three things: one, my foreknowledge of the inevitable two-shake sugar crash; two, I repeat, six bucks!; three, the Wild West Show starts in seven minutes, and I have no intention of missing it.

"Honey," I say. "You can't just quit a vacation. It's not that simple."

"Oh yes it is," she says.

She's still pouting as we spill out onto the boardwalk into the breathtaking heat, wending our way through the gathering crowd, past the General Store and the Saloon to the Leatherworks, where we jostle for three spots against the rail. Main is cordoned off through the heart of town. Shutters creak in the hot wind. Dust devils dance midstreet. Horses whinny in the Livery. Somewhere in the wings, adhesive mustaches are applied, squibs are concealed, and lines are hurriedly rehearsed as Old Doc dons his stethoscope and Bart buffs his badge and straps on his six-shooter. The tension is palpable. For some of us, anyway.

"I've gotta find a bathroom," Janet announces. "I'll be back."

She turns and begins inching her way through the crowd belly first, just as the first gunshot rings out. Suddenly, a body crashes through the railing on the second floor of Hank's Hotel. A buxom redhead bursts through the saloon doors.

"They got Gus!" she proclaims, falling to her knees. Her great chest begins to heave. "Oh, Gus!" she laments.

Here comes Old Doc hobbling down Main Street at a trot, as patrons spill out of the saloon and gather around Gus.

"They got me," says Gus through gritted teeth. "See to my mama, Darla. Send word to my people back in Laramie."

"He's gut shot," Doc proclaims. "Somebody round up the sheriff."

"Round up the priest while you're at it," says a gruff voice from behind the saloon doors. Now the Hyena steps out from the shadows, squinting snake-eyed into the sunlight, casting a long shadow down Main Street. He's wearing a sombrero and a serape and wielding a bottle of mezcal.

"You'll hang for this, Gomez!" says a bystander.

No sooner does Gomez draw his pistol in a sun-glint flash of silver than the bystander crumples in the street, clutching his chest. The squib fires late, and somebody's cell phone rings, but the effect is good enough.

"Don't worry," I whisper. "It's not real." But when I look down, Piper's not there.

"Honey?"

She's not behind me or along the rail to either side.

"Piper!"

"Shhh," someone says.

A cold hand grips my heart as I push my way back through the crowd, craning my neck to scan the neighboring storefronts. I see Janet navigating her way back from the bathroom. Before she can register my panic, she's upon me in front of the leatherworks.

"She's gone," I say.

"What do you mean 'she's gone'?"

"She was standing right next to me watching the show. When I looked down, she was gone."

"Jesus Christ, Ben."

"Check that way," I say. "I'll look up this way."

My panic hardens into something much denser, as I force my way through the throng, past the craft store. "Piper!" I call.

Frantic, I search the blacksmith, then the Sweet Shop.

"Have you seen a little girl?" I ask the clerk.

"What does she look like?"

Eight minutes later, I'm on the boardwalk in front of the livery, talking to two security guards.

"She's six years old. She's wearing—Christ, what the fuck is she wearing? She's wearing a dress. I think a red and white dress."

Janet trots across Main Street toward us, clutching her stomach as she bounces. All the color has drained from her face. She's been crying.

"I've looked everywhere," she says breathlessly.

"She'll turn up, ma'am," says the pudgy security guard.

"She can't go far," the skinnier one assures us.

"Why weren't you watching her?" Janet rasps, breaking down into tears again. "Goddamnit, Ben, why weren't you watching!"

"Calm down," I say. "What was she wearing?"

"A blue-checked dress," she whimpers.

"And you say her name is Piker?" says the pudgy one.

"Piper, with a *p*," I say. "Her face is peeling. One of her front teeth hasn't come in all the way."

As I'm describing her, I know with a terrible certainty that I'm never going to see my daughter again. That I've lost her. That somebody has taken her, forced her into a van, drugged her. Still, the hopeless search continues. Security personnel plumb the silver mine with flashlights. The schoolhouse is turned upside down. A half hour passes in a jangled blur as I dart frantically in and out of storefronts. To make matters worse, the Wild West Show has ended, and everywhere there is movement as the horde fractures and undulates, but there's not a blue-checked dress among them.

As hard as I try to push the thought from my mind, I can see the man who's taken her. He has a mustache. Sunglasses. A jagged little scar above his left eyebrow. He's wearing a sweatshirt in spite of the heat.

Suddenly, through the photo parlor window, I glimpse a dark head of hair and burst through the door. But it turns out to be a boy half Piper's age. My mind is playing tricks on me.

"Have you seen this girl?" I ask the photographer, thrusting a wallet-sized photo into his face.

Nobody's seen her. Not the woman in the Needleworks, not the old lady in the Candle Shop. Not the Chinese guy in the Boot and Saddle. My cell phone is running out of juice. The pudgy security guard continues to reassure Janet in front of the ice wagon.

The grim scene plays out in my head. There's no stopping it. I can see the van trailing a cloud of dust as it speeds out into the desert — there's not even a road where he's taking her.

At the far end of Main Street, I hurry up the hill through the cemetery toward the squat little Christian church. I push through the door. The place is empty. Still as a sarcophagus. Slants of sunlight swimming with dust. I walk down the aisle between the pews, feverish, heartsick, certain that my life will never be the same. Bile is rising in my throat. The room is starting to wobble. I'm going to puke. I double over, steadying myself on the last pew. Just when I'm about to lose it, I see her, asleep on her side on the bench with her mouth half open, her blue-checked dress pasted to her sunburned knees.

the edge

Highway 191 begins in the unassuming flatlands a dozen or so miles west of Bozeman, where it picks up the Gallatin River, running flat through sprawling pasturelands. Soon the mountains converge before us, and the road begins a winding ascent through the steep forested slopes of Gallatin Canyon. The snowcapped Madisons rear up to the west, buttressed by squat green foothills, while abruptly the craggy Gallatins crowd in on us from the east. The van labors in low gear, as we inch our way up the ever-steepening grade toward the Yellowstone plateau, a treacherous two-lane crawl along shoulderless overhangs. The vistas are among the most dramatic we've yet to encounter. Just over a guardrail, ominously buckled in places, strung intermittently with memorial wreaths, the world falls away precipitously into a bottomless tree-stubbled gorge. Mercifully, I'm unable to crane my neck. Above us on either side, the cliff faces are studded with sandstone and marred by recent slides. I'd grip the wheel harder if my bandaged hands would allow me.

In the backseat, Dot and Peaches converse with the familiarity of old friends, occasionally in hushed tones. Though Dot is younger, she is more worldly and does most of the talking. Peaches takes it all in like the gospel, her bright eyes shining above her cherubic cheeks. Now and again, I catch snippets of their conversation.

"Let me guess," says Dot. "Every time you bring it up, he talks about wanting everything to be perfect, right? He talks about some future where all the details are taken care of and the timing is right."

"Yeah, how did you know?"

"Because they're all that way — Ron, Kirk, my dad."

"What way?"

"Scared."

"Of what?"

"Of everything. So they invent a future where they've got nothing to be afraid of. It usually has to do with having more money."

Peaches cradles her belly in both hands, and looks out over the gorge. "Elton was gonna make us rich," she says sadly.

"Don't worry," says Dot. "He still will."

Beside me, Trev seems perfectly at ease. The transformation is remarkable. Never mind that our journey has been hopelessly derailed at every juncture, that we're overbudget, behind schedule, and have no clue where the nearest medical facility is located. Never mind that the dummy light is on again. Never mind that the man to whom he has entrusted his health is wrapped in gauze, wearing a neck brace, and teetering precariously on the edge of sanity. Trev is a rock.

"So, are you gonna come back to work?" he says to me, out of the blue.

"I mean, when this is over?"

"I'm not sure."

"What else would you do?"

"I have no idea." The fact is, I haven't given it a thought. I'm lucky to see my hand in front of my face in my current state of myopia.

Trev looks out his window at the cliff face hugging the shoulder, then rolls his head back toward me. "You gotta do something."

"Yeah, I know."

"My mom will be fine with it. It's my decision, really. Look, dude, you're old. This is serious. You gotta figure out what you're gonna do."

"Yeah."

"What did you do before?"

"Nothing, really. I wrote poetry."

"No, really, what did you *do*?"

"Worked some bullshit jobs."

"Like what?"

"Like I worked at a bookstore. And I worked for a place that painted parade floats. And I worked as a courier for a reprographics outfit. And I worked at a bakery for a long time."

"So, you were a baker?"

"No, I worked behind the counter."

Trev considers this, as though contemplating my employment prospects. "Parade floats, huh?"

"Yeah, the big inflatables."

"How come I don't know any of this stuff?" he says.

"You never asked."

Arriving at West Yellowstone is like arriving on the edge of the world. Squatting near the edge of a broad plateau stretching from horizon to horizon, the town itself, a collusion of local merchants straining to summon the western frontier with splintered storefronts and swinging doors, huddles around one wide thoroughfare running north to south. It's not so different from a certain ghost town. For all its hokey frontier airs, West Yellowstone really is about as rugged an outpost as you're likely to find in the West, hemmed in by a seemingly boundless wilderness, snowbound half the year, and eighty miles from anything else you could call a town.

Though it's late in the season, most of the hotels boast no vacancy. After three passes, we finally find a vacancy at the Roundup Motor Lodge on the edge of town. The room is sad but inexpensive, lit like an interrogation room. There's no art on the walls, no Bible in the drawer. And maybe it's me, but the ceilings feel low.

I shower with Trev. He sits rigidly in his shower seat, clutching the handrail, as I sponge the ghostly white skin of his back and shampoo his hair. Afterward, Peaches redresses my wounds, while Trev sits in his wheelchair before the mirror with a towel wrapped around his waist, running an electric razor unevenly over his face. When he's finished shaving, I put on his deodorant and carry him to the bed, where the girls look the other way as I dress him in clean cargoes and a black T-shirt.

In spite of my insistence that she needs to eat, Peaches refuses to join us for dinner, claiming she's not hungry. But I think she just wants to be alone. Dot makes one last attempt to persuade her while Trev and I wait in the parking lot under the huge night sky.

"Dude," he says to me. "Don't take this the wrong way — but would you mind if like, uh, you know, I flew solo on this one or whatever? The dinner, I mean."

"Ahhh, right, gotcha. I'll just grab a pizza and bring it back to the room. You have a key?"

"Yeah."

"You need to go to the bathroom or anything?"

"I'm cool."

"You warm enough?"

"Yeah."

"Got your wallet?"

"*Yes.*"

"Just call me if you need — "

"Go," he says, rolling his head back and waving me on with a little flipper motion.

I pat my own pocket for my wallet and cell and turn to leave.

"Are you really gonna wear that?" he says.

"What, the shirt?"

"The neck brace."

"Why, does it make me look fat?"

"You don't want the ladies feeling sorry for you."

"Sure I do."

"You don't. Trust me."

But the truth is, I don't care at this point what the ladies or anyone else thinks of me.

The thin air of the plateau is unexpectedly chilly. I should have worn a sweatshirt. But at least my neck is warm as I angle across the lot toward the main drag. A quick check of my cell tells me it's 8:35 p.m. Though my search for pizza needn't take me far (I spot the Wild West Pizzeria right across the street, it's red neon abuzz), I feel like stretching my legs. At Canyon, I veer south. Neither the glow of West Yellowstone nor the moon waxing yellow on the horizon is bright enough to wash out a smattering of cold white stars splashed across the night sky. A black pickup crawls past, trailing salsa music. A chorus of muffled laughter seeps out of the saloon up the street, where out front I can discern the glow of a cigarette cherry.

Otherwise, the town huddles warily in darkness, one eye open against the silent, patient menace of the wilderness, pressing in from all sides.

Stuffing my bandaged hands in my pockets, I walk past the darkened boutiques, past the hokey Trading Post, and the abandoned frankfurter stand, past the all-night retro diner, vacant save for a lone coffee drinker perched on a chrome stool at the end of the bar. Briskly, though I have no purpose, I stride past the desolate IMAX theater, past the visitor center, toward the far edge of town.

In the weeks and months following the disaster, those nights when I was courageous enough to stay sober but still too cowardly to end my life decisively, I used to walk like there was no tomorrow, no matter the weather nor the hour. Some nights I'd walk all the way down Agatewood, around the bend to Highway 305. I'd walk along the road's shoulder with the headlights at my back, north to the bridge, where I'd stand in the trade winds and peer between trusses out over the rail at the mutinous water seventy feet below. As if. As if seventy feet would even do the job. As if deep down I weren't too self-indulgent to ever remove myself from the corporeal realm, deny myself the fleeting luxuries of living on earth — the cheeseburgers, the sunsets, the bitter spoils of self-pity. As if I didn't deserve to die.

At the south end of Canyon, the town peters out, and the road ends abruptly in a wide tract of weeds and gravel. From there, the darkened plateau seems to stretch forever beneath the stars, studded with pines in the pale moonlight. Surely it is among the loneliest sights I've ever seen and somehow all the lonelier knowing that the little town is at my back. I venture a few crunchy steps off the sidewalk into the gravel, then a few more. After about thirty or forty steps, I stop and listen to the distant buzz of crickets. I turn and look back at the town. Even at 150 yards, it seems far away. I wouldn't have guessed it would have such a pull on me, this little postcard hamlet in the middle of nowhere, that it would call me back like this. Why should it? What promise awaits me there? On the other hand, the prospect of pushing farther into the darkness is at once thrilling and paralyzing. Obviously, I don't have the guts to go farther; maybe someday. Still, I force myself to linger, crossing my bare arms for warmth, digging my toe into the gravel and wishing I still smoked cigarettes. Suddenly a rustling in the weeds sets my neck hairs on end. All at once, the crickets stop. I spin around and peer into the void. Nothing.

Without further hesitation, I retreat hastily in the direction from which I came, as though something might be gaining on me. When I rejoin the sidewalk, I slacken my pace and begin doubling back through town toward the pizza joint. Passing the diner on the opposite side of the street, I see Trev and Dot in the window looking at menus, and I'm grateful, though I can't shake the feeling that I'm losing them both somehow.

When I return to the room, I find Peaches roosting on the edge of the bed with her head bowed, crying softly into a hand towel. Setting the pizza aside, I lower myself beside her and drape an arm over her shoulder, then begin to rock her gently back and forth as she clutches the towel. For a few minutes, we rock in silence. She sniffles and wipes her eyes.

Even in grief, puffy and ringed with red, her hazel eyes are lively, as she peers up into my face. "I don't want to be alone," she says.

I squeeze her tighter and clear the stray hairs from her face. "You won't be."

"But what about Elton?"

"Shhh," I say. "Don't worry about Elton. Elton will be back."

"But what if — "

"Shhh."

Sniffling, she searches me hopefully with her bright eyes. "What if I'm too — "

"Shhh," I say. "Trust me, kid. You'll be ready. Everything will change."

She sniffles once more, leaning into my assurances, but the fear hasn't left her, I can tell.

"There's nothing like it, Peach. Nothing even close."

And suddenly, it's not Peaches but me weeping. She unpins her arm and wraps it around my shoulders and gives me a squeeze.

"Shhh," she says.

promise

We're past the dogleg at Dolphin now, past the cedar snag and the doddering split-rail fence, easing down that final narrow stretch of Agatewood as Piper's voice washes over me. Just past the Birkland place, we hit the tract of potholes that act as our neighborhood speed bumps. Bob Williamson is out mowing his lawn on the rider, an iPod strapped to his thick waist. The Worths are apparently still down in Cannon Beach, because the Cartwright kid from down the road is there feeding the dogs, his blue bike sprawled in the driveway.

I glance in the rearview mirror. "Show me the booger," I say.

Piper brandishes her finger obediently. "Daddy, you're not *listening*," she complains as we pull up the driveway.

"I heard you, honey."

"What did I say, then?"

"You were talking about the octopus."

I pull to a stop in front of the garage and park on the sloping driveway.

"That was before! What was I telling you right now?"

Turning off the motor, I sigh. "Piper, honey," I say, passing her a piece of junk mail from the passenger's wheel well. "Please just wipe your finger on this envelope and unbuckle your brother, okay? Once we get the groceries in the house you can tell me whatever you want."

"Promise?"

"Promise."

nothing

In the morning, while the girls are in the bathroom with the water running, doing whatever it is girls do in the bathroom together, I pull Trev's covers back and begin to lay his clothing out on the foot of the bed — clean boxers, black T-shirt, khaki cargoes. Today we'll wind our way south through Yellowstone to the Tetons and make Jackson before dusk, where we'll deliver Peaches to her mother's house. By nightfall, we'll reach our terminus at Salt Lake and put Dot on a bus for Denver.

Trev remains conspicuously silent, watching the muted Weather Channel unfold over my shoulder as I finesse his arms through the shirt sleeves. By the time I slip the second gold-toed sock over his foot, it's readily apparent that he has no intention of volunteering any information about last night. I've no alternative but to fish.

"You guys were out late."

"Yeah," is all he says.

"So how'd it go?"

"Good."

"That's good. What did you guys do?"

"Talked."

"Just talked, huh?"

"Pretty much."

Scooping him off the bed, I could swear I catch a whiff of Dot's citrus-scented perfume on him.

"For five hours?" I say, nesting him in his wheelchair.

"Yeah, I guess. If that's how long it was."

"So, then, what'd you guys talk about?"

"Nothing, really."

"Nothing?"

"Pretty much. Just stuff."

I decide to wait him out, turning my attention to the television. Fifty-one degrees in Fairbanks. Sixty-three in Tacoma. Eighty-six in Redding. Without the interrogation, Trev settles into silence. Seventy-four in San Diego. Ninety-one in Phoenix. Sixty-eight in Denver. And it is in this silence that Trev finally reveals himself. Monitoring him out of the corner of my eye, I see contentment written plainly on his face as he settles deep into the silence and seems to gaze right through the television screen. And maybe it's the low ceilings or just the way he's sitting with his shoulders reared back and his chin held high, but he looks less frail somehow, bigger, and I suddenly know beyond a shadow of a doubt that he kissed her and that he doesn't want to talk about it — because like all young lovers, he wants to hoard the memory, hold it so close and contained that it can never escape him. I only hope she doesn't hurt him too badly.

"Oh yeah, I forgot to tell you," he says, at last. "He's here."

"Who?"

"The dude in the brown beater."

old faithful

Indeed, the Skylark has returned, less like a malignant shadow, and more like a ticket scalper that won't take no for an answer. Our pursuer picked us up in the tollbooth queue and holds steady two cars behind us, where he has little choice but to remain in the line of traffic as we crawl through the western fringe of Yellowstone, along the Madison River through dense pinewood flats. Within miles, the forest yields to rolling pasturelands, spangled with vast bison herds, strung out along the river to graze.

"What's the difference between a bison and a buffalo?" Trev says.

"Is this a joke?" says Dot.

"No, really. Is there a difference?"

"Beats me," I say. "Aren't they the same thing?"

"I think so," says Dot

"Elton would know," Peaches says.

I don't doubt that Elton would have an answer for just about anything. And who am I to decide what's best for anybody? Maybe it's better that Peaches just keep ennobling Elton in his absence. Maybe he'll pull through. Stranger things have happened. Let her believe.

We begin to veer south and detour through canyon country, where the Firehole River roars through narrow channels of crumbling rock, and scorched pines cling to the basin walls for purchase. Peaches is asleep by the time we pull over on the shoulder to watch the falls rumble down their craggy chute and splash down forty feet below. Just as I kill the ignition, the Skylark eases past us, and rounds the bend. Immediately, Dot jumps out to smoke.

"You wanna get out?" I say to Trev.

"Nah, I've got a good view right here."

"I'm gonna have a look."

I climb out of the van, ducking my stiff neck gingerly under the door frame. Dot's standing at the rail, smoking, as she stares out over the river. I station myself beside her, and take in the view.

"Pretty," she says.

"Yeah."

She takes a drag, exhales. "So, how come you're always leaning into my cigarette smoke?"

"What do you mean 'leaning'?"

"Like right now. You're sorta drifting closer and closer every time I take a puff."

"Hmph. Didn't realize. Miss it, I guess."

"Then why'd you quit?"

"Wife made me. Before we got married."

"That's lame," she says.

"Yeah, probably."

"Isn't that totally lame?" she says to Trev.

"I'm gonna stretch my legs," I say.

I trudge up the road a ways. I can hear Dot's voice as she talks to Trev through the open window, but soon the roar of the falls swallows it. About fifty yards upriver from the van, I stop to take in the view, sidling to the very edge of the precipice. Above the chute, the river runs braided around moldering snags, and the crumbling hillside rises toward the ridge at twenty degrees, stubbled with dead pines. I'm almost certainly going to need Forest to wire me some money in Jackson. At least a couple hundred to get me home. What I'm going to do with my life when I get back is still a complete mystery. I'll have two weeks to make rent. I've got an eBay account, the Subaru, a lot of plastic containers. I've got this neck brace, these tight shorts, a headache, and a few Cortázar poems committed to memory. So I've got that going for me.

Part of me just wants to stop right here. What's calling me back, anyway? Why not get a job in West Yellowstone selling buffalo turds? I could make clocks out of them. I could lease that vacant kiosk three doors down from the liquor store — maybe we could barter! I could rent a cellar somewhere and forget I ever was. Or why not just drop out altogether, ford that river, scramble up that hillside, and disappear over the ridge? But who am I kidding? Backing away from the ledge, I thrust my bandaged hands in my shorts pockets and amble downhill toward the others.

Dot is back in the van by the time I return, kneeling in her new station behind Trev. Peaches is still sleeping, her head slumped against the window, both hands flat on her belly for protection. I ought to wake her so that she doesn't miss the sights, but I figure she needs the rest. We continue to weave our way south through the canyon, past lava flows and nameless cascades, past colonnades of jagged rock pillars clinging like stalagmites to tapered ledges. The Skylark picks up our tail again where the loop rejoins the main road, easing in one car behind us. The scenery flattens out as we drop into the Lower Geyser Basin, and the otherworldly Yellowstone of postcards begins to reveal itself in the cracked and steaming flats. As far as the eye can see, the whitewashed earth is venting, burping, bubbling up from within. A giant caldera. A supervolcano. Somewhere a tour guide is saying something about the dawn of the world. But someday this belching cauldron may end the world.

"Holy crap," says Trev. "This is as almost as cool as the water tower in George."

"Pretty close," I say.

Dot is on her knees now, clutching the back of Trev's chair as she peers over his shoulder out the windshield. I've never seen her face like this, wide open in wonderment. For once, the world has exceeded her expectations.

The traffic slows as we approach Old Faithful. The gigantic parking lot is a clusterfuck of crisscrossing corridors, all of them full to bursting with cars of every conceivable make, from every conceivable locale. Even the handicapped spots are occupied. Crawling down a single line, I spot plates from Oregon, Arizona, Massachusetts, New Mexico, Alberta, Rhode Island, New Brunswick, New Jersey, New

York, and Florida. Somehow the Skylark manages to stick with us through the congestion, even finds a spot in the same row on the outer-outer fringe of the sprawl.

Dot begins unbuckling Trev as I lower the ramp.

Peaches finally awakens. "Where are we?" she says.

"Old Faithful," says Trev.

"Why didn't anyone wake me?"

"You guys go on ahead," I say. "I've got a few calls to make first. Meet you front and center."

"Aye aye, Captain," says Trev, who proceeds to execute a tight three-point turn in reverse, piloting himself onto the ramp, where he gives me the nod to lower him.

Once he's on the ground, the girls pile out after him, and together they make for the geyser. Watching them go, Trev rolling slowly down the center of the lane, shoulders back, head high, flanked by a girl on each shoulder, I don't have to see his face to know he's smiling.

Raising the ramp, I circle the van and fiddle with my cell phone for a minute, biding my time until the others are out of sight before I begin creeping purposefully up the lane in the opposite direction, stooping close to the bumpers to avoid detection. I have no intention of losing my temper. This may require some diplomacy. But I'm determined to get to the bottom of it. When I reach the Skylark, the driver is still in the car, rifling through a shaving bag. My knock on the window startles him, though his surprise turns quickly to alarm when he sees it's me, the guy who tried to tackle his car at twenty miles per hour. I must be even scarier with all this gauze and a neck brace. He reaches for the ignition, but I halt him with a one-handed yield gesture.

"Please," I say.

I take a step back from the car, where I beckon him to roll down his window. Warily, he obliges.

He's even more stubbled than before, wearing a Mariners cap that looks like someone kicked it there from Seattle, and the same loose-fitting shirt with ukuleles and coconuts on it. At a standstill, I can see the sunbaked crow's-feet bookending the sides of his face, and I can tell he's led an uneven life — good times and bad but not a lot of middle ground. He looks like a sportswriter who overslept his deadline.

"Look," I say calmly. "I know who you are."

"She told you, huh? That's a surprise."

"No, I just figured it out. It had to be Elsa."

He looks at me blankly. "Who's Elsa?"

"The woman who hired you."

"Nobody hired me."

Searching his face, I find genuine confusion there. "Who sent you, then? Janet?"

"Nobody sent me. I sent myself."

"Why are you following me?"

He squints at me, flexing his crow's feet. "I'm not following you. I'm following *her.*"

"Peaches?"

"Dorothy."

My first thought is perv. "What do you want with Dot?"

"What do *you* want with her?" he says. "You some kind of pervert?"

"I'm giving her a ride."

He gives me a long steady look, until he seems satisfied with the explanation. "I'm Cash Callahan."

He gives me a moment to let the information sink in, but it doesn't.

"She's my daughter."

My mind scrambles to make the connections. "Wait. But how . . . ?"

"I've been trailing her since she left Tacoma — she sure as hell hasn't made it easy. I've lost her twice already, and it's a miracle I didn't lose her in Missoula. I'm sure she's pissed as hell at me, but what's new?"

"She knows you've been following her?"

"She left me no choice, bro. I've got no control over her. Not that I ever did." He climbs out of the car and leans against the Skylark. Scanning the huge parking lot, he heaves a sigh.

"You smoke?" he says.

"Nope."

"Me neither. Sometimes I wish I did."

"Me too."

He scrapes absently at some rust under the door handle, stops himself, and jams his hand in his jeans pocket. "I can't tell her to quit smoking, bro — I've tried. She just smokes harder. I can't tell her who to date. I'm not even allowed to call her Dorothy anymore. All I can do is keep an eye out, and that's no small job. Christ, I slept in my car the last three nights. You got kids?"

"No."

"Hmph. Well, lucky you. It ain't easy, bro. Especially not teenage girls. But who am I to say? I've got no control of what Dorothy does in Denver. But the hell if I'm just gonna let my kid hitchhike halfway across the country. Just because she won't ride with me, doesn't mean I'm gonna let her out of my sight."

Cash kicks a little stone with the toe of his sandal. The pebble skitters a few feet across the pavement, takes a big hop, and clinks against the Range Rover parked next to him. He looks up at me thoughtfully, as though he's about to apologize for something. "So do me a favor, bro. Let me stick to you. Keep me on your radar, okay? I'll stay out of your hair, I promise. You won't even know I'm there. I don't wanna lose her."

He looks back down at his flip-flops and shakes his head. Talking to the ground, he says, "If anything should ever happen to her, bro, I'd . . ." He trails off.

I don't know anything about this guy beyond the fact that Dot's mother called him a deadbeat and that Dot says he's immature. When you get down to it, I don't know anything about Dot, except that her mother died, and Dot doesn't dress warmly enough. All I know is that this guy is willing to drive to the ends of the earth so that he doesn't get stuck holding the groceries, and I'm not going to stand in his way.

He's back to chipping away at the rusty Skylark. "The truth is, I lost her a long time ago, bro. I fucked up."

"It happens."

"Yeah, well I made a real fucking mess. And I may never get the chance to clean it up, and I can't blame Dorothy for that. Best I can do is not make it any worse."

Scraping at the rust, the poor guy looks abject with his stubbled face and his rumpled party shirt. You get the feeling he might blow out his flip-flop with the very next step.

"She used to think you were pretty cool," I offer as a consolation. "You know that, right?"

He looks up hopefully. "She said that?"

I nod. "She still wears the bracelet, doesn't she?"

"That turquoise one? Yeah, I noticed that. Darlene must've given it to her." He smiles and shakes his head again, and his smile fades immediately. "Or left it to her, I guess. I got it for Darlene in the early nineties. It was gonna be like an engagement thing. Bought it from some tripped-out desert sage at Burning Man. Dude had bones through his nipples and two different color eyes. Hmph. Seems like forever ago. So, what's your deal? You just drive around picking people up? You sure you're not a pervert?"

It's my turn to kick pebbles and shake my head. "Look, I didn't plan any of this, Cash, believe me. Not this trip, not these passengers, and definitely not what I left behind. I planned like hell for something else entirely. All this just happened."

Cash pats me on the shoulder. "I feel you, bro."

you don't understand

Listen to me: everything you think you know, every relationship you've ever taken for granted, every plan or possibility you've ever hatched, every conceit or endeavor you've ever concocted, can be stripped from you in an instant. Sooner or later, it *will* happen. So prepare yourself. Be ready not to be ready. Be ready to be brought to your knees and beaten to dust. Because no stable foundation, no act of will, no force of cautious habit will save you from this fact: nothing is indestructible.

Even if you glance over your shoulder in time to glimpse its arrival, if you manage to drop your groceries and throw yourself headlong at the destruction, you will be powerless to stop it. It will bear down on you like the devil until you feel your shoes surrendering their purchase on the grit of the driveway, until you shear the side mirror clean off the car with the force of your efforts. But the car will keep rolling. And you'll watch helplessly as the back wheel pins your daughter's red cape to the pavement, even as she reaches desperately to save her brother, who will disappear beneath the rear bumper. You will hear his frantic wailing as you attempt to wedge your own leg beneath the front wheel in an effort to stop the terrible thing. But you will not stop it. Instead, you will watch everything you love most in the world dragged over the edge of the incline with a terrible scraping, an irreversible yawning. And when you hear the sickening metallic clangor of impact, you will begin to forget everything you ever knew.

Afterward — how much time, ten minutes, an hour? — when the others have arrived in droves to see what your failure has wrought, you will pace and reel in utter confusion like a man struck by lightning.

You will not comprehend what has happened. Any attempt you make to order the universe will be desperate and laughable.

"I'm a stay-at-home dad," you will keep telling the gap-toothed EMT or the cop with the hairy knuckles or anyone else who will listen. "You don't understand," you will tell them, tugging desperately at their sleeves, and blocking their way. "I . . . I'm a stay-at-home dad."

"Sir," the hairy-knuckled cop will say. "We need you to calm down."

"But you don't understand. I — I'm . . ."

"Sir. I need you to sit down."

"The fingers."

"Sir."

"My wife will be home. We need the fingers."

"Yessir, we've contacted your wife."

You will grab him by the lapel and cling to him. "I-I didn't know. I-I . . ."

"Yessir, I understand. It was an accident. We all understand."

"No. You don't. The fingers."

"We've located the fingers."

"But I — I'm a stay-at-home dad."

And when he looks at you this time, you will see in his eyes that you frighten him, but you will not know why. Then you will get down on your hands and knees and begin to order the groceries, setting the cans right, gathering the wayward apples. You will retrieve a tube of Jimmy Dean sausage, which has rolled down the driveway and lodged itself beneath the hydrangea. You will see Janet at the curb, talking to a fireman with her hands covering her face. And before you can get to her, she will have left you already.

something else entirely

Having assured him that he'll stay on my radar, I bid Cash adieu and make my way at a leisurely stroll toward the geyser in search of Trev and the girls. Old Faithful is two minutes overdue by my clock. When I look back at Cash, he's rummaging around in the trunk of the Skylark, stowing a pillow, squashing down his sleeping bag, fishing out a backpack. I wonder if he's actually living out of his car.

When I look back a second time, the trunk is closed, and Cash is holding a flip-flop in his right hand, fiddling with the toe harness. Disgustedly, he hurls the sandal to the ground, just as a squat brown-haired family of four is passing. They cut a wide arc around the Skylark. Cash tips his dirty baseball cap at them, but they're all looking straight ahead, except for the little boy with the ice-cream cone that's too big for him, who gazes curiously back over his shoulder. Cash flips the kid off. The kid flips him off back.

About fifteen seconds later, a distant chorus of oohing and aahing rises from beyond the visitor center, as Old Faithful gushes with a rumble and a hiss. I can just barely see the plume over the peaked roof of the visitor complex. Beside me, the squat kid begins screaming and crying to beat the band. He's dropped his ice-cream cone, and his father is dragging him along at a trot.

Greeted by a gust of sulfur, I reach the sparsely wooded visitor area in time to see the geyser's gurgling retreat through the trees. No sooner do I begin cutting a diagonal path through the trees toward the viewing area than I see Dot break suddenly from the crowd and stop to periscope her head around the periphery. She spots me from thirty yards just as I clear the tree line, and she sprints the distance between us. She grabs me by the hand and pulls me desperately toward the crowd.

"Hurry," she says. "Something's happened."

volumes

Okay, so I'm the one not letting go of anything, I see that — do you think I don't see that? But somebody has to *not let go*. Somebody has to stay behind.

Here is Janet in the kitchen, clutching a single carelessly stuffed canvas bag amid a chaos of uneaten casseroles and unopened cards and half-packed boxes of children's clothing. It's ten days after the disaster, six days after the service, five days since her last shower. Her thick hair hangs greasy and lifeless. The pouches beneath her eyes droop clear to her cheekbones. She's been on the phone with her sister in Portland all morning.

"Where will you go?"

"Away," she says, as though from a great distance already.

"But you can't just . . . What about — "

"What about what?" She levels the question at me like a challenge. "There is no what, Ben."

But what Janet doesn't know could fill volumes. She doesn't know that the last look on her daughter's face was an entreaty. She doesn't know the confusion and panic that filled Jodi's brown eyes as he choked on his final breaths. She didn't touch them, damnit! She didn't lie to them! She didn't kneel beside their broken bodies and tell them everything was going to be all right, knowing that in a single bat of an eye the whole universe had jumped track, and everything was spinning inexplicably, hopelessly, irreversibly out of control. She was not forced to stand helplessly in death's way. She did not beat her head on the pavement, claw at her own eyes, scream herself raw, press her mouth to the slack jaw of her dead daughter, and try desperately to fill her lungs with life. She knows neither guilt nor blame nor the terrible truth. There *is* a what, there's always a what, and there will forever be a what as long as one person is left standing.

I'm certain now Janet started walking away long before the disaster. God knows, she yearned for more. I wonder at what point Bernard and Ruth began removing all evidence of me, striking me from the walls of the den, cutting me off at the shoulder? A week? Two weeks? A month? Some people fled quicker than others. Our friends with children wasted little time in effecting their retreat. Every casserole was like a good-bye — they didn't want their pans back. They didn't want to reckon with the ugly truth every time they packed a lunch box or buckled in their children. Up and down Agatewood, the neighbors heaved a collective sigh when the house went on the market. Nobody mentioned the moving trucks. Nobody inquired as to futures. Nobody even said good-bye. So what's holding me back? Why am I still standing in that driveway, still living in the hour of my destruction, when everybody else has left the scene? I'll tell you why: because what happened in the driveway was a revelation. In all the waking moments of my life, the disaster is the one thing that ever truly happened. Everything else is a lie.

"Sir, I'm going to need you to calm down."

"But you don't understand . . ."

"I'm going to have to ask you to step — "

"No, listen, I'm a — "

"Yessir, I understand, sir — you're a stay-at-home dad."

out of the frying pan

S ir, I'm gonna need you to calm down, sir," says the medic. He's a giant, maybe six foot seven, lightly stubbled, with a granite chin.

"Do you feel like you have to push?" he says to Peaches, flat on her back atop a space blanket with her knees in the air. She's panting, as the giant works her jeans over her ankles.

"I need you people to back off," he says, over his shoulder. Then, back to Peaches: "Do you feel like you have to poop?"

Before she can answer, she suddenly goes goggle-eyed with another contraction.

The giant eyes his wristwatch, then checks her pelvis and sees that she's bulging already. "Game on," he says. "We're not moving her. This kid's in a hurry. Are you full term?" he says to Peaches.

"She's due in eighteen days," I say.

"You the father?"

"No."

"Have you had prenatal?" he says to her.

"Yes," she says, wide-eyed. "The last was at six months."

"Is everything okay?" I say. "Is she all right?"

"Everything's fine, sir, under control."

"She's gonna have the baby now?"

"Yessir."

"Here?"

"Yessir. Could you hand me those blankets on the tailgate?"

"Isn't there someplace indoors we ca—"

"No time, sir. I'm gonna need you to calm down. Could you get me those blankets? And back these people off."

I think he's just trying to get me out of the way, because the people are already backed off to a forty-foot radius, except for a guy in a Marlins hat who beats me to the blankets on the tailgate and streaks toward the giant with them. Trev's on the perimeter with Dot, looking paler than I've seen him in months.

This is happening way too fast. Something must be wrong. Nobody has a baby this quickly. Piper was thirteen hours getting past the cervix — like she'd lost her nerve. Jodi was about half that, but every minute of it hard fought. Little Elton is a sprinter. Hardly have I knelt back down in the shadow of the giant before he's crowning.

Peaches is stoic. Or maybe this is easy for her. She's sweating like Sonny Liston after the twelfth round, but she doesn't look frightened or in pain as she clutches my hand fiercely and pushes with all her might.

"Keep pushing," says the giant.

"Is everything — "

"Everything's fine."

"You're sure?"

"Sir, I need you to calm down. What's your name, sweetheart?"

"Peaches," she says.

"Peaches, I need you to push — I mean really push, okay? When I count to three, I want you to push."

She bites her lip and nods.

"One, and two, and push!"

Peaches grits her teeth and pushes with all her might, but the baby makes no progress.

"Okay," says the giant. "We're going to try it again, Peaches. Even harder this time, okay?"

"Push like you're angry, Peach. Scream when you do it."

"Just like he says, honey — go ahead and scream. Okay now? Push as hard as you possibly can. One, and two, and . . ."

Again, she pushes, half grunting, half hollering, her face beet red with the effort, her knees trembling. But still the infant makes no progress.

"Okay, I need you to breathe, Peaches. Big breaths, okay, sweetheart?" I can see a glint of fear flash in his eyes. His wheels are spinning fast. He's talking faster. What if something goes wrong. What if he has to perform an emergency C-section with that puny kit of his?

"Big breaths now," he says. "Third time is the charm."

"C'mon, Peach, you can do it," I say, hoping she can't hear the panic that's crept into my voice. That old familiar feeling of calamity is starting to take hold. Something is going terribly wrong here. I'm in the driveway all over again, looking for something to order, something to hold on to, something to keep me from being dragged down by the undertow of terrifying reality.

Peaches grunts and pushes a third time, and it is not the charm. The baby is still stalled crowning. The giant is talking faster than ever, beginning to sweat at the temples. Suddenly something in me snaps, and I'm on my feet again, pacing wildly like a confused accident victim. I look around at the crush of people, their figures a colorful smudge. I feel like rushing at them.

"Get away!" I yell, and they all shift back on their heels but only a single step. I look at my bandaged hands, both of them, and I don't know why, as dully another countdown rings in my ear. "One, and two, and . . ."

Suddenly, Peaches looses a great open-mouthed roar, and turning, I see baby Elton makes his appearance, a side presentation with a thick head of dark slick hair.

"That's it," the giant says, reaching for the bulb syringe. "You're doing great, sweetie."

With the force of a vacuum, the terror leaves my body all at once, and the ache of gratitude fills the breach. Again, I can feel my feet on the ground, discern individual faces. "You got it, Peach," I say, tears streaming down my face. "Keep pushing! You're almost there!"

Little Elton's pinched red face is grimacing as he emerges. The giant continues to suction furiously with his right hand as Elton corkscrews his way out smoothly past the shoulders into the medic's guiding left hand. The instant he issues his first phlegmy cry, the crowd seems to draw in closer, and a few people ooh and aah. He's tiny, maybe six pounds, but ostensibly healthy in spite of a conical head that seems to regain its shape before my eyes.

"He's beautiful," I lie.

The giant clamps the cord a half foot from the baby's belly, then clamps it again an inch or two higher.

"You wanna cut the cord?" he says to me.

And the next thing I know, I'm clutching the blue disposable cord scissors, looking down into Elton's face, with the scissors poised between the ligatures. He's the image of his father — the same beady eyes and weak chin. I wonder if he'll have his business acumen. I look at Peaches, dazed and a little green, smiling like someone who doesn't know any better.

"Go ahead," says the giant.

I snip the cord. The giant sweeps the baby out from under me before I can even move the scissors, wraps him in a reflective blanket, and begins swaddling him in another. And just like that it's over. I look dazedly out at the crowd, which has already begun to disperse, shuffling in a herd toward the front of the viewing area — except for Trev, who whirs toward the center of the circle, with Dot beside him, just as the giant puts Baby Elton to Peaches's chest, then waves the ambulance through.

boxes

For a few minutes after the ambulance has parted the crowd, wending its way through the parking lot toward the main road, Trev and Dot and I stand in place, stunned, speechless. Checking my watch, I see that the delivery took just over an hour.

"Um . . . wow?" says Dot, finally.

"Didn't see that one coming," says Trev, still a half shade paler than usual. "Did that just happen?"

"Seriously."

"What now?" I say. "We follow her, right?"

"I guess I better call my dad first," says Trev. "Let him know we're gonna be late."

Trev whirs off in the direction of the visitor center. He stops about halfway, where he wrestles his phone out of his side pocket, arches his back, and hoists the phone to chest level. He pitches his head to one side and speed-dials Bob.

"You hungry?" I say to Dot.

"No."

"Me neither. You wanna sit down?"

We make our way toward the benches in front of the visitor center, passing Trev, who nods when I signal our destination.

"You've got blood on your shirt," Dot says.

Arriving at the nearest bench, we plop down shoulder to shoulder and fall silent, watching the newcomers file in from Nebraska, Ohio, Alaska, Saskatchewan. I have no idea when Old Faithful is due next, but the restlessness of the dense crowd gathering at the rail suggests she's due to blow soon.

"You talked to him, didn't you?" Dot says.

"Who?"

"C'mon," she says, looking off in the other direction.

"Yeah. I did."

She blows her bangs out of her eyes, proffers her last cigarette from her jean vest, and begins patting around for matches. "Now I suppose you're going to try to make me go with him, aren't you? You can't do that, you know. I'm an adult."

"I know you are, and I'm not. It's none of my business. But I am gonna let him follow us, Dot."

Unable to find a match, Dot contemplates her unlit cigarette for a few seconds. Suddenly, she snaps it in two. "Filthy habit, anyway," she says, stuffing the pieces in her pocket. "So, what did he tell you?"

"Just who he was and why he was following."

"Yeah? What else did he tell you? Did he tell you I tried to seduce his friend?"

"No."

"Did he tell you I stole fifty bucks out of his wallet?"

"No."

"Did he tell you the reason he's driving that piece of shit is because I totaled his Subaru?"

She begins scratching absently at her denim skirt, as though she were scraping dry ketchup off it. "And just so you know, I didn't really try to seduce his friend. I just made that up."

"Good one."

"That's because he doesn't have any friends. At least, he never sees them. They're all married. Like normal people."

Halfway across the clearing, Trev is still on the phone with Bob. He's actually smiling.

"So, what else did he tell you?" says Dot.

"Not much, really."

"C'mon."

"He told me that bracelet used to be your mom's."

She looks away in the other direction again. "Yeah. So I lied."

How badly I'd like to see a picture of her mom. How badly I'd like to have seen the two of them together. "I wouldn't call it a lie."

We fall back into silence. The geyser is beginning to gush and splash a bit, showing signs of what the pamphlets call preplay. Dot scatters some loose tobacco with her toe.

"My dad died when I was in college. I was never very close to him, though."

Dot's hands are fidgety, like she's wishing she had that last cigarette back. She's picking at her cuticles again.

"Looking back," I say. "I wish I had been."

"Been what?"

"Closer to him."

"Mmph," she says, turning her attention back to her feet, and tracing a squiggly line in the dirt with her toe. "So, what was your dad like, anyway?"

"Sort of a Ward Cleaver type."

"Who's Ward Cleaver?"

"Never mind," I say, waving it off. "I'm dating myself. Let's just say my dad wasn't a passionate guy. He liked to read the paper. He liked to pack things neatly in boxes and label them — that was his idea of a good time. He was kind of set in his ways."

Fidgeting now with a tube of mascara, Dot spins it between her fingers, screwing and unscrewing the cap. "Not my dad," she says. "I *wish* he'd set some ways for himself."

"Part of your dad probably wishes that, too."

"Yeah, maybe so."

"It's not easy getting old, you know. Things become a lot less clear."

"I guess I wouldn't know. I'll have to take your word for it."

Then, in the ensuing silence, Dot does a strange thing. She reaches for my bandaged hand and presses it into her own and squeezes it. And she says something totally unexpected. I could hug her for saying it, even if she's just saying it to make me feel better.

"I'm sorry about what happened. Trev told me. I'll bet you were a good dad," she says.

west yellowstone redux

For the first time in this oft-delayed, endlessly diverted voyage, we're actually traveling backward — back to West Yellowstone to stay with Peaches at the clinic, until her mother arrives from Jackson to take her home, where she and Little Elton will begin a new life.

As we retrace our path through the lower basin and into the canyon, I imagine the nursery as Peaches described it. A sunny little room with southern exposure, smelling of calendula and baby powder. I imagine Peaches's mom, a generously proportioned Mother Hubbard type, rocking baby Elton in a corner as he clutches at the generous folds of her frilly old-lady blouse, cooing blissfully to the tune of a music box. I imagine Peaches trying to catch a cat nap on the sofa. Even in her punchy state of exhaustion, in her baggy sweats and frumpy bathrobe with dried spit-up on the lapel, she glows. When she wakes up twenty minutes later, still exhausted, she will miss Baby Elton already. Her body will ache for him. Every time he cries at his inability to express himself, every time he coos while clutching at her breast, every time he follows her with his nearsighted gaze as she leaves a room, her body will ache for him. And with the thought of this aching, all the wonderment and humility and stupefying awe of parenthood comes flooding back.

The Family Clinic is located on the south end of town on a wide, dusty thoroughfare not unlike Canyon Street but without all the frontier pretense. The edifice, squat, unadorned, four shades of faded brown, with long tinted windows, looks less like a medical facility and more like a place where you'd attend a transgender support group, or an indoor flea market. Somehow, Cash has managed to beat us here in the Skylark, where he's parked right out front, one arm out the window, listening to a warbling Guess Who cassette. He nods as we pass, looking a little crestfallen when Dot ignores him. But then, as though she can read his mind, she stops in her path momentarily and turns back to him, arms akimbo.

"Hey, Dad. The seventies called."

"Yeah?" he says, hopefully.

"They want their technology back."

Cash smiles — he'll take what he can get.

The clinic is actually quite sunny on the inside. New carpet in the lobby. Freshly painted corridors. Cheerful receptionist. Peaches is once again in high color, propped up in a hospital bed in a powder blue smock with her hair tied back. She clutches Baby Elton to her chest. His tiny blue and white striped beanie cannot belie his still-misshapen head. He's a hairy little guy. His breathing is a little raspy. He's got a wide flat nose, no lips, and a prominent brow ridge to offset his father's beady eyes and weak chin. On his forehead, he's got one of those blotchy wine-spot birthmarks. He's gonna need some really cute outfits.

"He's perfect," I say.

"He looks like Elton," Trev says from the foot of the bed.

"I think he looks like Peaches," says Dot.

I think he looks like Gorbachev — but I don't say as much. These things have a way of working themselves out. Piper was an odd-looking baby, even through fatherhood's rose-colored glasses. It happens. But somehow homeliness makes them all the more precious.

Elton stirs, clutches at Peaches's smock. She liberates her left breast, and he suckles greedily. She strokes the dark downy hair at the nape of his puny neck as we watch him feed in silence. Now and again, the nipple eludes him, and we hear his desperate suckling, as he gropes and bats at her chest. She smiles and guides his little mouth back to the nipple, hushing him with a loving stroke. I'm watching this girl become a woman right before my eyes.

"Maybe we'll come see the Tetons next summer," I say cheerfully.

"Totally," Trev says. "Elton might be home by then."

It'll never happen, and we both know it.

Peaches's mother arrives late in the afternoon. She's not the fleshy Mother Hubbard type I imagined but a small, hard, sun-baked little woman you could crack walnuts on. She looks about fifty. Clearly a no-nonsense type. Self-reliant — no purse, no wedding ring. Probably just what Little Elton needs in the way of a grandmother. No frilly old lady blouse, just a cotton work shirt with a western stitch, and a pair of bootcut jeans that look like they've been ironed. She's got a firm handshake, and her bony little bird hands are calloused on the inside.

"I'm much obliged to you, Mr. Benjamin. Thanks for seeing to my Peaches."

"It was my pleasure. Call me Ben."

"I'd like to reimburse you for all expenses, Mr. Benjamin."

"No need. I wouldn't think of it." The truth, of course, is that I've got thirteen dollars cash, and my credit card may bounce with the next purchase. I'm dreading the prospect of hitting Forest up for a loan, though I know it's inevitable.

"You will take my money, Mr. Benjamin. I'm a stubborn woman."

She produces a wide leather billfold from her back pocket and removes a crisp pair of fifties and three twenties. When I balk, she tuts me and presses the bills firmly into my hand.

Before we can say our good-byes, both Peaches and Little Elton have slipped off to sleep, Peaches with her jaw set, as though fighting it, and Elton with his little mouth twitching as he dreams of the nipple. They're beautiful — even if he does look like Gorbachev. I want to physically take hold of this moment before it escapes me. I never want to say good-bye to anybody ever again.

Leaning over the bed, I plant a kiss ever so lightly on Peaches's forehead. She doesn't stir. I think of the Wyoming sun slanting through the window of a circus-themed nursery, and I tell myself that everything will work out fine.

another long haul

It's dusk by the time we emerge from the clinic. Out front, Cash is asleep in the driver's seat of the Skylark, clutching a half-eaten sub, his other hand on the wheel. Dot pounds on the windshield as she passes, startling him awake. Hurriedly he rewraps his sub. We've got four hundred miles to Salt Lake City, and I intend to have us there by midnight.

We drive south toward Ashton in the darkness, with Cash's dingy yellow headlights glowing in the rearview mirror. To the west, vast rolling potato fields stretch out in the moonlight toward the horizon. Once in a while, the dark form of a grain elevator whizzes past, while somewhere up ahead of us, the backside of the Tetons loom in darkness. Trev and Dot are both asleep by the time we reach Rexburg. I could sleep like a baby myself, a thought I'm forced to chase away time and again. It's been a hell of a long day, a long week, a long couple of years. And Salt Lake City is still a long, lonely stretch from here. I crack the window to stay awake, and I tighten my neck brace as the wind flaps and flutters in my ear. Wishing I smoked again, I steady my gaze on the never-ending white lines, taking a small comfort in knowing those headlights behind me belong to Cash.

I'm already beginning to fade by the time I pick up I-15 north of Idaho Falls, but I manage to power on for another hour or so before hunger and fatigue finally compel me to stop at the Sizzler in Pocatello, ten minutes before closing. Trev and Dot awaken when the van motor goes silent.

"Where are we?" says Trev sleepily. "We're not here, are we?"

"Pocatello," I say.

He angles his chair forward slightly with a whir. Dot unfastens his buckles as I lower the ramp, and the three of us pile out of the van, Dot yawning and stretching as she ducks under the threshold of the sliding door. We take a window booth that looks directly out on Cash, who's remained in the Skylark, where he's eating the rest of his gas station sub and listening to his warbly Guess Who tape.

"I can't stand it anymore," says Dot.

"What?"

"Look at him. It's pathetic. I'm pretty sure he's been eating that cheese sandwich since yesterday."

"Actually, I think there's meat on it," I say.

"I'm seriously starting to feel sorry for him. Who has a tape deck still?"

She looks right at him, but he can't see her through the tinted window. She shakes her head woefully. "I mean, he's been sleeping in the car the whole time. I just like can't believe he's actually following me the *whole* freaking way. I thought he was totally full of shit. He's crazy. Who does that?"

"A parent."

"Well, I can't stand it anymore." She stands up and marches down the aisle toward the exit.

"Where's she going?" says Trev.

"To yell at him, maybe?"

Momentarily, Dot reappears outside the window directly in front of us, where she taps on the Skylark window. Cash rolls it down, and Dot begins talking a mile a minute. I can't hear her voice.

"What was he like?" says Trev.

"Honestly?"

"Yeah."

"He seems like an all right guy to me. Musical taste notwithstanding."

"I think she really likes him," he says. "I just think he embarrasses her a little. And she wishes he'd man up, you know? I can relate. Don't tell Dot, but I kinda feel sorry for him."

Out the window, Dot has coaxed him out of the car, where he's doing the talking now, looking down at his feet. She takes him by the wrist and tugs at him until he submits, allowing her to drag him toward the restaurant entrance. A moment later, they're both sidling into the booth across from me, with Trev at the head of the table.

"Hey," Cash says to me, then gives Trev a little nod. "What up, bro?"

"Not much," says Trev. "Just gettin' my Sizzle on."

"Right on," says Cash.

"You've got mustard on your shirt," Dot says to her father.

"Bummer," he says, without bothering to investigate. He goes straight for a menu.

The waiter looks like a retired pensions and actuaries man, paunchy, with a gray comb-over, short sleeve button-up with a pen protector, a name tag that says HOWARD, and thick black rubber-soled loafers. He's not waiter material. Maybe he's the manager, because anybody but a manager would be put out that we've arrived just minutes before closing, and nobody but a manager would offer to restock the salad bar, which even at a distance, has a sad aura about it.

Cash orders the Malibu chicken. Dot and Trev both order the shrimp alfredo. I order coffee and the signature steak, emphasizing the rare, because something about Howard suggests that he's not a man who understands rare. As soon as he walks off with the menus, Dot retreats to the ladies' room. Once she's out of earshot, Cash turns to Trev.

"So, you taking good care of my daughter?" he says.

"How about you?" says Trev.

Cash smiles appreciatively, scratches his neck. "Tough job, right?"

"Nice work, if you can get it."

Cash nods knowingly, and flips his coffee cup over, just as Howard returns with the coffee. I follow suit, and the three of us sit silently as the cups are filled.

Dot returns, sliding in next to her dad.

"What did he say about me?"

"Nothing," says Trev.

"I told him how when you were seven years old you wanted to be the surgeon general," Cash says.

"I never said that."

"And how you were going to write a constitution for the house pets and how your mom was going to ratify it."

"You're making that up."

"I had to look up ratify," he says. "Maybe I should tell them about the infamous Barbie boycott of 2000."

"Do tell," says Trev.

"Just stop," says Dot, socking him on the shoulder playfully. I'm guessing she likes the attention. "Oh fine, then," she says, waving it off. "Tell them whatever you want. It's probably all made up, anyway."

Cash tells us about Dot's childhood propensity for the xylophone, about her love of chinchillas, about how she always insisted on cutting her own hair. Trev is riveted by it all. Howard arrives with the platters, bumbles through the service, and bids us adieu. Sure enough, my steak is tougher than a new saddlebag, with maybe a quarter inch of pink in the center — rare like a mosquito in the Everglades. But the rice is decent, in a TV dinner sort of way, and the cheese bread, though oily and slightly off-color, is strangely satisfying.

Cash, meanwhile, inhales his Malibu chicken, nodding enthusiastically throughout. Trev skewers the shrimp out of his alfredo one at a time with his fork while Dot picks around the edges of her plate, rearranging the pasta more than eating it. I can almost feel Trev's heart breaking as he watches her — stealthily, or so he thinks — spindle fettuccine around her fork.

After dinner, once we're back out in the night air, Dot stops in front of the Skylark, spinning the ring on her finger. "So, I think I might ride with my dad for the next stretch," she says, a little apologetically. "Help him stay awake."

"That's cool," says Trev, but he can't hide his disappointment. The next stretch will probably be the last stretch, which means he's got nothing to look forward to but a good-bye. Dot can see he's forlorn, but she's not going to start pitying him now.

"So, we'll see you at the next stop," she says.

"Cool."

As Dot climbs into the Skylark, I hear her say, "Can we at *least* listen to a different tape?"

The final long dark stretch to Salt Lake City is mostly silent. Trev is awake the whole way, gazing dully out the window, as the mile markers fly by faster than ever. I do my best to cheer him.

"Five to one your old man's fly is down when he answers the door. What do you bet he's got a bucket of KFC waiting?"

"Probably," he says.

A little after midnight, the outskirts of North Salt Lake appear twinkling on the horizon and within minutes begin to fill the darkness until they're crowding in on both sides of the interstate. The time has come to cut the cord again. Signaling well in advance, I ease off the interstate, and Cash follows me a few blocks down a frontage road, until I pull over in the tiny lot of a power equipment rental joint, where we park on opposite sides.

By the time Trev wheels down the ramp, Cash and Dot are already awaiting us at the bottom. The night is cool, a touch of autumn in the thin desert air. Even perpetually underdressed Dot has her arms folded across her chest.

"Well," she says.

I give Cash a nod on the sly, and we duck out in tandem, walking the fifty feet to the curb, where Cash leans against a flagpole, and I stuff my hands in my pocket. Off to the west across the interstate, a low flying jet descends, its wing lights flashing.

"So what's wrong with him?" says Cash.

"MD."

Cash considers the diagnosis, looking down at his duct-taped flip-flop, and shaking his head. "How bad is that?"

"Pretty bad."

"How bad?"

"No telling, really. They can slow it down, but they can't stop it."

"Life's a fucking class A bitch," he says, his tone resolved more than bitter. "Seems like a hell of a nice kid. Funny. Smart."

"He's a peach," I say. "And so is Dot. You've got a great kid there. She's gonna grow into herself, you watch."

He shakes his head and smiles sadly. "Well, then, maybe she can teach me a thing or two."

Cash pushes off from the flagpole, and we begin drifting back toward the van.

"Thanks again, bro," he says.

"My pleasure. And I mean that."

We pull up halfway, in time to watch Dot lean down and give Trev a long, awkward kiss. Trev's arms are sort of in the way. His head is reared back at a funny angle. But it's not just him. Watching Dot bend down to him, tentatively, as though she's afraid she might injure him, it strikes me that she isn't as experienced as she'd have the world believe. When she stands upright after the kiss, she immediately folds her arms again.

"You've got my number," she says, backpedaling toward the Skylark.

Cash and I shake hands.

"Be safe," I say.

"Later, bro."

The Skylark is already pulling out of the lot as Trev mounts the ramp and maneuvers himself into place. For the first time in days, I buckle him in without Dot's assistance — crouching in back to wrangle the straps around the axle before ducking out and circling around to the passenger's side to secure the front. I'm gonna miss that kid in more ways than one.

the hide-a-bed incident

Bob's condo is off the Belt Route within rumbling distance of the airport. He occupies the bottom floor of a dirty gray duplex with a dead lawn. There is a wire reindeer out front listing badly to one side.

"Gotta be Blitzen," I say.

"Welcome to Casa Bob," says Trev, whirring up the walkway, "where every day is Christmas."

I'm proud of Trev. He's been surprisingly upbeat in the half hour since his good-bye kiss. Maybe because Dot's texted him twice already.

At the front steps, a sturdy access ramp of three-quarter-inch plywood has been erected, with twin strips of wide-grip tape running parallel up the center. The apartment is dark, inside and out. Stationed on either side of the front door is a large ceramic planter with a dead plant in it.

I ring the bell and wait. Ten seconds pass. I ring it again, clear my throat, wait. Still nothing.

"Try knocking," says Trev.

I rap on the door. We wait.

"Maybe he ran to the store," I say, rapping again.

"At one a.m.?"

"He's probably waiting up for us. So maybe he got thirsty or something."

Trev fishes his phone out of his pouch and dials Bob. In a moment, we can hear the cell phone ringing from within. Then, faintly, a groan. I rap harder on the door. Another groan.

"Bob, you in there?" The phone is still ringing. Now I'm knocking like a cop, with my fist. "Bob, open the door!"

A third groan, and then Bob's voice calling out something inaudible.

"What? "

"Va doe if umucked!" Bob bellows.

"What did he say?"

Trev shrugs.

I press my ear to the door.

"Va doe if umucked!" Bob shouts again.

"Something about the door," says Trev.

"If umucked!" proclaims Bob.

"Try the door," says Trev.

The door is unlocked. I push through, stepping into the darkened apartment. Before I can find a light, I hear Bob's voice again, still a little muffled.

"Va mights to va veft ova doe."

I snap on the overhead light, and there's Bob mounting the sofa. His folding wheelchair is overturned halfway across the room. His good arm is wedged in the bowels of the couch, and his arm cast rests unnaturally against the side of his head. His face is buried between the couch cushions.

"What the hell?" says Trev, wheeling across the threshold.

I right Bob's wheelchair and kneel to assist him, very carefully extracting his good arm from the depths of the sofa bed. Once his arm is clear, I rotate his body, until he's looking up into my face. He smiles sheepishly and looks down toward his lap, which is soaked.

"Yeah," he says. "Sorry about that. Think you can lift me back into the chair?"

The instant I heft him three inches off the sofa, he hoots like a barred owl, and his eyes begin to water. I ease him back down against the sofa, where he looks like he might pass out. All the color has drained from him.

"You've got to support the leg," he says, gasping for breath. "The leg."

This time, I get him under the leg cast with one arm and around the back and under the armpits with the other. I lift him slowly, looking down into his face for signs of discomfort. But for some grimacing and a few cringes, I manage to nest him in his chair without further incident.

"Thanks," he says with a great sigh of relief.

"You okay?"

"I think so. Everything feels about the same. Face is kind of itchy."

"What the hell were you doing, Dad?"

"Trying to fold out the hide-a-bed, make it up for you guys. Damned strap's way down on the inside, behind the cushions, and I got caught leaning too far. The chair slid out from under me. Got stuck, couldn't move."

"How long ago was this?"

"I don't know. What time is it?"

"One ten."

"About four hours ago."

"Four hours!" says Trev.

"Why didn't you yell for your neighbor?" I say.

"He's deaf."

"Oh, right."

"What happened to you?" Bob says to me.

"He hurt his neck in Missoula," Trev says.

The apartment is dumpy but orderly. Despite the glaring overhead light and a menagerie of colors splashed about — from the pale blue carpet, to the dull yellow La-Z-Boy, to the custard-colored sofa bed — the place is dark. A murky fishbowl on the end table catches my eye. Inside, a lone tenant describes sluggish circles endlessly, his big mouth slowly opening and closing.

"That's Mr. Baxter," says Bob, following my gaze.

"Why do you call him Mr. Baxter?"

"I dunno," he says. Wheeling in a half circle, he nearly takes me off at the knees with his clunky leg cast. "Ope. Sorry. Keep forgetting the damn thing's there. Well, I better get out of these wet drawers."

"You need help?" I say.

"Oh no. I can handle it."

Bob tries to maneuver between Trev and me, but there's no room. Trev backs up, I slide over. Bob runs over my foot on his way past.

"Ope," he says. "Sorry about that. Say, maybe you could give me a hand with that hide-a-bed."

"Got it," I say.

"Welcome to Utah, fellas."

"Thanks, Dad. Sorry you peed your pants."

Bob rolls off into the bedroom and with considerable effort manages to shut the door. Almost immediately, there's some bumbling with a stuck drawer, and something crashes to the floor.

"Nothing to worry about in here!" he calls out. "Bottle just fell off the bureau is all. It didn't break — no biggie!"

I turn my attention to the hide-a-bed and start feeling around for the strap. "So what do you think?" I say, fishing around behind the couch cushions. "You glad we came?"

Before Trev can answer, his phone beeps, and he breaks into a wide grin. Another text. He cranes his neck and bows his back, then lowers his arm like a backhoe, scooping his phone out of the pouch. Hoisting the screen to face level, he squints as he reads the text.

I locate the hide-a-bed strap, give it a tug. The folded mattress rears up on its spring base. I kick out the legs and smooth the mattress and unfold the clean bedding as Trev struggles fiercely to manipulate his tiny keypad.

"Look at you, Mr. Text."

"Texting is the shiz," he says just as the phone slips from his grasp, careens off his knee, and scurries across the floor.

Circling the hide-a-bed, I stoop and retrieve the phone and hand it back to Trev. "You want me to type something?"

"Nah. I got it." He raises the phone and begins the agonizing business all over again. It's bad enough he doesn't have a flip phone.

Bob soon reemerges in a cloud of aftershave, clad in dry khaki Dockers and the shirt I gave him this summer. Wheeling past me into the living room, where the hide-a-bed allows for only a narrow passage, he jostles the end table, setting the fishbowl to wobbling. The water heaves and laps up over the rim, but Mr. Baxter doesn't seem to care. Nothing seems to stir Mr. Baxter. Even when Bob pauses to pepper a few precious flakes of krill into the water, Mr. Baxter just lets the food float on the surface. I'm guessing he's bat-shit crazy from turning circles in that murky little bowl his whole life, and that he doesn't care anymore whether he lives or dies.

"This is Mr. Baxter."

"Yeah, we know," says Trev.

Who can blame Bob for being nervous? He's been riding the pine for years, waiting for this opportunity to get back in the game with Trev. How many buckets of chicken and crummy motel beds has he endured with the hope of arriving at this moment? How many red-eye flights from Sea-Tac on the heels of defeat, knowing that he'd gladly do it all again for the opportunity to redeem himself? Now Bob's finally got that chance. What Bob doesn't know is that he can relax. His son is in love, and next to that vast awakening, there's nothing momentous about their reunion. Trev is willing to forgive anything as long as those texts keep coming.

"Hey, Dad," he says, punching ponderously at his keypad, his head back. "You got anything to drink?"

"How about some root beer?"

"That'll work."

"Ben?"

"Sure, what the heck."

Bob spins, clipping the hide-a-bed with his chair, wheels over my foot again, and bumps the end table again, sloshing Mr. Baxter around in his bowl.

"Tell you what," I say. "Let me grab that. You two can play catch-up. How 'bout you, Bob? Root beer?"

"Why not?"

I retire to the kitchen and start searching the cabinets for glasses.

"So, who you texting?" I hear Bob say.

"Just a girl," says Trev.

I locate the glasses, a bachelor's assemblage, which includes a mason jar and a partially melted blue plastic tumbler.

"You mean like a girlfriend?" Bob says.

"Yeah, maybe. We haven't really gotten that far."

Bob's next question is lost in the hum of the ice box as I'm greeted by an arctic blast of freezer-burned vapor. Excavating two bags of frozen peas, some hamburger, and a Lean Cuisine, I locate the ice near the back, buried beneath some link sausage and a turkey pot pie. The cubes in the half-empty tray have an opaque, shrunken aspect to them, and almost certainly they'll taste of frozen hamburger. But at least they're cold. Closing the freezer, I can hear Bob laughing.

"Well, that's what it looked like, seriously," says Trev.

"That's bad," Bob says. "I wish I could have seen it. What else? Tell me about Missoula."

"Missoula. Oh man. I wouldn't even know where to begin."

"Tell me everything."

And as Trev begins telling his dad everything — Peaches, Elton, the Skylark, the Yeti, Scruggs, me streaking across the lot of the C'mon Inn, I linger in the kitchen, clinking the ice cubes in the glasses methodically, one at a time, refilling the tray, nice and level, clearing a spot among the frozen whatnot, reorganizing the goods as I go. When I can't stall any longer, I uncap the warm root beer gradually, letting it hiss, watching it froth up jubilantly, as though it's excited at finally being released.

the biggest pit in the world

Trev and I are are rudely awakened at eight in the morning by an alarm. Not the mindless bleating of a digital alarm clock but the frantic squealing of a twelve-volt fire alarm. Shooting upright on the hide-a-bed, I hear the unmistakable hiss of scalding oil, the clang of cast iron on linoleum. Then Bob.

"Ope! Uhhh — need an assist in here!"

I leap from the mattress, swing around the foot of the bed, past Mr. Baxter and into the kitchen, where black smoke billows from the range. An iron skillet is ablaze, a tongue of flames lapping at the hood. On the ground, another skillet smolders next to several broken eggs. Bob is in the middle of it all, clutching a spatula in his good hand. Even in the thick of the smoke, I can smell his spilled aftershave from last night. In a frenzy, he swings around to address me, nearly knocking me off my feet with his unwieldy cast. I sidle past him, snap a dish towel off the stove handle, wrap it around my hand, and dive in for the burning skillet. When I've got a firm hold of the handle, I swing the flaming skillet in a wide arc toward the sink, drop it in the basin, and slam the cold water on full throttle. The skillet chuffs and hisses like a steam engine as the flames fizzle and a new wave of smoke overwhelms the kitchen.

I snap off both burners, snatch the remaining skillet off the linoleum, and drop it in the sink with the other.

Bob's still clutching his spatula in the middle of the kitchen, an embarrassed grin tacked to his face. "Nice," he says, loud enough that I can hear him over the squawking alarm. "That's what I call grace under pressure."

"You too, Bob." I throw the kitchen window wide open, and the smoke begins funneling out into the overcast day.

"So much for country breakfast," he says.

"What's going on in there?" says Trev.

First I disarm the alarm. Then I dress Trev. Then I mop the kitchen floor and fan the room until the smoke clears. Following a breakfast of toast, I set Trev on the toilet and return to the kitchen to wash dishes as I await his call. When he beckons, I wipe him, lift him up, cradle him in my arms, hoist his pants, and set him in his chair, whereupon I give him two swipes of deodorant, set his electric razor out, squeeze a curlicue of toothpaste on his brush, and place it on the edge of the sink where he can reach it. Then I retire to the living room, where I begin wrestling with the hide-a-bed.

That's when disaster strikes. After feeding Mr. Baxter (who still hasn't touched his last measly flakes), Bob swings around abruptly.

"Oh, incidentally — " he says, grazing the fishbowl, which wobbles off the edge of the table, tips and shatters on the wood floor.

Mr. Baxter, whom I've sorely misjudged, is flopping furiously for his life on the nearby throw rug. For the second time this morning, I'm grace under pressure: I scoop Mr. Baxter up, hurdle one of Bob's outstretched legs, and dash to the kitchen with Mr. Baxter wiggling crazily in my clutches. I snatch the mason jar out of the cupboard, drop Mr. Baxter in, and fill it with water. He remains perfectly still for a few seconds, as though he's dead or in shock. I tap the glass.

"C'mon, Mr. Baxter. Move."

Nothing.

I tap the glass again. "C'mon, let's go."

Lifting the jar to my face, I look Mr. Baxter square in the eye. He looks at once stately and constipated, like Winston Churchill. He doesn't move, doesn't open his mouth, doesn't blink — but then he's got no eyelids. He just stares wall-eyed through the glass right past me. I tap the jar again. Still nothing. I give it a little shake. Nothing. I'm about fifteen seconds from flushing Mr. Baxter when Bob rolls into the kitchen and peers over my shoulder.

"Is he . . .?"

"I don't know." I give the jar another shake, and Mr. Baxter splashes up against the side of the jar, lifelessly.

"Does he blink at all?"

"I don't think he has any eyelids."

Now Trev wheels in with his electric razor in hand.

"Is he . . .?"

"We're not sure," says Bob.

"It's looking that way," I say.

Though Mr. Baxter is showing no signs of life, he's not floating yet. I jiggle him again.

"This is my fault," says Bob. "Everything I touch turns to shit."

"Or breaks," adds Trev.

Suddenly Mr. Baxter stirs, swimming a slow circle, then stops, staring right at me. He opens his mouth and closes it. Opens it again, closes it.

"Whoa," I say, breathing easy. "Gave me a scare there, Bax."

When I set the jar on the counter, I set it right up against the backsplash so Bob can't knock it over. Mr. Baxter is more active now, circling counterclockwise in a tight radius. But by the time he turns eight or nine circles in the mason jar, he looks disconsolate again, stops, and stares at the three of us grouped in the kitchen.

"I'm worried about Mr. Baxter," I say.

"I think we can help him," Bob says.

Within the hour, we're off to Bingham Canyon. I've buckled Trev in the van and strapped Bob in the backseat with his broken leg propped on the cooler. Though Bob has already seen the Biggest Pit in the World, he's nonetheless excited.

"That's the beauty of it. It just gets bigger," he says.

On our way out of town, Bob directs me to the Wal-Mart Supercenter in South Jordan. In the rear of the store, he selects a five-gallon hooded glass aquarium with fluorescent lights and a bio filter. He adds a two-pound bag of glowing blue gravel, a colorful array of lily bulbs, and an underwater plant. And to top things off, a sparkly white castle.

We're navigating our way toward the checkout with our oversized cart, through a wilderness of egg beaters and baby clothes, picture frames and garden hoes, camping stoves and dinette sets, greeting cards and coverlets, when I suddenly decide there is something I simply must have.

"I've gotta grab a few things real quick," I say. "I'll catch up with you guys at the van."

Bob peels off three twenties. "For the aquarium," he says.

When I arrive at the van, Trev and Bob are waiting at the foot of the ramp. I stow the aquarium in back. Thunderheads are stacking up on the western horizon. The air is sticky. My neck brace is beginning to stink. Lucky for me, you can smell Bob's aftershave in Ogden, so I'm not likely to offend anyone.

Driving west through the thinning suburbs, we leave the valley behind and snake our way through the arid foothills, toward the Oquirrhs, broad-shouldered brown mountains, mottled with green like a skin rash. Bob tells us it won't be long before they're covered in snow. I can still see a narrow strip of the Salt Lake Valley in the rearview mirror.

What is now a pit was once a mountain, so arriving at the Bingham copper mine is something like arriving at the rim of a tremendous caldera. We pay our five bucks, park the van, and make our way across the dusty lot. We walk down the causeway toward the viewing area, where a placard informs us that at two and a half miles wide, and three quarters of a mile deep (and getting deeper by the day), the Bingham pit is the Biggest Pit in the World by a wide margin. Along with the Great Wall of China, the pit is one of only two feats of human engineering visible from outer space. If the Bingham pit were a stadium, the placard informs us, it would hold nine million people. Emerging from the causeway and rounding a corner, I catch my first glimpse of the copper mine, and indeed, the great yawning chasm resembles nothing more than a stupendous amphitheater, its striated walls descending steeply in countless rows toward the ever-deepening bottom, where even now the great loaders and crushers churn up a slow rising dust.

"Big hole," says Trev.

"What did I tell you?" says Bob, wheeling closer to Trev. "It's something, huh?"

"Kinda scary."

Deep in the pit, running a dusty line along a terraced wall, a parade of giant trucks, minuscule from our vantage near the rim, belch and heave their way toward the crusher.

"Glad you came," says Bob, patting Trev on the back with his good arm.

"Yeah," says Trev. "The pictures don't do it justice."

"Out here, I mean. To see me."

"Yeah, I know what you mean. So, do you think they'll just keep digging forever?"

"As long as there's copper. Look, I know I haven't been — "

"Dad, stop."

"I was young. It really wasn't about — "

"Dad, stop. It's okay."

"I'm gonna get a Coke," I say.

I wander down past the visitor center, past the gift shop, past a line of viewfinders, and a gigantic truck tire with a placard. When I've left the crowd behind, I find a quiet stretch of rail, dig the hard pack out of my jean pocket, and strike it three times briskly against my palm. I twirl off the cellophane strip, remove the gold flap, and tap out a smoke.

Fuck it. I'm tired of wishing.

I light up, inhale, and lean on the rail. Exhaling slowly, I peer out over the ledge. There it is, so deep you probably can't see out of it: the Biggest Pit in the World. It's so goddamn deep it's hard to fathom that there's anything anywhere but just a great big hole in the ground. And for the first time in what feels like an eternity, I'm not in it.

I fish my phone out and dial Forest. He answers on the second ring.

"Hey, buddy. It's me," I say.

"Benji boy."

"Look, I've got a couple of favors to ask."

the longest haul yet

Already the chill is burning off as the sun beams just above the eastern horizon. It's 6:30 a.m. and we're a day behind schedule. Bob and Trev are wheel-to-wheel curbside, as I stuff the last of the bags willy-nilly in the back of the van and force the hatch shut so that Trev's big black duffel is pancaked against the rear window. God help us if somebody needs the Tums, because I haven't a clue where they are back there.

Bob and Trev are having a moment, or at least Bob is doing his best to make it a moment, while stuck to the heel of his outstretched cast, three squares of toilet paper stir gently in the desert breeze.

"You know," he says gloomily. "Leaving was the biggest mistake of my life."

"Would you just stop," says Trev.

"I'm really sorry about everything."

"Yeah, I get it, already. Stop," he says with an edge of impatience. But when he sees Bob looking a little crestfallen, he softens up. "Look, just bring me some chicken, and we'll call it good."

Bob brightens. "You're on," he says.

Easing the van away from the curb, I watch Bob in the rearview mirror as he wheels to the middle of the dead lawn and attempts to right the listing reindeer. Look at you, Bob, setting your house in order at last.

Trev and I skirt the the reservoir in silence, speed across the flats for hours on end, over the border to Twin Falls wordlessly, until somewhere around Boise, I'm moved to speech.

"Seems like you let him off the hook easy," I say.

"Yeah, well, it was time, I guess."

And that's the last anybody says of it, about the last anybody says of anything, as we shoot through the high desert of northeastern Oregon — a landscape as scorched and ravaged as anything in the Mojave — past Baker City and La Grande with the sun burning fiercely at our backs. We've no desire to stop and, so far, no need. At the junction, we pick up the gorge and snake our way through Pendleton and The Dalles, with nothing but a quick stop for lunch at Biggs Cafe. We haven't got time for the Stonehenge replica at Maryhill, no time for the commemorative placard atop Sam Hill as we hurry west. And while I'm not sure what propels Trev onward, for the first time since we set out on this journey, I know where I'm going, and I wish I could say it were home.

a king

Don't think for one minute that hitting a softball is like riding a bike. If you think you can succeed on muscle memory alone, you're wrong. You've got to stay within yourself. You've got to be in the moment. You've got to maintain your poise. You've got to resist temptation, no matter how slow it is moving. Sounds easy enough — if you're a monk. I'm willing to concede that when you're doing it right, hitting feels like riding a bike.

Back in those fat days when Forest scrawled my name mechanically in the three-hole — right in front of his own name — back when tattooing the sweet spot of a softball seemed effortless, before I began striding too early, before I started dropping my back elbow and lunging at bad pitches, before I started getting completely mental in the box, Janet used to bring the kids to my late games on Wednesdays. They'd stand at the backstop as I strode to the plate clutching my bat. Jodi, at eleven months, in snug shorts and a bulging diaper, doddering on chubby legs as he clutched the chain-link fence for balance. Wide-eyed, no doubt, when I sent a frozen rope into the power alley or a screaming meanie past third.

"Go, Daddy!" Piper would shout as I darted down the line and rounded first.

And pulling into second base at an easy trot, I felt like a hero when I heard my teammates lauding me from the dugout with a chorus of cheers. I felt like a king when I peered back at my family behind home plate: Piper clashing famously in rubber boots and a leotard. Janet looking wholesome and relaxed in a pullover sweatshirt and flattering jeans. Jodi with drool streaming down his chin, flashing his new bottom teeth like a jack-o'-lantern as he garbled his approval.

A king, I tell you.

And maybe that seems sort of sad, sort of pathetic — the spectacle of some unemployable stay-at-home schlub whose wife gives him an allowance, standing astride second base with two bad knees as though it were Mount Everest. But it's not. What's sad is that I can't bring any of it back. What's pathetic is that after all this time, I'm still trying.

close enough

I suppose it's a convenient place for a rendezvous, if not a little desolate. But after a 400-mile drive, with 180 miles to go, I'll take convenient. The Supercenter is in North Portland Harbor, right off the interstate, just shy of the bridge. What was once a mall is now vacant, its bleached walls and streaked awnings wearing the weather poorly. The shrubbery has gone to pot. The trash bins are heaping. The doors are chained shut. Somebody's tagged the glass with white spray paint. It's almost sad to think the place may be haunted. I'd hate to be a ghost floating around in there amid the gutted racks and the empty hangers.

Beyond the mall stretches a vast gray sea of vacant parking, maybe five hundred yards across, like a great concrete bay ringed with hulking superstores: Pier 1, Old Navy, Babies "R" Us. From a quarter mile away, I can see Janet's silver sedan, idling alone near the middle of the lot, her headlights spearing the gloomy dusk, a little cross-eyed. I park the van about eight spaces up the row from her and grab the manila envelope off the floor between Trev and me.

"You're okay with this? It might take a few minutes."

"Just leave the window cracked," he says. "I'll bark if I'm feeling needy."

Leaving the van to idle in the gathering darkness, I crack the window, adjust the radio and heat to comfortable levels, and step out of the van into a mud puddle. It's spitting rain again, and cold — uncharacteristically cold for the season.

Walking the eight long spaces to Janet with my head down, I resolve myself not to dig up old bones, not to make any speeches, not to make her suffer any more than I already have. With a deep breath, I duck into the passenger's seat of the idling sedan. The heat is on full blast, the wipers squeak slowly.

"Hello, Ben."

"Hey."

She looks tired and doubtful as I hand her the papers. She sets the envelope in her lap without inspecting its contents.

"Is this for real?" she says.

"It's for real."

We agree that this exchange warrants a short silence. We both gaze straight ahead, across the empty lot, toward the distant lights of Babies "R" Us. We used to drive all the way to Tacoma for Babies "R" Us. Our old lives were all but made of colored plastic.

"Thank you, Ben," she says at last.

"Sorry about the wait. I just needed some — "

"No need to explain," she says, more like an entreaty than a free pass. "What happened to your neck?"

"I sprained it, I think. Or pulled it. Whatever you do to a neck."

"Have you seen a doctor?"

"Not yet."

"What about your hands?"

"I fell."

She shakes her head. The same woeful head shake I've seen a thousand times. "Oh, Ben, what's going to happen to you? You need to take care of yourself."

"I just took a vacation, didn't I?"

"Ben, really."

I look over at the idling van, its exhaust plume steaming in the cold air. It's getting dark. I should have left a dome light on for Trev.

"You smell like cigarettes," she says.

"Yeah, I started again."

"That's too bad."

"Yeah, I guess."

She smoothes the envelope in her lap and turns to me. "Ben. You know, this is really about me, okay, not you. I've tried to tell you this right from the start. Things only got nasty because . . ."

"Janet, I get it."

"You do?"

"Not really. But I'm ready to live with it."

And the truth is, I do get it, or I'm starting to. Janet needs a new context. Janet can no longer live in relation to me or what's left of me. She can no longer navigate a world with no signposts, no living landmarks, only colored plastic ruins. She cannot live on a borrowed light that only grows weaker with each passing day, cannot walk among the lengthening shadows of her dead.

She turns from me and looks out the side window toward Pier 1. "I've said some horrible things, Ben. Things I didn't mean."

"Welcome to the club."

"I mean about what happened."

"I know. Fuck, I know. So have I. I'm so sorry."

"You don't owe me any apologies."

"But I do."

"You don't."

"Goddamnit, it was my fault. I was there. I caused it."

"It happened. It was an accident," she says decisively, clutching my knee. And as she does, an old grief wells up under my ribs, as though for the first time, rumbling up my chest like a herd of buffalo.

"Shhh," she says.

But that only makes it worse.

"Ben, it's okay."

"You know what kills me?" I say, wiping my face and choking down my lump of grief. "What really kills me is the thought that if I'd been more successful at something—Christ, at anything—I never would've been a stay-at-home dad in the first place. This never would've happened."

"And if I were a more successful mom, I would've been at home with the kids, is that it? No, Ben, you can't think like that anymore. We're way past the if stage here—past the why stage, and the how stage. We're in the *is* stage, Ben. Best that we both look straight ahead for a while."

She releases her grip on my leg and pats the manila envelope. "I realize how hard this is for you, and I'm sorry I left. I didn't mean to, I tried not to, but I did, and I'm sorry. I had to, Ben. I'm not asking you to forgive me."

But I do. The truth is that suddenly I feel lighter, I feel like I can breathe deeper than I've breathed in years. Maybe all I wanted was an apology. I wipe my face dry and give a throaty sniffle, swallowing the last of my grief — at least for now.

"Ain't no thang," I say.

She smiles sadly and pats my knee. Without unbuckling, she leans in for an awkward embrace. I breathe deeply of her, fill my lungs greedily with the scent of her. I could hold her forever, long enough for her stiff body to slacken, to melt into mine. Even with my screwy neck, I could hold her forever. But Janet doesn't have that kind of time.

"Good-bye, Ben," she says, easing away from me. "Take care of yourself."

"I'm gonna be okay," I say. "Don't worry about me."

Buoyed somewhat by the suspicion that I actually might be okay, that like Janet, I might find a new context for myself, I duck out of the car and take a deep breath of the cold wet air. The daylight has faded completely now. The lights of the stores look almost inviting.

"I still think that Sunderland guy is a putz," I say, and close the door.

Janet smiles apologetically through the glass.

I'm smiling, too, as I cover the eight spaces in long, brisk strides and hop back into the van. I find Trev with his chair angled back slightly, working clumsily away at his tiny keypad in the dark.

"Sorry about the wait, bro."

"No worries," he says, without looking up. "How'd it go?"

"Not bad."

"That's good, right?"

"Close enough."

Janet is inspecting the papers beneath the dome light. It kills me to know her heart is beating fast. But I'm also glad for her. I wing a wide one eighty and angle across the lot toward the access road, looking everywhere but behind me. It's troubling how big and dead this place is. Suddenly, I want to run from it. I hang a right at the exit and barely beat the signal.

I ease the van onto the interstate headed north, listening to the thrum of the wipers and the swish of the tires, knowing with every molecule of my being that I love Janet, that I still want to be with her, that in spite of everything, I still want to make it work. Because I still care deeply — about Janet, about my kids, about Forest and Trev and Elsa and Bob and Dot and Peaches and Little Elton and even about Big Elton. I'll never stop caring. But the thing about caring is, it's inconvenient. Sometimes you've got to give when it makes no sense at all. Sometimes you've got to give until it hurts. It's not easy, and it can be downright thankless, but if you can do it, and you don't mind working for squat, they're still offering classes at the Abundant Life Foursquare Church right behind the Howard Johnson in Bremerton. Tell them Ben sent you.

ACKNOWLEDGMENTS

I'M GRATEFULLY INDEBTED to so many wonderful people for their help on this novel that I'm sure to forget somebody, and for this, I apologize in advance. Let it be a testament to the extent of my indebtedness.

A million thanks to my friend Case Levenson, for being such a huge inspiration and hilarious companion. I'm ever-so-grateful to my wife, Lauren, for all her support and encouragement, and for lighting up my world with her smile. For sharing their expertise in their respective fields, I thank Dave Coatsworth and Dale Duffy. For their early readings and amazing editorial insigts, I thank Michael Meachen, Shelby Rogers, Dennis O'Reilly, Keith Dixon, Brock Dubbles, Mike Tassone, and Mark Krieger. For their unending support, Beth Branco and Carmela D'Amico. For their amazing advocacy in the field, Kurtis Q. Lowe, Phoebe "Gassy" Gaston, Matt "Don't Call Me Jake Gyllenhaal" Wickiser, John Majeska, and Frazer Dobson.

To my amazing friend and agent, Mollie Glick, and her stalwart assistant, Kathleen Hamblin. Also, Stephanie Abou and Hannah Gordon Brown for all their hustle. To my Internet associates and partners in crime, Dennis Haritou, Jason Rice, Jason Chambers, and Brad Listi. Also, Richard Nash for always being in my corner.

To my whole family and my wife's whole family, for their love and encouragement. You don't choose your family, but I'd choose all of you if I could.

To my incredible friends—you know who you are. I'm blessed to have you. My door is always open.

To indie booksellers everywhere for their part in bringing my stories to the world.

At Algonquin, the greatest publisher any writer could ever hope for, I thank Craig Popelars, Kelly Bowen, Michael Taeckens, Sarah Rose Nordgren, Michael Rockliff, Katie Ford, Jude Grant, Brunson Hoole, Steven Pace, Elisabeth Scharlatt, Peter Workman, Ina Stern, Lauren Moseley, and everybody top to bottom at Workman and Algonquin. Unlike my family, I did choose you, and you were among the best choices I ever made.

And finally, a million thanks to my dear editor, Chuck Adams. Yo, pops, thanks for being my champion and advocate, and somebody to look up to.